BEFORE HER EYES

May the life that flashes before your eyes be filled with joy

Rebecca

By

REBECCA FORSTER

Before Her Eyes
Copyright © Rebecca Forster, 2010
All rights reserved

Though certain elements of this novel were suggested by actual events, it is a work of fiction. All characters, whether central or peripheral, are purely products of the author's imagination, as are their actions, motivations, thoughts, and conversations, and neither the characters nor the situations were invented for them are intended to depict real people.

FOR

For my Dad, Arch Forster
and my Father-in-Law, John Czuleger

Many thanks to Jerome
and Arizona Police Chief
Allen L. Muma for his insights

BEFORE HER EYES

Dove Connelly's Bedroom
<u>2:17 a.m.</u>

Dove Connelly caught up the phone on the first ring even though it was set so low as to make the sound virtually mute. Any other human being in a deep sleep wouldn't have heard it, but Dove wasn't any one else.

First, he didn't sleep all that deep anymore. Then there was the thing he had in him: it was his sixth sense that let him hear and see what others didn't, anticipate what others couldn't.

Most people respected his talent, some thanked God for it and others who weren't so law abiding steered clear of it. His wife, Cherie, would swear that she would be forever faithful because he would know her intentions even before she strayed. But that was before the unthinkable happened. Now, if Cherie spoke of that sixth sense at all, she did so with regret, sad that the gift had forsaken Dove when they needed it most.

Tonight Dove's wife didn't move when he pushed aside the covers and got out of bed. He put the phone to his ear, padding along to the kitchen in bare feet, wearing only old sweat pants, having no inkling that he'd be putting on his uniform any time soon.

"What is it, Jessica? Hogan boys tear up the tavern again?" He kept his voice low. The house wasn't big.

Jessica Taylor started to speak but all Dove heard was the news catching in her throat. In all the years he had known her, Jessica reported to him using a scale of verbal sorrow, outrage or downright disbelief that gave him a clue as to enormity of the crime that was waiting on him. This night, for a layer of a second, she was speechless. Dove's blood ran cold; as cold as it had run all those months ago when another crime was over and done before he knew it had even begun.

"Talk to me, Jessica."

"Oh God, it's a bad 'un. Bad as anything." The woman pulled in a breath and it went no further than the middle of her chest.

"What and where?"

"One of ours, Dove. Paddy Johnson was drivin' home, saw the lights at the Mountain Store and figured Fritz was hostin' one of his poker parties like he used to." Jessica breathed deep again and this time it went all the way in to her gut. "Paddy stopped into the store thinking to pick up a hand, Dove. He went into the store and found Fritz dead. Head splattered all over the back room. I'm so sorry."

"Ah, Jesus."

Dove put a hand to his face. There were no words to express Dove's shock and sorrow. Bowing his head, covering his eyes did not make this news easier to take. They were talking about Fritz, a jack-o-lantern of a man:

solid, round, possessed of a smile that cracked his face in two and lit up even the darkest times.

Dove remembered Fritz passing hot coffee to him on a bitter morning. Dove could still hear Fritz's good words even when there was nothing good in his own life to speak of. Fritz was Dove's best friend and confessor, the only one who knew what had really gone on in the sheriff's home. Fritz was fond of reminding the sheriff that he carried the spirit of the bird his mother had named him for. Dove. Peace. Fritz had tried so hard to help Dove make peace with his demons.

Now Fritz was gone and Dove was shamed he slept through the man's dying. That he didn't feel his friend's need was as close to a sin as anything he could imagine. There would come a time for personal reckoning. The time wasn't now. Now was the time for Dove to do his job.

"Where's Paddy?" Dove asked flatly.

"Says he's sittin' in his truck waitin' on you. He called from the store but didn't want to stay inside." There was a beat before Jessica asked: "Want me to let the state boys know?"

"Give them a call but I'm not waiting on them, Jessie."

"Alright, Dove."

"Ring up Tim and get him out there. Call Nathan, too."

"You going to trust Nathan with this?" Jessica asked tentatively.

"I trust him, Jessica. You make the call," Dove directed. Then he thought again. "And Bernadette. We've got to let Bernadette know."

3

"I'll see to it, Dove," Jessica offered but he had already changed his mind.

"Never mind. Not yet. I'll go out to the store first. There's always a chance Paddy is wrong." Dove clutched for something that would make this better. The straw he came up with was speculation. It was a short one, a ridiculous dodge, but it was what he had. "Besides, if Bernadette's awake she'll know something's gone down. Can't be as close as those two have been all these years and not know."

Jessica murmured something Dove couldn't quite catch. It sounded like 'hallelujah'. He was about to ring off when she stopped him.

"Dove, you think he could have done it himself? I mean, it's been hard on him with Bernadette and all."

"No," he snapped. "Fritz wouldn't have left us with that on our mind."

"You're right," Jessica agreed. "You just do what you've got to do, Dove. I'll be by the phone ready to help with whatever you need."

"Jessie?"

"Yep?"

"Lock your doors. Keep your eyes open. Is your gun loaded?"

"Dove, whoever did this is probably gone. Besides, I can take ca…"

"You do it, Jessica," Dove snapped. "One friend gone is enough. I won't have another."

Dove rang off. He kept his thoughts so close there wasn't room for his huge sorrow. He dressed in the near dark, the small light in the bathroom casting only the faintest glow. Cherie saw that his uniform was laundered good as any city cop. She reasoned that if Dove's size didn't make people think twice before coming down on him, his starched and pressed uniform would. Even in these big mountains where so much law was made just by two people meeting up together, a fine uniform made a difference.

Dove put his gun in his holster and his jacket on over that. He slipped his knife into its sheath and took his hat off the peg. It was only when he went to kiss his sleeping wife that he paused.

Cherie was a powerful draw and it used to be he couldn't be in the same room without wanting to touch her. Yet, her brow was furrowed as she struggled inside her dreams and it caught him up short. Those dreams were a place Dove didn't want to go — he couldn't help even if he got there — so he reached out and put his hand on her head. It didn't ease her worry. It was a bad night all around.

Dove stepped back but the bassinette was in his way and he was forced to look at the baby. The girl's eyes were open. Big eyes still blue from birth even though four months had passed. He prayed they would change dark like his and Cherie's. Maybe if her eyes changed everything else would, too. But she looked up with those blue eyes without seeing him; Dove turned away as if he couldn't see her.

One of the cats stretched when he took the keys to the car. Its yellow eyes followed him as he stepped into the small room off the kitchen. A basket of cleanly folded laundry sat atop the washer. It smelled of baby powder and pink cream. The scent made Dove gag but it didn't stop him from staying long enough to check the security control panel.

The lights were lit green, each window and door of his house wired so that an alarm would sound at Jessica's should anyone open them without a code. The indicators for the alarm pads that were buried around the perimeter of the property pulsed red. Finally, Dove flipped on the floodlights ringing his cabin home. That done he retraced his steps and opened the back door.

Outside, Dove saw his breath and gave the black dog no more than a glance as he walked by. The creature was all muscle, pointed ears and snout. He had teeth that could rip a man to shreds. Dove swung himself into his car, fired up the engine, switched on the headlights and headed out.

It was two thirty-five in the morning.

My name is Tessa Bradley.

I am, I have been told, a very beautiful woman.

Most men believe they would die happy if they could touch me; women have said they would kill to be me. I don't see what the fuss is all about, but then I have lived inside this skin long enough to know that life balances everything out.

While these looks of mine have earned me a few brass rings, there is always something on the back end to rub off the shine. Tonight that something is a gun pointing at my back. The heavy barrel drags over my spine to hurry me on. I do my best but I'm confused by the shadows as we move among the trees. I'm afraid and fear slows me even more.

"Bitch."

The muzzle hits me between the shoulder blades. I don't expect it because we've walked a fair way in silence. I fall hard to the cold ground. I play possum, wanting a minute more to figure out why I'm here, who these men are and why they hate me.

"Get up."

Boots come into view. They are thick and worn. They belong to the man with the shaved head. He is the dog who grabbed me when we met up at the front door of that general store off the highway.

"Get up. Get up."

His accent is so thick the words sound like 'giddy up'. Tired of waiting on me, he swings his boot. It connects with my gut. Swallowing my cry of surprise and terror, I roll away and cup my body around the blow. It wasn't hard enough to knock the breath out of me; it's knowing he did it that makes me sick. What he's done brings back memories.

"Hold your horses," I mutter.

I struggle to my hands and knees. I glare at him through a curtain of light hair. He doesn't see the hatred in my eyes but I know he feels it. A man no more turns his own eyes my way than I feel what he feels. Usually it is his lust stamping me like a branding iron. In another place this man might think of me that way, but here I am the enemy and I don't know why. I get to my feet. My ankle wobbles in my high-heeled boots. That sign of weakness gives the man with the gun courage.

For each step I take back he gets bolder and comes forward. My body convulses with fear and cold but mostly fear. An owl hoots. A wind ruffles the tops of the trees and runs over my cheek. The bright moon comes out from behind a cloud and I see a little better. A pinecone falls with a 'whump'. Neither of us turns at the sound. We only have eyes for each other even though there are three of us on this mountain: me, the man with the gun, and a younger man. That man is silent. He stops a little ways back.

His shoulders are slumped. His hair is long and curly. His hands stick deep in the pockets of his old coat. He seems weary but I'm not fooled. Weary only means he isn't going to put himself out one way or another. Slowly he turns his head and stares off into the darkness. His face in profile looks like a wolf gone too long without food. He leans toward the gunman, putting in his two cents in that language I don't understand.

The tattooed man shakes his head. Like a terrorist, his scarf hides him from the nose down. I see only the top half of his face. Shaved head. White scar through the tattoo on his temple. His small eyes skate over the six flawless carats of diamond on my left hand, my jeans, my cashmere sweater. I am a woman people will miss and that makes him nervous.

"What do you boys want?" There it is. The voice I thought I lost is back. I ratchet it up a notch. "Come on you bastards? What? Money?"

The man with the gun darts a look at his companion. The weary man smirks. He understands alright but money means nothing to him. That's downright scary. To most people, money is everything.

"Is this about Jake?"

My voice shakes. Not that it matters. They aren't interested in how I feel and they aren't inclined to answer my questions. The younger one speaks urgently, gesturing, unable to take his eyes off me now. I am not surprised. Someone once told me I'm most beautiful when I'm afraid. If that's true, I must look like a goddess because I am scared shitless.

The one with the gun argues with the other one, biting off his words like tough meat as his eyes flicker and his arm straightens. His knuckles go white and his finger tightens on the trigger the way my daddy's used to when he meant to shoot. The gun points at my face. My hand comes up, fingers spread wide. I always thought I didn't care about my face, but I do. If he blows my face off what will anyone remember about me? How will anyone know me?

Sweet Jesus.

I pray, even though it has been my experience that Jesus isn't paying much attention to what's happening down here on earth. A tear creeps out of the corner of my eye. Reflected there I see things: Jake and Charlotte, mug shots of my lovers, ugly truths beneath the rocks that litter the path of my life.

I don't want to see all of my life passing before my eyes. It's not time and I'm not ready to admit this is the end.. Understanding that, I'm not afraid anymore. Instead, I'm just friggin' ticked when I look at the ugly man square on.

Him and me, we make peace with our decisions at the same time. I see it in his eyes but he misses what is in mine. Bad call on his part. I scream 'no' just before I hear a click, an explosion and another scream. I feel heat and smell smoke. My shoulder is hot/cold with hurt. The dark in the mountains turns bright white. I have been blown to the ground but not to kingdom come. Half blind, I scramble up but the short one is on me.

I kick. I scream. The gunman's scarf pulls away giving me a glimpse of the sad excuse for a man he is: weak jawed and scarred. His teeth are bad. He is nothing but we are the same. We live by our props. Without them he is a bully and a thug. Without mine, I am nothing but a gawky piece of Texas white trash. The difference between us is this: I'm wanting to live more than he's wanting me to die.

The weary man is suddenly animated. He screams, too, as he dances around us. The man on top of me twirls my sweater into his fist and pulls me off the ground. He cracks me across the jaw. My lip splits. The taste of my own blood makes me crazy. I beat at him. It is then I feel something bite into my palm. My car key is still in my hand. I have me a weapon and that means I have a chance.

Clawing at the grip on my throat with one hand, I work the key into position with the other. Viciously I drive it into my assailant's eye. Gore and blood covers my hand and splatters my face but I don't stop. I twist the key. And twist. And twist. His howls deafen me. His hands fly up as he throws himself away.

He is hurt.

I am free.

He rolls on the ground.

I am standing. The third man bends over the first.

I am gone.

I run for my life.

I fear what is ahead, but I fear what is behind me even more.

Fritz's Mountain Store
2:58 a.m.

Dove stopped off the road when he got to Fritz's Mountain Store and paused as he always did when he came upon a crime scene.

It wasn't just the uncertainty of what he would find that made Dove's heart beat faster, it was the hope that this call would bring him up against the man he intended to kill. But he knew if he met up with anyone tonight, it would probably be the person who murdered Fritz. No matter. Dove had a bullet waiting for him, too.

Pulling on the parking brake, Dove left his high beams shining as he got out of the car. He planted his feet hard on the ground and kept the door as a shield between him and whatever was out there.

Every lawman had a name for what came next. Dove called his settling the *feel* and the *notice*. The *feel* came first

— or at least it used to. He opened his mind, hoping to feel if someone was in the shadows, if there was still danger lurking about behind the building. In this instance, it took no special talent to know there wasn't a living soul inside that lit-up store. What worried Dove was that he wasn't picking up anything at all.

His eyes roamed the perimeter of the grounds. There could be someone hiding in the woods. A maniac might be crouched in that Range Rover parked to the right of the porch. Or, like the man Dove hunted, this monster might have simply gone away, pleased with his night's work.

Dove didn't know what to think anymore, he couldn't rely on that sixth sense of his. It had been shocked out of him, driven away.

Evil had been incomprehensible a year ago, now Dove took it for fact. He would be a fool not to admit there wasn't some fright in that. Still, it wasn't enough to scare him off so Dove closed the door of his patrol car, palmed the big flashlight shoulder high and kept the *notice* close as he walked out wide of Paddy's dilapidated pick-up. The truck was parked between him and the building. The inside light was on. The driver's door was open. Dove could just make out two feet on the ground. That didn't mean those feet belonged to Paddy. Could be a man waiting to kill again.

It was the man himself all right and he sat like he was contemplating something deep. His feet were spread apart, his hands were on his knees, his shoulders were sloped and his head hung between them. Paddy's dinner and the last three beers he had drunk were puddled on the ground in front of him.

"You doing okay, there, Paddy?" Dove's deep voice was velvet in the dark.

"Hell, no, Sheriff," Paddy muttered. A rope of spittle hung from his lower lip. Dove gave over a handkerchief.

"Okay. See anybody? Touch anything?"

Paddy shook his head and wiped his lips as Dove gave him the once over. The man flinched and swatted at the light in his eyes, but Dove kept it steady. There wasn't any blood on Paddy's hands or body. There was some on his shoes. That was to be expected if he had stumbled on the scene, unaware of what was underfoot. Paddy's clothes weren't torn. His hands weren't scratched up and neither was his face. His expression radiated shock not guilt. Dove swung that bright light into Paddy's truck. A shotgun was slung in the back of the cab.

"What are you shootin' there, Paddy?"

"Buckshot." He cut his eyes toward Dove. "And you don't need to be asking me if I killed Fritz. He was my friend. I thought he was yours. You could at least look sorry."

Stony-eyed, Dove listened. Used to be he would have showed some heart, but now Dove understood there was no real safety in his woods. Knowing that changed the way Dove lived; it would probably change the way he died.

"No need to question what I'm feeling. Best you be thanking your lucky stars you didn't show up any earlier or there'd be two of you lying in there," Dove reminded him. "So go on home, Paddy. Keep quiet, you hear? Least 'till I get to Bernadette."

Paddy nodded miserably as he climbed into the truck cab. Dove was already walking toward the store when Paddy stopped him.

"Sheriff? There was something. Ain't much. Just some back lights going over the ridge."

"Remember what they looked like?" Dove asked.

Paddy shook his head.

"Not now. Maybe later if I think hard. I just remember them riding real high. You know how you can get fooled up here. Coulda been someone driving right past the store instead of pulling out," he said miserably.

"You never know. If you can think how those lights were laid out I'd appreciate you getting back to me," Dove instructed.

Paddy was reaching for the door handle when he paused again. He thought twice about leaving the sheriff alone. Dove had made it pretty clear that being alone was what he preferred these days but you never knew if he was just shy about asking for some help.

There wasn't a man nor woman who didn't wonder what had got into him. It was like he was hungry for something there was never enough of; like he needed to rest but was afraid to stop moving. Dove's eyes went to strangers as if he wanted them to be trouble, even hoped they would be. Still, when a man found himself on a ledge that was just a little too narrow for his boots, he might need some help getting across the chasm. Lord knew Dove had done it often enough for others.

"Want me to come with you, Dove? It's hard to look at." Paddy was almost sorry he offered when he saw Dove's broad back tightened up. But when the sheriff looked over his shoulder he was his old self. There was even the hint of a grateful smile.

"Tim's on his way, Paddy. You go on home now. I'll see to Fritz."

Dove retraced his steps and closed the door of the truck. Paddy pulled out of the dirt lot and onto the road. He went slow, like a one-man funeral procession. Once he was gone, Dove took up the *notice* in earnest.

The earth was wet and soft with a spring cold, just solid enough for footprints to show clear. The snow that still remained was nothing more than dirty ice. Paddy's footprints went walking to the store and running back. The Range Rover tracks were even and straight. They came off the road and stopped near the porch just to the right of the front door.

To Dove's left were other tracks, the ones from Paddy's truck being the freshest. Underneath those were ones made by another car. That vehicle was heavy. The tires were set wide, deep treaded and not necessarily new. The car came in like it should, driving up tight to the side of the porch on the left. On the way out, though, it skidded before hitting the highway hard. Even from where he stood, Dove could see the mud and dirt and gravel kicked out, the rubber lay down on the pavement.

Careful not to step on the tire tracks, he went toward the building, his eyes still on the ground. He saw where the big car parked and noted two sets of footprints heading to the back of the store. It seemed one set came back the same way; another came out the front. The ones in front were messed up, unclear as if the person couldn't keep his balance. Drunk? Hurt? These were tracks made by men, of that he was sure.

Dove turned the light on the Range Rover and checked out the dealer plates. He shined the beam inside just long enough to see that it was empty. Stolen more than likely. Dove passed it by and traded his flashlight for his gun. There was a chance he was dead wrong about what was waiting.

Inside, though, all was quiet. The cash register was closed. The jerky packs hung on their hooks; the cigarettes were stacked nice in the niche beyond. Nobody had touched the candy. The shelves to his right seemed untouched. Dish detergent and Alpo, crackers and cereal were all neatly lined up. They would do inventory later when Bernadette was up to it. Dove could hear the hum of the refrigerator where the beer and soft drinks cooled. The ancient coffee maker percolated and that meant Fritz hadn't been dead long.

Dove moved on.

The first sign of blood was by the newsstand. He stepped down real careful, pausing at the doorway that led to the back room. With his arm against the door he leaned his head in and took a good look. There was the big freezer to the left and boxes piled up to the right in the back storeroom. On the floor between the two lay Fritz.

Lurching across the unfamiliar ground I stumble and fall against a tree. Breathless and cold, gulping air, I look for an easy way out. There is none so I fill my lungs and run faster, crashing through the forest, cutting and scraping and bruising myself. My shoulder is on fire but it is nothing compared to the pain those men will cause if they catch me.

I scramble up the hill, clutching the key tighter. The flesh from my attacker's face will be evidence in a court of law. I will see the one who touched me burn in hell because, if nothing else, I know I didn't ask for this. At the store I only wanted cigarettes; for some reason those men wanted me.

I go slower.

I must be cautious and smart.

I stop.

Like a prairie dog, my head goes up. It snaps this way and that. My nostrils quiver. I smell danger but I don't know where the stench is coming from. I try hard to see through the deep, deep dark but the moon is fickle. It comes in and out until I feel I'm in my own Grimm fairytale.

I make out shapes of trees and rocks — or am I wrong? Are those men standing still over there? Crouching down? Lying in wait? The forest has fallen quiet as if waiting to see what will happen next. Because of this extraordinary silence I believe I hear boots on loamy ground, hands carefully pushing aside branches. I think I can hear the tattooed man's good eye moving as he spies for me and the younger man whispering commands in that language I hadn't heard before tonight.

My breath is sharp when I take it in. I don't know how to let it out. I back step. My ears prick.

Bastards.

I hear a click and a crack.

Cowards.

I turn into a rustle and whirl around at the sound of a scrape.

The whimper is mine. The fight still flares but fear is smothering it and the flame is going out.

Things move around me. I'm found. They are here.

No! They are there behind the stand of saplings.

No, over near the old growth.

No, no. They are looking 'round the corner of that white-faced boulder that glints in the palest moonlight. Their voices come from above me and under me and beside me. But how? How could they be everywhere?

I start to run again but suddenly the earth gives way, crumbling beneath my weight. I fall like people do in dreams: slowly, lightly, my lips drawn into an 'O' of surprise. My arms lift, my hands reach for a branch, a rock, anything to break my fall. The dream stops as suddenly as it began.

I tumble fast; faster than I ever thought possible. I claw at the dirt to save myself but the world is slippery. Colors and shapes rise up and twist in my eyes like the turn of a kaleidoscope. Ten thousand wings beat the air as a flock of birds tries to pluck me up into the sky. They fly away without me. Gone over an ocean. The rush of waves can be heard and I believe I will be washed to a friendly shore. I can hear hope. I can taste it. But the sound of it is faint and the taste of it short-lived. It falls from my ears and my tongue as the wave pulls back, the birds fly on, the colors fade and I am left battered and broken.

The world snaps.

I am lost in black.

Fritz's Mountain Store
3:23 a.m.

The tremor that racked Dove was swift moving, cauterizing his insides all the way up to his heart. Better that he was dead to the *feel* because what he was looking at was a damned cold killing. Fritz had taken one good shot up close. His face was gone. One ear was intact, the other hung by a thread. A piece of jawbone stuck through the bottom of the chin.

The person who did this might have taken some pleasure in watching Fritz bleed out because it was obvious he hadn't run around in a panic. In fact, the shooter had leaned over the body. Dove could just make it out, a little lump of something in the blood. He would get it but he would not hurry. No sense making a mistake that could be used to the killer's advantage down the road.

Stretching further, he peered around the boxes. The back door was open and right there that was odd. Fritz wouldn't have left it that way and wasted heat. He could barely afford to keep this place going much less pay for Bernadette's woe off what he took in. The inside of the store was almost warm despite the door being open.

That brought Dove to wondering why Fritz hadn't closed up on time. Maybe the day just got away from him or maybe he had heard something and gone to investigate. Fritz could have opened the back door because he was expecting whoever had come. The coffee was fresh. Could a friend have done this thing?

Dove stayed quiet, wishing he could connect with whatever was left of Fritz. A glimpse of the truth was all he needed. Since there was only silence and the smell of death, Dove retraced his steps intending to go 'round back to the open door but the sound of a car pulling off the highway stopped him. His heartbeat fast, his body went taut. The butt of his gun was slick with the sweat off his hand yet fear was the furthest thing from his mind. What Dove felt was excitement and happy anticipation.

He wanted the killer to come back. He prayed for the chance to claim that pound of flesh.

Moving slowly, Dove listened for the sound of doors closing. He heard one slam. His wife's face flashed into his mind. The baby's cry sounded in his head. Fritz's voice was there, too. Dove ignored them all. Nothing would interfere with what he had to do if this was the time. But it wasn't the killer. Dove could see just enough to know that it was Tim Hoag's van parked near the road.

Holstering his weapon, Dove walked out onto the narrow porch and watched Tim gather the tools of his trade. He looked worn out, walking slow, hunched over under the weight of the body bag until he caught sight of Dove. That's when Tim put a spring in his step and called out like he was headed into town for a brew. Dove knew it was for his benefit that Tim put on the show.

"Coroner's a thankless job, Dove. Good thing it pays nothing or I'd be real disappointed."

Tim hoisted the unwieldy plastic bag over one thin shoulder to get a better grip. He squinted up at Dove even though he should have been able to see clear as day through those Coke-bottle lenses. In a few years the doc would be legally blind but for now, as he liked to say, he could see everything he needed to. From his pocket, Tim pulled out a pill bottle and shook it.

"You need a little something to calm you there, Dove? Been noticing you're a bit on edge lately and this thing tonight won't help you any."

Dove shook his head. The pills went back in the pocket of Tim's plaid jacket.

"You're in a better place than me then. I had to take a few, I can tell you." Tim lamented his weakness then perked up in a bid to stave off the inevitable. "You're probably too tired to get riled about anything what with the new baby and all. She being good, is she?"

Dove nodded again and turned his back. Tim kept talking.

"God, Dove, you're going to talk my ear off one of these days." Tim gave the sheriff's shoulder a neighborly punch as he stepped onto the porch. "Nothing like a baby in the house to make you feel old, huh, Dove? Well, you are an old cuss. Not Cherie, though. No, siree. How you ever got that beautiful young thing to take you on I'll never..."

"Doc, do you mind? Fritz is in there getting cold," Dove said, not wanting to make small talk.

"So he is. As we all will one day." The body bag slipped from his shoulder. He was holding his black doctoring kit tight in his hand. "I'm sorry, Dove. It's just an old man blathering. Something like this – so senseless, you know. I'll shut up and get to it. I'm thinking just the basics, Dove. I'll get a temperature. Give you a general report on the condition of the body."

"That's good. Nathan's on his way. You wait for him to give you the go ahead before you move Fritz, okay?" Dove instructed.

"You'll have no trouble from me. I have a great deal of respect for Nathan. Some people might not think he's worth his weight because he's self taught, but I can tell you, if reading your profession was good enough for Lincoln, then by George..."

Tim stopped without so much as a look from Dove. The need to hear himself talk even got on his nerves at times. He sighed deeply.

"Well, be that as it may," he said on the rewind. "I have a lot of faith in young Nathan's abilities. When he has all his pictures, I'll get Fritz over to the morgue in Jerome. Hate to take him so far, but it can't be helped."

"I don't think an autopsy is going to turn up any surprises. The way it looks, Fritz didn't have a minute to defend himself. Bag his hands anyway, just in case there's something to scrape."

"Happy to, Dove." Tim reached down for the body bag again.

"And go at him from the right. There's some stuff I want Nathan to pick up on the left." Dove clapped Tim on the back. "I'll get some evidence bags."

They parted ways: Tim inside the store, Dove heading outside. He never made it to his car because when he got close the Range Rover threw off something quick and powerful. It came at him like the smell of smoke in dry woods; a seductive whiff that made a man pay attention. Dove attended to it because a fire left on its own could destroy everything in its path. A controlled burn was something else. He didn't know which one this was so he went back to the car. Sadly, the *feel* left Dove as fast as it had come upon him. Still, he gave the car the once over.

The temporary registration taped to the side of the window told Dove that Jake Bradley of Bleden Town owned the car. Bleden Town was on the North Slope. Technically the community was in Dove's jurisdiction but there wasn't much call for his service. The people who lived there hired out their security, buried their indiscretions and shipped their troublemaking children off to cities as big as their problems. Dove figured if anyone in Bleden town wanted to blow the face off a poor grocer they'd hire that out, too.

He opened the passenger door and lighted up the interior. There was a woman's mink-lined jacket in the back and a book of matches on the passenger side floor. Two cigarette butts were in the ashtray. Between the front seats was a dual cup holder and in one section there was a Styrofoam cup with a Starbucks sleeve. In the gulp of coffee left in the bottom a butt floated like a tadpole in stagnant water. It was a different brand than the two in the ashtray. Before Dove could look closer, Nathan arrived and Dove abandoned his search.

"You made good time," he called as Nathan came to join him.

Though Nathan was of age, he seemed more a boy. It was in the awkward way he stood, the fragility of his body that seemed to sway under its own weight. Nathan's fingers were long and skinny as chicken bones, his nails bitten to the quick. Pale blue veins marbled his bisque colored skin. Those pond-water eyes of his were always wide open as if looking for monsters under the bed.

Now they had a monster and Nathan, curious, brilliant and self-taught in the ways of forensics, wasn't sure he wanted to look. His eyes sparkled in the shine of Dove's light. His white/blonde hair was stuffed under a woman's hairnet. He seemed paler than usual.

"You got all you need, Nathan?" Dove asked as soon as the boy came to a stop.

"I think so." He hiked the bulging bag in his hand and raised up on his toes. His eyes darted toward the store and back again. "Damn, Dove, there's a hell of a lot of tracks here. I don't have enough dental stone to cast 'em all. Is it okay if I take some paraffin out of the store if I need it? Or plaster if Fritz has it?"

"Take what you need. Just log it. Okay, let's go," Dove directed but Nathan hung back. Dove cocked his head, and he lowered his voice. "You ready, Nathan?"

"I'm not sure."

"You are. Don't worry."

Dove caught the young man's eye, dispensing some courage the way a priest gives penance: short and to the point. Nathan pulled up his chin and squared his skinny shoulders. He nodded once then followed Dove, chattering as they picked their way across the parking lot.

"Is it bad, Dove? I mean, I've never actually seen a murder in real life. Everyone knows I learn things from books and videos, and, well, this is Fritz. Whatever I do it will be important when we get to court. I'll have to talk about what I find. I could screw up. I could let Fritz down. I just don't know that I have what it takes."

Dove stopped short and swung the beam of his light at Nathan's feet. He had to be careful what he said to the boy or he'd lose him before they got started.

"Nathan, you're smart and you're careful. Because it's Fritz, you're going to do your job extra well. No question in my mind. You go ahead and own that, Nathan." Dove waited a beat for that to sink in before he told the rest of the truth. "Knowing you've got the courage in you, I won't lie. It's bad. Worse than anything you ever saw in a book and because it's Fritz. Understood?"

Nathan nodded and fell in step again, walking like a Lost Boy trudging off to a gruesome Neverland. When they reached the store, Dove shined the light on the back of the building. Nathan reached into his bag and took out a pair of latex gloves. He put them on with a snap, touched his hair net and pulled open the door. For a second he kept his eyes front and center. His lashes fluttered just before he looked down and saw Fritz.

Nathan threw himself back and out through the screen door. It slammed open hard then slammed back again. Frantically, he fumbled for a paper bag. Fast as Dove could turn the light to see what the boy was doing, Nathan buried his face inside the bag. He threw up with such force Dove thought the bottom was going to blow right out. The boy heaved three times, raised his head, and then buried it in the bag once more.

When he was done, Nathan held the sack of vomit in one hand and reached into the duffle with the other. Delicately he pulled out a tissue, patted his lips clean, folded the Kleenex and dabbed at his brow. Finally, he dropped it into the waste bag and turned the top down in three even folds.

"Sorry," he muttered.

"No need." Dove moved close enough to lay his hand on Nathan's skinny back. "Done it myself. I just wasn't so neat about it."

"Really?" Nathan set the package aside on the edge of the porch to collect later.

"No lie."

Dove stopped there. No need to talk about the last time, the worst time. Nathan blinked a time or two, ran his tongue over his teeth and changed to a new pair of gloves.

"Okay, I'm ready now…" He flashed a shaky smile only to have it fade when they heard a frantic call.

"Dove! Dove!"

Nathan started but Dove grasped his arm to keep him from running.

"It's just Tim."

"Yeah. Oh, yeah, I recognize his voice now. He sounds scared." Nathan breathed a sigh of relief mixed with concern. His hairnet had creeped up over one of his big ears.

"He's just excited. You start work and I'll see what Tim needs."

"Where in the hell are you, man?" Tim was standing in the doorway of the store just as Dove came round the front again. "There you are. Spooked me for sure thinking you left me here alone."

"I was putting Nathan to work. Are you alright?"

"I'm fine. I'm fine. But look."

Tim handed Dove a purse made of good leather and gold fittings. It was expensive and new, just like the car and the coat. A woman wouldn't leave any of it behind willingly.

"Where'd you find it?" Dove asked, opening it up.

"Just inside the door here."

Tim pointed as Dove looked inside the purse. He took out a wallet and unsnapped it. Even for Dove the silence that followed was deep so Tim got on his toes to see what the sheriff was looking at.

"She's a pretty one," the old man whistled reverently.

Dove ran his thumb over the picture as if to wipe away a haze that was keeping him from recognizing this woman. It didn't work. He knew her but couldn't place her even when he saw her name. Familiarity was deep in her eyes and evident only because the driver license picture was a raw one. Overexposure clear down to the soul. That's what you got with a government photo. Then it dawned on him that what he recognized was in those eyes of hers. It was pain. A deep hurt. Same as he carried.

Dove checked out her description: very tall, blonde, very thin. The address matched the car registration. Her name was Tessa Bradley. He lifted his eyes and gazed out toward the place where the vehicle with the wide-set tires had spun out. Then he followed the road north where Paddy had seen the disappearing backlights of a car. Finally, his eyes flicked over the unclear footprints just off the porch.

"You and Nathan take care of things here, Tim. I've got some people to wake up."

I blink my eyes open only to have them close again. I was dreaming about that time I was working in the Virgin Islands. Dressed in a Dior gown, I lounged under a striped tent that had been erected on the beach so I wouldn't get hot or tired. I waited on some prissy photographer to finish fooling with his camera. I waited on the sun to get to just the right place in the sky. I waited on some woman who was supposed to touch up my make up. Charlotte was beside me, young and unimpressed with any of this.

We hadn't spent more than a bucketful of days together since Jake had brought her to live with us. She made me nervous because I didn't understand her curiosity. I wasn't one to question what went on in life. Things were what they were. Yet, Charlotte, my child, was interested in things no self-respecting nine year old should be interested in: chemistry and bugs, politics and world peace. We didn't talk about the one thing she was interested in most — why she lived with me now after we had spent so many years apart.

If she asked I would have told her the truth. I tried to get her, failed miserably and gave up. Yep, I was a quitter. A scardy cat. You'd never guess it to look at me but I spent most of my life afraid of my mama and just about everyone else. It was Jake who managed the impossible. But that day she didn't care about the big picture. Charlotte wanted to know why shaved ice gave her brain freeze. I pretended I didn't hear because I felt stupid sitting there all decked out like the Empress of Nothing. Charlotte was better than me, smarter than me, more beautiful than me in ways that counted and she had brain freeze.

As I come to my senses, I realize that was a long ago day. Charlotte isn't here. I'm alone in a forest and the only frozen brain is mine. My head rests on a flat rock and that rock is awash in cold water. My long blond hair floats in it. When I move the pain in my head is so great sparkly starbursts pop behind my eyes.

I stay still, catching my breath. The night has passed and left behind an oppressive grey shell of a day. It is so odd that I can't put a time to it. Above me the forest is dense; the incline from which I fell is steep. I can't imagine how I survived but now that I have it's time to take inventory.

My legs feel light; my left arm feels like a horse has stamped on it. My car key is tight in my right hand. I manage to sit up. The pain takes a long time in settling. When it does I look around to see what's what.

Behind me the creek widens to a river. The forest across the way is no more inviting than it is on this side. I have no clue where I am but the good news is that people will be looking for me. My car is at that store. My purse is there. Those men are probably locked up already and have told the police where I am.

Yet, when I scoot my rear tight against a big rock, I see the truth. I am on my own and that's not looking like the best thing to be. My feet are swollen so I can't take my boots off. My wrist is purple and black, puffed-up big so that the diamond bracelet of my watch cuts into the skin. The crystal is shattered; the hands stopped at two forty. I can't bring myself to take it off even though I should. This watch was the first thing I bought that wasn't necessary just to survive. I will keep it a while longer to remind me that good things come to those who survive.

I find a dollar and a lipstick in my front pocket, my cell phone is in the back one. I hope to see the little reception symbol lit up like a Christmas tree but the screen is dark, the battery dead. This little lifesaver – the best money can buy or technology can provide – is nothing but a hunk of metal. I hide my despair behind disappointment because that makes despair manageable.

It takes me a few tries to stand. I test my legs, working them a little, forcing myself to agree with the pain and to find my balance. When I am steady as I can be, I listen for one of two sounds: those men or civilization. I hear neither. Then it dawns on me that I hear absolutely nothing: no wind in the trees, no babble from the stream, no birds singing. I don't hear the tap of a woodpecker or the skritch of a squirrel skipping across the ground and up a tree. Even my own breathing is swallowed up by stillness and that scares me. I have to get out of here, find someone, and find help.

Pulling the wet collar of my sweater higher I weigh my cell phone in the palm of my hand. With a twinge of regret, I wedge it between the rocks and painstakingly paint an arrow on the dark screen with my lipstick. The arrow points downstream. If the bad guys find it I will deal with them; if the good guys get to it first they will know I haven't given up and they won't either.

That done, I find a stout branch to be my crutch. I bend down as best I can and kiss the top of that cell phone. A kiss for luck. I am leaving behind something of mine and it is harder than I thought it would be. Finally, I start to walk. I wish I could say each step is easier to take than the last, but it isn't that way at all.

Bernadette's House
4:30 a.m.

Dove's woman, Cherie, was waiting out front of Fritz's house as he had asked her to be. She stood with one arm draped around the porch post, leaning against it, gazing at nothing in particular. Her blond hair, red-tinged and braided, fell to the middle of her back. Her fair skin was peppered with freckles and Dove believed he could see each one of those little spots the minute he caught sight of her. He couldn't, of course. No one could until they got close. It was just that Dove carried every inch of Cherie in his mind's eye: those freckles, her dark eyes, those wide full lips, her heart-shaped face.

When she heard the car, Cherie pushed herself off the post and tracked him in. She greeted him solemnly the way she had the day they met.

That day her father had near cut off his leg with a chain saw. The old man bled to death before help could come. Cherie handled herself well; impressing Dove like no woman had impressed him before. She was tiny but strong, sexy but modest. Her grief was private. The day of the funeral Dove charged her not to blame herself for her father's death.

"It was meant to be," she answered in a voice that sounded as if she was comforting him.

Cherie repeated that phrase when they took their vows but that time there was a smile on her face. Her east coast schooling was forgotten as easily as the ten years between them. Everything according to Cherie happened as it was meant to be. Hard to imagine that was the case with Fritz, though.

"Hey, Dove." They took hold of one another. Dove buried his lips in her hair.

"Does she know?" he asked.

"Not unless someone called before I got here." Cherie pulled away, leaving her arm wrapped around her husband's waist as they walked toward the cabin. "I put the baby to sleep in the back room, Dove. I thought we might be staying awhile."

"That would be good, if you can manage."

Dove let his wife go. He took his hat off then put it on again. There was no comfortable way to be in a situation like this. He reached for the doorknob. Cherie put her hand over his.

"I'm so sorry, Dove. I know Fritz was a true friend. I'll miss him, too, but I understand what he meant to you."

Dove took comfort in the feel of her small hand on his big one. He kissed her, appreciating the sentiment that needed no comment. He opened the door for her but Cherie let him go first. She closed it softly behind her.

Dove whispered, "Will you wake Berna…"

"No, need, Dove."

Together Cherie and Dove turned. Fritz's wife, Bernadette, stood in the bedroom doorway. There was so little of her these days she could have been a shadow on the wall. Dove barely noticed the dark sweat suit she wore or the black cotton scarf on her head. All he could see was the glitter of her eyes. It looked like the brightness of fever but it was just life taking its sweet time burning out. Her sickness was horrible, the news to come more horrible still.

"Fritz isn't coming home, is he, Dove?" she asked weakly.

"No, Bernadette, he isn't."

"How?"

"Shot," Dove answered honestly. "Probably a robbery, Bernadette."

He held her gaze out of respect for the strong woman she was. It was hard as anything he had ever done. Bernadette seemed to be considering Dove's speculation. Finally, she spoke.

"Well, then. I guess this is a blessing since he never could stand to see me suffer. Now he won't have to watch. Yes, I suppose that's what this is. A blessing..."

Her thoughts feathered into a sigh and her head seemed heavy with the news. She rested it against the doorframe then faded away into the darkened room she and Fritz used to share. There was nothing there for her now. All the things that kept her alive were in the living room: the hospital bed and IV, the pills and the monitors. Dove and Cherie stood side-by-side, looking at the empty space where Bernadette had been. Then the baby began to cry.

"I'll get her," Cherie said quietly.

"I have to go," Dove answered and that gave Cherie pause.

"You should hold her, Dove. Just for a minute. She needs you to do that. She feels the sorrow, too, even if she's so little."

Dove's eyes flickered toward the sound. Cherie waited as something ugly crackled off her husband. He caught it back before she could say anything. Dove put his hand on her shoulder and leaned down to kiss her cheek.

"I have to go. There are other people to see. It's my job."

He left Cherie to Bernadette and the baby. He hadn't lied; there was another family to see. The news wouldn't be as bad as it was for Bernadette but it sure as hell wouldn't be good. The baby would have to wait. There was just so much grief Dove could take in one day.

Jake Bradley's Lodge
5:20 a.m.

Dove drove to Bleden town with the lights on, the siren off. He arrived at the rich man's house with the pink blush of dawn. The big lodge materialized through curtains of leaves, underscores of branches and dense walls of holly.

It was made of logs the size of ten men around and showcased whole walls of thick, clear glass. The front door window was stained in forest colors. Three stone chimneys punctured the slate roof. Soft lights on the eaves illuminated bits and pieces of an impressive deck that wrapped around the house like a shameless woman: naked wood, sensual curves, it begged to be walked on.

Dove didn't particularly want to be a rich man but that didn't stop him from appreciating the things rich bought. That feeling was gone by the time he took the first slate step that led to the front door. Sorrow was sorrow, he decided, no matter where it squatted and money didn't mean caution wasn't called for. A man was dead, a woman missing. It all could have started here so Dove kept his eyes open.

He was shoulder high to the edge of the deck when he paused, aware that he was being watched. Slowly he checked out the deck, finding the watcher far back, pulled into a chair, huddled under a blanket. When Dove didn't move and his gaze didn't waiver, that person got up. It was a woman and, even though she was covered head to toe in a blanket, Dove Connelly recognized her. It was Tessa Bradley, not missing at all but safe at home. He started to smile, almost voiced his relief and then Dove saw his mistake as the blanket slipped from the woman's head.

Her hair was short, dark and curly, not long and blond. This woman wore flannel, not mink. She came at Dove sure footed and silent. Her shoulders were back, her spine straight. She stopped at the rail and looked down on him.

"Is she dead or what? My mother, I mean."

When Charlotte was three my mama told her that I was dead.

My mother might as well have let me have it square in the head with a shovel when she gave me the news. The only reason I went away, the reason I worked my butt off and sent money back home was for Charlotte. But mama said the baby didn't know who I was from one visit to the next, what with me looking so different every time I came back. Besides, my mama said, it was her doin' all the work. Her changing diapers and feeding the baby and listening to her cry. She was the mama, really.

I was mad as hell when she said that, but I was also still a kid. I did what other people said I should do: mama who bore me, Simon who said he loved me and Peter who promised he could make my life better. I was just supposed to walk the road; they would tell me when I got to where I should be. According to my mama, my road led me away from Charlotte.

Now I've reached the end of this road I'm walking and I feel like a kid again: breathless and distrustful of my instincts. What if I make the wrong choice and do more harm than good? I did that with Charlotte; I can't afford to do it again. Especially here. Especially now. It is my life in the balance. If I don't make the right choice now I will never get back to Charlotte. I will never be able to explain the bad choice I made before.

My stomach gurgles. My shoulders are so heavy they sag low. Like Aunt Ruby's boobs, I figure they'll never get back up where they belong. I stop and rub the one that hurts. That doesn't make it feel any better, but it's no worse either. It is a waste of time to fret about years gone by. Things I didn't do. Things I should have done.

I catch some dry snow on the tip of my tongue. I listen for the drone of a plane, the growl of an off-road vehicle, the sound of dogs barking as they pick up my scent. I hear none of these things. That makes me sad. Is no one looking for me?

The creek has played out. Since it's a crap shoot which way to go, I choose the prettiest. To my right the trees grow to a canopy of yellow/gold leaves on one side and white on the other. The branches move so the leaves twirl and flutter like fairy wings. I half expect to see little fairy faces looking down on me as I get close to these magical trees.

I walk under this canopy like a princess bride wishing Jake and Charlotte were here to see this. Charlotte would name the trees before she turned her camera on them; Jake would draw a face on one and pen an oh-to-the-sharpest-point caption about root-bound politicians thinking gold grew on trees. They are so smart, the two of them.

Impulsively, I reach up and snap a small branch feathered with golden leaves. I put it in my pocket intending to press it in a book and give it to Charlotte so she will know I understood her for a minute.

I push my hair back. My neck hurts. I'm exhausted and anger comes out of nowhere. Suddenly, I blame Jake and Charlotte for my circumstances because it feels better to blame someone. Funny how fast the heart turns when it's left to its own devices.

One more step. Two.

A flurry blows up. I turn my head and close my eyes. When I open them again I am like Dorothy transported to Oz by a tornado of snow. Right in front of me is an opening in the mountain. At first I think it's a mirage, but it's not. Timber is stuck at right angles in the ground and another one is set like a keystone above a door. In the next second my walking stick becomes a divining rod that drags me forward. I have a big smile on my face because I am positive I am saved.

"Hey y'all! Hello!"

Ridiculously, I call out as if I expect someone to answer. No one does, of course. I trip and sprawl across the entry. That shuts me up fast. I roll to my side and onto my back, holding my poor hurt leg. The snow has turned to tiny hail. It hits my face like a good slap from a bad friend so I don't stay down.

When I'm standing again I see it is railroad tracks that have tripped me up. The rails are bent; the ties are split. They are too narrow for a big train and they run into the mountain, not away.

It's a sign if there ever was one. There have been others before me, others who might be coming back. Hefting my stick up I hobble forward, grateful for the shelter even as I am troubled by the dark that engulfs me.

Outside the Bradley Lodge
5:26 a.m.

"You're Tessa Bradley's daughter?"

35

"You can't tell? You must be the only one on this earth who can't."

The woman misunderstood Dove's surprise. It wasn't the way she looked that took him aback; it was the fact that there couldn't be more than fifteen or sixteen years between the two women.

"Is Mr. Bradley home?" he asked, taking in her red-rimmed eyes, the angry twitch at the corner of her lips.

"Inside. He's worried sick." Dove tipped his fingers to his hat, meaning to go on to the front door but she mirrored his steps and slowed him down with her talk. "I think it would be better if you told me first. Whatever news you have, I should hear it first. I'll know how to help him then."

"It would be best if I speak to the both of you at the same time," Dove answered, noting that she was counting on the news being bad. In fact, it seemed she would welcome bad news. Dove thought this was a strange thing for the woman to feel about her mother.

"Please, just say it. She must be dead. Why else would a uniformed cop come here?" Charlotte kept moving along with Dove. Nervous energy flew off her like water off a shaking dog. "What did she do, sheriff? Drive off a cliff? Oh, God, did she hurt someone else? How selfish…"

"Charlotte!" A man's call silenced her.

The woman jolted. Her shoulders pulled back, her chin cocked up like a pure bred on a choke chain. She colored high on her cheeks but she wasn't deterred. Her eyes narrowed and became hard as flint.

"She was selfish," the woman insisted. *"Leaving all night. Never calling. Letting you…"*

"We'll worry about what your mother is or is not later." He *walked part way across the deck. Charlotte looked over her shoulder and followed his progress with hungry eyes. She stepped back to let him pass then closed tight in against his shoulder. The man was pale and tired looking. "I'm Jake Bradley, Sheriff. You have news about my wife?"*

"The owner of Fritz's Mountain Store is dead from a gun shot blast." Dove paused. The news of Fritz's death meant nothing to either of these people. It was to be expected, he imagined, they were waiting for the other shoe to drop. They were waiting to hear if Tessa Bradley was dead, too. Dove had no choice except to go straight on. "Your car is in front of the store. Your wife's purse was left in the front seat. She's missing."

"Missing," Jake Bradley whispered just as his knees buckled and Charlotte Bradley rushed to catch him.

Inside Jake Bradley's Lodge
<u>5:43 a.m.</u>

Exquisite rugs covered the bare wood floors of Jake Bradley's house. They were Navajo and they were old. Dove knew that because there was Navajo blood in him. It showed in the cut of his cheekbones and nose, in the red/brown of his skin. There were other things in his blood, too. They were reflected in the lightness of his eyes and the softening of his chin, the slight bit of gold in the near-black hair he wore long. Indian, though, was the thing people saw and they tried to make it most important to him. It wasn't and never would be. A man didn't define himself by qualities he had no control over.

Still, the rugs were beautiful and Dove appreciated them. Jake Bradley noticed nothing as he hurried through the house and up a staircase. When Dove got to the studio on the second floor Jake was already rummaging through his desk. He was dressed in casual clothes. Expensive leather moccasins, a big sweater made of cashmere that he had thrown over a fine cotton shirt. His slacks were pressed. Fine wool if Dove had to guess.

Charlotte had settled near the drawing table. She had left the blanket behind and Dove saw she dressed as plain as she talked: a worn flannel shirt, a T-shirt under that, jeans and hiking boots that weren't just for show. She was a beautiful woman in workingman's clothes. Dove stood square in the middle of the room and figured out real fast who he was dealing with.

Jake Bradley: syndicated political cartoonist, satirist, and conscience of the country. Wasn't a day went by that Dove didn't take a look at this man's work and admire the clarity with which he viewed the world; the brevity, objectivity and sharpness with which he commented on it. It had crossed his mind that a man like Jake Bradley could explain what had happened to Dove and his family and set his mind at rest. Now Dove wasn't so sure.

It wasn't just that he was older than Dove would have thought; it was that Jake Bradley was fretful, fearful, strangely aggressive and timid all at the same time. Dove took into account that he had just been told of his wife's disappearance. That kind of news could cut a man down real fast, didn't he know, so Dove reserved judgment.

"Here they are, Sheriff. Forty of them. Here." Jake spun smoothly on the tiny wheels of his well-worn office chair. His hands were full of envelopes: big and small, white and colored. In his haste to help, he lost his grip and they scattered across his lap and onto the floor. Charlotte fell to her knees and collected them.

"God, this is a nightmare. I never thought it would come to this," Jake fretted.

Charlotte handed Dove a stack of envelopes then went in search of those under the drawing table. A few were still clutched tightly in Jake's hands but Dove had enough to work with. He opened one and scanned it. Then another and another before he read aloud.

"You are not God's creature. To spread lies and untruths thru the use of commentary. I shall cut off your fingers and your hands. Stop. Vile untruths…" Dove put that one aside. "You are worse against a fine woman who serves this grate country. Stop now or I take your head from…" Dove paused and looked away from the letters. "Scary stuff, Mr. Bradley. I'd say you've got an enemy."

"So much hate. For what? An opinion? A cartoon?" Jake lamented. One hand went to his face and his fingers pressed into his mouth before he spoke again. "Usually I disregard the mail. But I couldn't ignore these – these vile, hateful things. I never thought he'd find us here."

"He didn't find you here." Dove held up an envelope. It bore an east coast address. Jake waved away the implication.

"People write to my syndicate in New York and they forward the letters," Jake explained. "That doesn't mean he isn't here, in California, or just across the border in Oregon. Those letters are why we left New York. We literally fled."

"How long ago was that?"

Dove scanned the precisely folded paper as he talked. It was plain, wide ruled and torn from a spiral binder. The handwriting was unique, defined and purposeful. Some included bold, graffiti-like doodles. All the while, Dove was aware of Charlotte Bradley's cool scrutiny.

"Two years." Jake inched forward in his chair. "Look at how they are written. See how some of the words are misspelled; some are out of context. It's as if English is a second language. There's no specific motivational thread. Sometimes it seems as if there are religious overtones, sometimes the person is just mad that I exist."

"Is the threat always specific to you?"

"They never mention Tessa specifically, if that's what you mean."

Jake handed off his letters to Dove and shot out of his chair. Unable to sit still, he paced. Dove pulled out two more.

"The return address on these is in a town on the California/Oregon border. Not more than three hours from here."

"They come from all over the country." Charlotte interrupted as she pointed to the letters. "That paper can be bought in any Wal-Mart. It's the same with the envelopes. The FBI doesn't even test them anymore. They told us to call if something changes." Those eyes of hers lay boldly on Dove. "I'd say something has changed, wouldn't you?"

"Yes, ma'am." Dove held Charlotte's gaze briefly. When she didn't back down he asked, "Why didn't you call my office when Mrs. Bradley didn't come home last night?"

"Sometimes my wife needs to be alone. She . ." Jake began.

"My mother doesn't tell us about her business." Charlotte interjected.

"Tessa is independent." Jake corrected.

"Do you know if your wife ever visited this town?" Dove indicated the envelope again.

"She's been all over the world. She probably doesn't remember half the places she's been," Charlotte answered again.

"Have the letters been coming with more regularity since you moved up here?" Dove had his notebook out and his pen at the ready.

"No. There is no real pattern," Jake answered. Dove looked to Charlotte for confirmation.

"I don't know. I live in Sedona. He wouldn't have told me, anyway." She nodded at Jake Bradley. "He never wants to worry me."

Jake was close enough to grasp her hand and pull it to his lips without thought for Dove. There wasn't a whole lot of room between those two for Tessa Bradley to squeeze into. Dove figured it was that way in some families. This situation seemed odd, though. Charlotte Bradley wasn't his idea of daddy's little girl.

"What about friends?" Dove asked.

Charlotte shot him an annoyed look as she got up off the floor to busy herself at the desk in the corner of the room.

"She knew the tradespeople here but there were no friends to speak of. Her work was in New York. She had friends there, of course," Jake said.

"The man who died, Sheriff. Was he young?" Charlotte asked suddenly.

"Thirty-four."

"What did he look like?" Casually, she looked over her shoulder with those sharp eyes of hers. She snapped a rubber band around her fingers.

"Ordinary. His wife is sick. He was a good friend," Dove responded.

Charlotte raised her chin slightly, as if to let him know she found him naive. Dove took exception to that. In fact, Dove took exception to Charlotte Bradley.

"Did he have children, Sheriff?" Jake asked.

"No, sir. He didn't.

"A small blessing." Jake muttered. "What happens now? What can we do to get Tessa back? How can we find her?"

"I need phone bills to start. Land line and cell phones. I'd like Mrs. Bradley's and both of yours."

"Mine won't help. I don't live here. Remember?" Charlotte drawled. She seemed to have decided that Dove needed to be put in his place. What she didn't realize was that he was already in it.

"My memory is good, ma'am. But your mother might have used your phone or called you from somewhere that can help us. Unless you have a valid objection, I'd like to have your phone records."

Charlotte was about to object when Jake overruled her.

"Of course, Sheriff. Charlotte? Your mother's and mine are in the downstairs office filing cabinet." Jake looked at Dove. "How far back do you want them?"

"Three months is a place to start. And I'd like to have a picture of her. Something not so fancy as these." Dove indicated the stunning pictures of the missing woman that seemed to fill every inch of her husband's office. He had never seen so many pictures of one person in such a small space.

"I'll find one." Charlotte left the room without a backward glance. Dove waited until he could no longer hear her footsteps then he got down to business.

"Mr. Bradley, I'm not discounting what's in these letters, but I need to look close to home, too. Is there anything that could connect the owner of the grocer and your wife?" Dove asked.

"No. I'm positive of that. Nothing," Jake insisted.

"Have either of you seen any strangers here? Any unusual traffic coming up your road? Maybe someone around by the river out back?"

"Not that I'm aware of."

"Would your wife have told you if she had?"

"She would have taken care of it herself. Tessa wasn't afraid of anything. Naturally, that could be a good thing, considering. I mean, whatever happened to her Tessa will keep her wits about her. You can be sure of that."

Jake ran a hand through his graying hair. He pulled his lips together until they very nearly disappeared. Deep lines cut from his nose to the corner of his mouth. His forehead was high and his hair thick. There was a modernity about him, a cutting -edge intelligence about his appearance that made him look wise in pictures. This morning it all added up to old and tired. Dove would not have imagined this man married to a woman who looked like Tessa Bradley. Yet she had chosen him and that left

Dove to wonder if Jake Bradley was special, lucky or had been played for a fool.

"Did you fight with your wife, Mr. Bradley?" Dove's pen was poised so that he could look at the man when that question was asked.

"No." Jake answered too quickly, colored too fast. He was not a good liar and sure enough Dove's silence drove him to elaborate. "I meant we didn't fight last night. We've been going through a rough patch because of this move. Considering who she was and what she did, this place must have felt like prison."

"What kind of work does your wife do?"

"You're joking, aren't you?" Jake swung his head and cut Dove Connelly down with a serrated look of disdain and superiority. Before that look could slice Dove up, the other man's expression gave way to astonishment, awareness and regret.

"I apologize. My reaction was uncalled for. I thought everyone knew who Tessa was."

Dove noted the use of past tense again. He filed it away with all the other information: wealth, notoriety, outside threats, inside dysfunction, a daughter who preferred to be her father's close friend and her mother's enemy.

"I still need to know," he insisted.

"My wife was one of the highest paid fashion models in the world. She couldn't go anywhere without causing a fuss," Jake answered. "My wife is so famous she is only known by her first name in half the world."

Dove nodded. He obviously lived in the other half that didn't know her from Adam. It was to be expected.

There wasn't much call for fancy clothes or fashion models up this way.

"So maybe someone set this up to get her out of the business?" he suggested.

"Professional jealousy?" Jake laughed sadly and shook his head. "Maybe ten years ago but not now. Her career was essentially over. I thought being away from New York would give her some clarity. It didn't and we fought about it."

"I'm surprised she couldn't get work."

Dove raised his pen, indicating the pictures. Jake's eyes followed. He waved away Dove's comment with a bitter gesture. Then he thought again and picked up a photo in a filigree frame. He held it out for Dove to admire but when the sheriff put out his hand to take it, Jake moved back. Look, don't touch. Dove followed the rules.

"That's what she looked like in her prime. A modern day Grace Kelly." Jake Bradley's eyes softened as he remembered the old days. He was lost in them for a moment then brought himself back to what he considered an ugly present. "She's forty-six now and Vogue wants twelve-year-old children who look like they bobbed up from the bottom of the melting pot. Nobody recognizes quality like Tessa's anymore. They call her for spreads that appeal to women of a certain age. Such a waste."

Jake ran his fingers around the frame, lost in thought even though he continued speaking.

"Anyway, about a month ago Tessa got so moody I thought she had hit bottom and was regrouping. I realize now she was depressed. Her spirit was broken. It's awful to watch a beautiful woman suffer."

Dove flinched. Cherie came to mind but he wasn't inclined to compare notes and neither was Jake Bradley. He swiveled toward the windows and stared out toward the trees for a long while. Then, slowly, he looked over his shoulder, raised an eyebrow and floated an idea.

"Sheriff, what if Tessa staged this? Her abduction, I mean. What if something went wrong but all this was really just an innocent bid for attention?"

"If she did that, sir, your wife better pray I don't find her," Dove answered.

Jake Bradley's eyes went flat, closing off any chance Dove had to read what was in them.

"You're right, of course. It would be unconscionable. A man is dead. Speculation isn't the way to help, is it? Action is what we need. I'll come with you. I want to look for Tessa." Jake started to rise only to have Dove stop him.

"My boys are out, Mr. Bradley. They know this mountain. You look around here. She might have left some clues about where she's been driving out to. Look for business cards, match books..."

"Tessa doesn't smoke. She quit years ago," he said quickly. Dove almost smiled. Small things could be so telling.

"Collect anything you think is important." Dove put his card on the drawing table, not ready to discuss what was found in Mrs. Bradley's car. "Call some of those New York people. Maybe they know what's been on her mind. I'd also like the name of your contact at the FBI." When Jake hesitated, Dove insisted. "Sir? I need the name of your contact."

"I haven't talked to the FBI for a very long time," Jake said. "They won't know anything."

"The last name you have is fine. I'll take it from there," Dove assured him.

"Alright, then. Brian Drake. He's in the Oregon office," Jake said, only to add: "I'm sure he's long gone, though."

"Guess we'll see." Dove was almost done. He put a hand on the stack of letters. "What makes you think a man wrote these?"

Jake's eyes widened, "I just assumed. We always talked about 'he' – the FBI and me. I suppose a woman could have written them. I just never thought about it."

"Okay, then, I'll call if I hear anything."

Dove turned to leave but Jake stopped him.

"Sheriff? Tessa. She's very special."

"So was the grocer," Dove countered. "And I mean to treat them equal."

He was on the stairs when he heard Jake Bradley call out once more, his voice faint and already sounding hopeless.

"One way or the other, bring her home."

Dove didn't stop. He hadn't heard anything that needed answering so he walked through the lodge without a look at any of the fine things. No more than twenty minutes had passed and he was back on those slate steps. As he left the house behind he saw Charlotte Bradley waiting in front of him. She watched him come, making no move to meet him half way.

"Here. The phone bills and a picture. The picture was taken the summer my parents moved up here. We went into town for that Fourth of July parade."

She shoved a manila envelope at him when he was close enough to take it. Inside was a family photo: Tessa Bradley without make-up, smiling, leaning over her husband's shoulder. Charlotte grinned while Jake bear hugged her from behind, his arm across her throat; her hand holding tight to his arm. Jake Bradley could have been husband or father to both of them.

"It's a nice picture," Dove noted. "Who took it?"

"The man from the feed store in Bleden," Charlotte moved so she could look over his shoulder. "Tessa looked so happy then."

"You all did," Dove said.

"I thought we were." There was regret in her voice. Charlotte Bradley had some feelings for her mother after all.

"I'll get it back to you." Dove put the picture back in the envelope. When she didn't move Dove lowered his voice and spoke plainly. "I don't have time to guess what's on your mind, ma'am."

"I don't want him to know." Charlotte cocked head toward the house.

"You'd best be worrying about your mother first."

Charlotte flushed. Her chest rose and fell. Still she didn't speak. With no time to waste, Dove stepped around her. Charlotte Bradley pirouetted and put her hand on his arm.

"Alright. Okay. Someone has been coming here. A man."

"A friend of yours?" Dove asked. Charlotte shook her head as she bowed it.

"A friend of my mother's."

I was at my lowest when Simon Hart came upon me in Corallis. He said:

"Tessa?" He stopped like he'd seen a ghost. In a way I was. I had died and come back as someone else. Then that smile just broke through like the sun and Simon said: "Hot damn, Tessa. What happened to you?"

I smiled. I probably blushed. He looked at me like I was his favorite candy and he sounded like he wanted to know everything. So I told Simon about Peter Wolfson, a New York photographer who found me clerking at Dollar-Rent-A-Car.

A mother for a year already, tired to the bone, I was in no mood for the fancy, trash-talking man who rolled in late one night. He wanted a fancy SUV and we didn't have one. The kid at the desk did his best to explain we only had so many SUVs, but Peter went nuts. He yelled and screamed but when Peter called the desk boy a lazy fat ass, something inside me snapped. I told him to apologize or I'd come over the counter and kick his butt.

You would have thought I flashed the Pope the way Peter reacted. The poor, fat, stupid boy I worked with backed up so fast I figured he'd go through the wall. The little girl assistant who followed Peter around like a scared puppy nearly fainted. Peter, though, wanted to fight and that's when I really got pissed off.

"You little bitch," he said. "I want to see the manager."

So I answered, "That would be me."

It was a lie but the manager was out having a bang with the woman from the restaurant two doors down. I didn't care what would happen to me if anyone found out I'd misrepresented myself. I just didn't want him abusing the fat boy again. Then I told him, "You're using up more of my time than I like. Now, you want this Saturn compact or you want to walk wherever you've got to get to?"

The girl assistant, my chubby mate and me, we all waited on him. I think I was the only one breathing. He decided he wasn't going to fight us all and finally threw in the towel.

"I'll take the Saturn."

I punched a few buttons on the computer.

"Thank you," I snapped.

"You're welcome." He said that like he was spitting on me.

I raised my baby blues. I looked right at him. I dangled the keys to that Saturn from my fingers.

"I meant you should say thank you."

He didn't, but it was enough that everyone heard me. When it was over, I went back to the break room, put my feet up, wished my breasts weren't so full of milk, lay my head back and wondered if things would ever get better.

Peter came back for me a week later. I left my parents, that miserable town and my baby behind. I was going to be someone. When I was, I would come back for my Charlotte. I'd give her the world.

I asked if Simon ever thought of coming back for me. But he only laughed sweetly. Or it seemed sweet to me right then. He asked me if I had a kiss for an old friend and — since it looked like I was doing good — could I see my way to buy him lunch and some cigarettes. I only heard him ask for a kiss. I gave it to him. My eyes were closed. My lips met his cheek. I breathed him in.

I was a girl again.

I'm thinking about those times to remind me that everyone takes advantage of an opportunity including me. Behind me, the snow falls in earnest and the wind kicks up to point out that I'm not doing much with the opportunity I have at hand. I need to go deeper into the mine to get warm so I use the smooth wall of the tunnel to guide me.

Eventually, after what seems like forever, the narrow passage opens up to a big room. Light must come in through fissures in the rock because I see a little better in here. What I see makes me hopeful.

A pick ax rests against one wall. On the ground next to it is a drill. The pick ax is sharp and heavy; the drill is an old hand tool. A wooden cart sits upright on the tracks that were laid to this point and no further. I'd like to crawl inside and roll home but this thing isn't going anywhere so neither am I.

My knees give out before I have time to feel sorry for myself. I clutch the cart to keep from falling. When it moves the back wheels catch on something soft. I'm on the ground in the next second with my hand under the cart, searching for whatever it is. When I find it, I scramble backward, hiding in the corner as if I am afraid someone will take it from me.

It is a rucksack; a treasure.

Old, dirty and dun colored, the flap is held in place with small, rusted buckles. My fingers hurt so bad I'm sure I'll never get them open. Finally, one comes loose. Then the other is undone, too. I half expect to see Genie smoke come out. If it does, I'm ready with my wishes: keep me safe, get me out of here, get me home.

Since there is no Genie, I settle for what I find: a box with three matches, a piece of paper that can't be read because of the gloom. I push the sack from the bottom and feel from the top but there is nothing more. I am crushed but what did I expect? Resting my head against the rock, I close my eyes and count my blessings: I am alive and I am sheltered.

When I open them again I am rewarded for my attitude adjustment. Hanging high up on a hook above me is a good old-fashioned lantern. I stand up. I take that stick of mine and poke at that lantern 'till it falls. When it does I scoot around, whooping like a dog in a field of gophers. I look for cracks in the globe. There are none. I give the lantern a shake. I hear the slosh of fuel. I smell the kerosene. I twist the scorched wick up. I dig for those matches in my sack.

I'm in business.

Outside the Bradley's Lodge
7:02 a.m.

"I knew she wasn't happy here, but an affair with some mountain man? I thought Tessa had some standards."

Charlotte sat heavily on the bumper of Dove's big car. Ignorant of her insult, she planted her feet, clasped her hands and was all business as she gave her opinion of her mother.

"What do you know about him?" Dove asked.

She shook her head. "We didn't talk about it."

"So she didn't specifically say she was having an affair?"

Charlotte's eyes snapped up at the sound of the sliding glass door opening. Dove positioned himself between the house and the woman, cutting Jake Bradley off from her line of sight, annoying Charlotte.

"No. I just said she didn't talk about it. Besides, she didn't have to." Charlotte shrugged. "Tessa was beautiful and he was a man. Certain things came easy for Tessa."

"So she didn't try to explain where she'd been or cover up to keep you from speculating?"

"Tessa?" Charlotte barked a laugh. "She never explains anything, especially to me. I used to ask her questions all the time just to get her to talk to me when I was a kid.

She'd just sit there like she didn't hear me. I wasn't even sure she liked me."

"And now?"

Dove looped his thumb at his belt and gave a quick look to the deck. He didn't see Jake Bradley but he had an idea he was lurking there, just behind the big doors. Still, he gave his full attention to Charlotte.

"Sometimes I'm scared that I'm like her. But I'm really not." She sat up straight, her balled fists rested on her knees. "I would never, ever cheat on him. Tessa didn't know what a good thing she had."

"Do you always call your mother by her first name?"

"Your provincial is showing, Sheriff." Charlotte flashed an honest smile showing Dove a softer, prettier face.

"Maybe your mother had car trouble and this man gave her a hitch," Dove suggested.

"You've seen her car. It was new. Besides, she stayed in after that and drove her car the next morning. No, he picked her up and she knew him – hard as it is to believe." Charlotte's mouth twisted cruelly. "This guy was raunchy, Sheriff. Not like a rocker or one of Tessa's fashion groupies. You know how they can look – they work at looking down and out. Chic grunge. But this one was real poor. In the city I would have thought he was homeless. He got out of the car and chased after her a little. Then she turned around. One damn look from her stopped him cold."

Charlotte snapped her fingers before letting them fall to her lips. Long and graceful, they rested there as she mused.

"You've never seen a woman like my mother, Sheriff. She can stop an elephant in its tracks with that look. This guy didn't have a chance. He just stood there with his mouth open and watched her leave." Charlotte dropped her hand. "I wish I could control my life that way."

"You're giving your mother a lot of credit. Nobody ever controls their life," Dove assured her.

"You sound so positive."

"I am."

If control were possible Fritz wouldn't be dead, Tessa Bradley wouldn't be missing and Cherie... Well, Dove would have stopped it all. Every last bad thing that had come to his mountain.

"Well, then we'll have to resign ourselves to a wild ride, won't we?" Charlotte lamented.

"Suppose so." Dove took out his notebook. "Was that the only time you saw him?"

"No. I was in Corallis two days after that. He mistook me for Tessa. We're about the same height and he couldn't see my hair under my hat. I didn't realize he was talking to me. He yanked my arm hard so I got in his face. Self defense classes, you know." Almost playfully Charlotte stiffened her hands into a karate motion yet her expression remained dead serious. "The man was trash. The thought of him touching Tessa was just – not good."

Charlotte shuddered then noticed Dove's pen and paper. She stood up, wrapped her arms around herself and she chucked her chin, giving him permission to start writing.

"About five ten or eleven. Late forties. Dark hair. Long. Waves. Thinning. His clothes were old: a corduroy jacket, jeans, workman's boots. His face was kind of long.

Very creased. I suppose he'd be handsome if he cleaned up. You know, in the way that Tommy Lee Jones can be handsome? Only this guy wasn't Tommy Lee Jones by a long shot."

"Eyes?" Dove asked.

"Bluish/grey. Oh, there was a scar across his forehead." Charlotte drew her finger down the left side of her brow. "Minor, but noticeable."

"You saw a lot," Dove commented.

"I'm a photographer. I'm used to registering detail."

"Then you're in the same business as your mother?"

"Hardly. I work for National Geographic. Nature shots. Tessa and I have a very different idea of what's beautiful." Charlotte laughed wryly. She was becoming impatient. "It's cold. Do you want to finish up? "

"Whenever you're ready."

"Okay. I saw his car that day when he brought Tessa back. It was light blue and beat up. An SUV. Four door. Front bumper was missing."

Her voice trailed off as she thought about what she wanted to say.

"Look, I'm not proud of this, but I went after him in town. I made a fool of myself, yelling, asking what he wanted with Tessa. I don't usually get emotional – especially about her – but there was something about him.

Dove waited for her to put that something into words but there was only embarrassment, then disappointment, then frustration.

"This may sound weird, but I got the feeling he didn't know what I was saying. He looked so – stupid. Like I frightened him. He ran away. I started after him but realized how ridiculous that was. I mean, what was I going to do if I caught him?" Charlotte shivered. She waved her hand. "Anyway, I didn't see him get into his car that day."

"Does your mother speak another language?" Dove put his notebook in his breast pocket.

"She knows enough French to get her down the runway or to order champagne. That's it. That's all I remember. Oh, except we were standing on the main street right near the stop light if that means anything."

"It could. I'll get on over there and check it out."

"Good. Thanks." Charlotte nodded gravely. "I hope it helps. No matter what I think about Tessa, I don't want her to be hurt."

"I understand." Dove lied. He had a long way to go before he understood the Bradley family.

"Fine. Then I'll let you do your job." Charlotte started away then looked back. "You're not going to tell him, are you?"

Dove looked up at Jake Bradley who watched them from the deck now. He had forgotten about the man was there but Charlotte had not.

"Let me find this man first. If he knows something then I'm going to have to bring it back here."

"Okay, but give me a head's up. You've got my cell number in the envelope. I want to be with him if she's run away with that guy." Charlotte looked hard at Dove. "If you don't find him, you keep it to yourself."

"You're father's a lucky man to have you care about him so much."

"That's a matter of opinion," Charlotte countered.

When it seemed there was no more to say he opened the car door, put the notebook in his pocket and tossed his hat onto the seat. He was half in when Charlotte called to him. She was standing on the slate riser like it was a stage.

"Jake's not my father. I thought I should tell you before someone else did."

Fritz's Mountain Store
8:41 a.m.

Lonely. Worn. Fragile as an old woman abandoned by the side of the road. That's what Fritz's Mountain Store looked like. Yellow tape was strung around the perimeter. Inside that, old man Davis rested on his haunches waiting for molds to set in the tire tracks and footprints. Cars were parked on the other side of the road and a few people were waiting for their marching orders.

Dove was parked fifty yards down and across from the store. One leg was curled up and his notebook was balanced on his knee. There would be things he needed to be reminded of when he had time to think: Charlotte Bradley's devotion to her stepfather, her anger toward her mother, those letters, the phone bills, the man in Corallis. He found himself distracted by a more urgent thought, though, and that was of Fritz himself. The last hours Dove spent with Fritz had been selfish, spent on Dove's worries and troubles. What had he failed to notice about Fritz? What?

"Dove. Dove!"

He started and the notebook fell between the seats. His right hand instinctively went toward his gun but there was no need. It was only Nathan knocking on the window with his knuckle. His face was so close Dove could see the downy whiskers Nathan kept trying to coax to a beard. Dove opened the car door and got out.

"I'm glad you're here." Nathan danced back to give Dove room.

"You've found her?"

"Sorry. No. Just reporting, Dove. There's a bad front coming in late tonight or tomorrow. Oh, and the state boys aren't going to be sending up search and rescue before that. I did everything I could to convince them but it's a no-go. I mean, I really tried, Dove," Nathan said.

"You talk to Bob Taylor?" Dove asked.

"Yep, the man himself. He says he's sorry, Dove. He'd like to oblige but he's spread thin because they've got a couple of lost kids up his way."

"Is it anything that might link up to what we've got here?"

"Nah," Nathan let his head swing right then left. "They've been missing almost a week. One of 'em is a retard. The mothers keep saying they know the kids are alive. No way they are, of course. Not in this weather. I mean who could stay out at night..." Nathan bemoaned false hopes and wishes as he looked off into the woods. It wasn't until he noticed that Dove hadn't taken kindly to that observation that he back-pedaled. "But that's not saying our lady won't be just fine, Dove. An adult has resources, kids don't."

"I wouldn't count on this adult feeling that resourceful either. This lady's a world famous New York model. Her husband's big time, too. Ever hear of Jake Bradley, the political cartoonist?" Dove asked.

"He lives up here? Damn." Nathan whistled, duly impressed.

"Yep. And he's had some trouble with a stalker so we're going to be looking out for ten things at once. Did you call the new sheriff in Corallis?"

"I didn't, Dove, if you want to know. They don't have any air power or nothing and I figured that's what we'd need…"

Nathan had skipped ahead on the conversational road only to realize Dove was lagging behind. The big man's eyes were on the tree line where Cherie was handing out coffee. Nathan cast him a wary glace. It didn't take much to see Dove wasn't happy.

"Cherie wanted to help, Dove. I didn't ask her to come on down here. I swear, I didn't even so much as suggest it."

"I told her to stay with Bernadette," Dove muttered. Then he scolded Nathan. "And I've told you, I don't want Cherie near our business."

"I said that and she said she'd handle you." Nathan shrugged self-consciously. Much as he didn't want to tangle with Dove, Nathan sure didn't want to mix it up with Cherie. Everyone knew she gave as good as she got even though she was a bitty little thing. "Sorry, Dove but that's what she said. Besides, she told me Bernadette wanted her to leave. Cherie was probably scared to go back to your place alone. Women can get spooked, you know that."

"Yeah, I know that." He watched a second longer then went back to Nathan. "How many men have you turned out? Who's up there?"

"Five so far. I set 'em out in a fan formation." Nathan spread his arm and gestured toward the forest. "We got the two Braimen boys on the tail end and Aaron's got his dog out. I used the jacket from the back of the Range Rover for scent. I didn't want to let the dog get into the car 'cause I didn't know how many people had been in there…confused…"

Dove listened with half an ear. Cherie had turned her back and Dove saw the papoose. Only a bit of the baby' face showed between the swaddling and the knit hat. Much as he didn't want Cherie here, Dove wanted the baby gone more.

"Dove, does that seem right to you? I figure the percentage isn't high southeast. Those tracks spun out and headed north from here so I sent most everybody up that way. Out and north. What do you think?"

Dove shook himself out of his reverie, forcing his attention away from Cherie and the baby.

"You're positive the one that went off the road is the same vehicle that left here?" he asked.

"No way to be one hundred percent sure. We've got a good cast on the tire marks here but up there – look." Nathan pulled out a hand drawn map and pointed to a black 'X'. "This is where a car went off road fast again, through a bank of snow. I've got pictures, and near as I can tell it was the same tires, but the snow was mostly crystals, so it's a best guess. That's why I sent the search party that way. Only now I'm thinking maybe…"

"Don't second guess, Nathan. A man makes the call he has to make. You stay with that." Dove pushed back his jacket and looked at the ground eager to be on his way. "Anything else?"

"I'll have more on the shoe prints tomorrow. Most I can tell you is it looks like three people if you discount Fritz and Paddy's prints. Two men go in the back. One lady goes in the front. One man comes out the front and one out the back. Figure the woman was lifted off her feet."

"Did you get prints off the Starbucks cup? What about inside the car?" Dove asked as they started to move again.

"Yes, sir. Got some that look real clear. Already faxed 'em into the state boys. I got some off the back door and a whole bunch on one of the boxes in the storeroom, too."

"I want a photo as soon as possible if there's a hit. If they can't do it, try Portland PD. Okay?" Dove held up a hand in answer to someone who called out a greeting then he finished with Nathan. "If you don't have anything by ten, get Jessica on it."

"You won't have to ask twice about anything, Dove." Nathan hopped foot-to-foot like a kid who just remembered what he wanted for Christmas. "Oh, and Paddy drew out the back lights of the car he said he saw going north. I'm thinking I'm looking at a Ford. SUV from the height of the lights, but I don't think it's a new model from the sketch he brought me. I won't know for a bit, but it's something to work with."

"Good. I'm especially interested in a blue SUV. Older model. Run down anyone within thirty miles who has anything close to that."

Dove started to walk in earnest now but Nathan was on his heels, still not finished with his report.

"A couple more things, Dove. I took the liberty and checked with the highway patrol. They stopped two cars going down the mountain and onto the freeway fast last night. One was a kid and his girlfriend; the other was a middle-aged woman who just had a fight with her husband. Other than that, it was quiet."

"So, whoever did this would have had to drive down the mountain like law-abiding citizen right past those officers," Dove mused.

"They'd have to be harsh sons of bitches, Dove. Especially if the woman wasn't part of it." Nathan agreed. "If they had the woman wouldn't they be nervous? Kind of noticeable?"

"You'd think, Nathan," Dove mused. "Maybe the state boys didn't see anything because whoever did this didn't leave. Maybe, they're still on my mountain."

"And the woman?" Nathan whispered.

Dove hesitated. He wanted the *feel* so bad he could taste it. There was a warming in his brain but it didn't spread. Still, there was something.

"She's here," Dove concluded quietly.

Mesmerized by the big man with the long black hair, Nathan could barely breathe. His belief in Dove's sixth sense was so strong it didn't matter that common sense should have been the order of the day.

"Well, then, I guess I better get to work and see if we can find out what happened to her." Nathan said. Dove nodded but before they parted he had to know.

"Is Fritz good, Nathan?"

"Yes, Dove. Tim is taking good care of Fritz."

I dream of Charlotte and Jake while I sleep. Mostly, though, I dream of Charlotte. I know what's in my head isn't real but it's better than the place I'm in. I choose to stay there, my mind roaming around this fantasy world.

I see the duvet on my bed at home; I feel the crisp cotton that covers my pillows. Jake is beside me and his hair sparkles silver in a shard of morning sun that has sliced through the shutters. Charlotte is home, sleeping in the room next to ours. She is newly with us and already calls Jake daddy. I leave my bed. I am completely happy as I move through my home. That happiness, in and of itself, is proof I am dreaming. The other proof is, in my dream, my feet don't touch the floor.

Before I can get out a giggle of pure delight at this amazing turn of events my brain pops. The channel changes.

I am swimming, treading water in a lake of melted glass. It is warm and thick. It is easy to stay afloat. When I look down, I see my reflection there in these waves of liquid glass. It is all so very pretty.

Charlotte hovers over the lake with her back to me. She is grown and takes a picture. Her bulky camera has an old-fashioned flashbulb attached to a huge silver reflector. It goes off like an atom bomb. Blue spots dance in front of my eyes. When they clear, I am looking at an ancient photo. It is black and white and the edges are scalloped. It is a picture of me as a child. Charlotte is in the photo with her arm around me. We are grinning. My child and I are children together.

This is a great dream until her arms tighten around me.

She grabs me hard. Charlotte is angry. She doesn't want me to be happy. I am waking and she is gone. There is no lake of glass or comfortable bed. I am lying on hard earth inside a hollowed out mountain. Dust covers me, not a quilt. I clutch an old knapsack for comfort, not a soft pillow. A man's hands are on me, not my daughter's.

My eyes fly open and I see his shadow in the dying flame of my lantern. I'm heavy with sleep so my defense is pitiful. Like a reel of film breaking and spinning free, my body reacts. I snap away but he comes after me. My sweater stretches, tearing the dried blood around my bullet wound.

My head explodes.

I grunt and grab my stick. I swat and sob and dig in my heels. He stays at me. His hands are everywhere.

"Don't touch me. Don't touch me there."

I don't know if these are words or the meaning of my whimpers and cries. I lose my grip and my walking stick flies toward the little wooden cart. My eyes roll back in my head because I have seen who it is. It is the man with one eye. No. It's the old man with the long grey hair. It doesn't matter. Either one is my nightmare. I cannot watch. It's enough to make my face pull inside-out as if that will keep him from recognizing me. I whip my head down and bury it in the dirt, curling up like a pill bug waiting to die – but I don't.

Seconds tick by. Minutes. I raise myself on one elbow. Cautiously, I uncurl and sit myself up. My hands shake as I put them on my face. I am not inside-out. I laugh but the sound is too close to hysteria so I stop. I spit out dirt. I lift my lantern and look for proof that all this was my imagination. There is none. The dirt floor is packed tight and I can't make out if there are footprints or not. The light flickers. I haven't much time. I don't want to be here, in the dark, cornered, easy pickings.

Setting aside the lantern, I crawl toward my stick. The mine feels like a tomb.

If I die here I will mummify.

I pull myself forward again.

An archeologist will discover me and call me The Mine Maiden.

One more inch and the hurt in my legs, my neck, my shoulders brings tears to my eyes.

The archeologist who finds me will think I was someone special because my jewels will still encircle my bones.

Finally, I grasp the walking stick and pull it close to my chest. I lie in the dirt. Exhausted, I stare at nothing.

They will put me in a glass casket in a museum. People will look at my pathetic, inside-out face for eternity.

I laugh.

I am losing my mind.

I gotta go.

Jerome Morgue
8:50a.m.

The water Tim washed the body with was warm. He poured it from a tub instead of spraying Fritz down. Tim used a soft cloth to clean out the wounds. He arranged the body modestly and spoke gently as he took pictures of Fritz's poor face — or lack of it — and limbs and trunk. Tim pointed the camera at the bottom of Fritz's feet and the palms of his hand. He muttered apologies as he picked shot out of Fritz's body. The doctor chattered on, sharing with Fritz all the good memories of him.

He knew all these mutterings and cooings would be on the tape he had activated when he walked into the room. There would also be the sound of weeping. Tim didn't care about that. Finally finished, he put away his tools, covered Fritz with a sheet and put him to rest in a climate-controlled room.

When all that was done, Tim catalogued his evidence bags. Fritz had carried with him three dollars in bills and twenty-seven cents in change. He had a crumpled piece of paper with a telephone number and a receipt for gas. He had another list in the breast pocket of his shirt. That piece of paper was so bloody Fritz could only make out bits and pieces of the phone numbers: Bernadette's doctor, the pharmacy, the mortuary. Those were the only ones he recognized.

That piece of paper was still moist with Fritz's blood. Tim ran his finger across the bottom line nearly erasing the mortuary number. Then he began to pray and then he began to cry in earnest. He sank to the floor, put his back up against the table upon which Fritz had been laid out and cried until he had nothing left inside him.

After that, he called Dove and told him what he found.

Then Tim cried some more.

The Road to Corallis
9:50 a.m.

Dove kept his foot heavy on the gas. Corallis wasn't a stretch and the speed wasn't going to get him there all that much sooner, but he had the need for it. He was not feeling kindly toward Cherie. She had dared him to put her back home when there was a woman missing, a man dead and work to be done. Dove argued it was for her own safety but she would have none of it. So he left, driving fast, reminding himself that he knew she was an obstinate woman when he married her.

Dove settled with it by the time he was a few miles out of Corallis. He slowed and dialed the FBI. Brian Drake was still active but out in the field on the California side. Dove left his contact information and rolled to a stop at the light on Corallis's Main Street where Charlotte Bradley had confronted her mother's friend. Then Dove set thoughts of Cherie aside and smiled. He looked at the Starbucks sign on the building on the corner of Main Street and Pine. The cup in the car had come from here.

He was getting somewhere.

Bernadette's House
9:55 a.m.

In high school, Bernadette reigned as Ice Queen over the winter ball. Thirty-two of her classmates, and anyone on the mountain who wanted to dance, were invited.

Bernadette wore a red taffeta dress. Darlene, owner of Darlene's Custom Beauty, piled Bernadette's chestnut curls high to show the paste tiara off to its best advantage. The local newspaper ran a picture and mentioned how perfectly suited Bernadette was to a crown and a fancy do. She wore that tiara when she danced with Fritz and when they made love in the back seat of his car after the dance was over. On her wedding day, Bernadette's mother attached her veil to the tiara. For fifteen years it was perched atop the television until Bernadette couldn't bear to look at it any more.

A month after finding a lump in her breast, three weeks after learning it was in her bones and two weeks after starting chemo and radiation Bernadette packed that tiara away. Thankfully, those lousy little mutant cells had not made their way to her brain. She still thought clearly. Fritz, on the other hand kidded himself that it was business as usual.

Even when Bernadette came out into the living room, naked as a jaybird, wet as a hen, holding half her hair in her hand, Fritz still didn't get it. He had wrapped her in a towel, sat her on his lap and pulled out the rest of her hair like a mama cat grooming her kitten.

Fritz never said a word about the cancer and that riled Bernadette. She screamed at her husband while pointing out the ravages of the disease. Shock kept him mum, but that didn't make it any better. What Bernadette didn't understand was that Fritz simply couldn't imagine the world without her. What Fritz didn't understand was that Bernadette would have appreciated a chance to tell him she couldn't picture a world without her either. And, if he wasn't going to do anything about it, if God wasn't going to step in and give her a reprieve, then damn if she didn't have faith in herself to make things right.

Now she was thinking that faith had been misplaced. The chore she set for herself was proving harder than expected. She lay on the floor of the shed, open boxes all around her, too tired to move. The scarf over her bald head barely kept out the chill. She thought she heard critters underneath the floor, but she knew better. There was nothing but the cold earth there and the only thing keeping her from lying underneath it was her will to live.

Sighing, Bernadette rolled onto her back and put her hand on her empty chest. There were times it surprised her to find her heart still beating when half of her wasn't there. For a second she wished someone would find her, help her back to bed, discover the secret of what Fritz had done but Bernadette knew that wouldn't happen.

They were all out looking for the boogieman – the one who had shot her man dead. They wouldn't find him because the boogieman knew just how far to run and how low to lie. He knew just when to show up and what candy to dangle. That creature may have misjudged poor, dumb Fritz but he wouldn't be misjudging anything or anyone else.

Moving onto her side, Bernadette rested another minute then rolled onto her stomach. Lying with her cheek on the smooth wooden planks, she put her palms down and pushed. By the time she got her back up against the wall, Bernadette was panting and the world was spinning. Still, she set to her task again: pulling paper out of one box, methodically tearing it into pieces and putting it in another box. She did it because Fritz would have wanted it that way.

Outside the air is fresh. The snow has stopped falling. It didn't stick and the ground gives under my feet. A white cloud sits atop this mountain like a lazy cat. I feel better now that I've had a rest, now that I'm in the open again. I set the lantern on the ground, hunker down to turn it off. It is then I see something amazing. The hands on my watch have moved. I'm not sure if I was in that mine for one minute or one minute and a day but I am sure that my watch now says forty-one minutes after two. Damn, if this isn't a sign. I am not going to die in the middle of nowhere. I'm going to be safe. Time is moving on and so will I.

Smiling now, damn pleased with the situation, I look up to scope out the forest and that's when I learn that safety has an expiration date. I hear the crack of a rifle shot. My heart leaps, stops and leaps again. The fog muffles the sound and I can't tell where the shot comes from. I hang on to my stick and stay close to the ground looking for the best place to hide. All I see is white. That means all they see is white. Staying low, I move with the fog, keeping in the thick of it, crawling away from where I think the sound has come from.

Another crack.

Where the hell is the damn shooter? A best guess is all I have left and my guess is that he is behind me. I gather up my courage and struggle to my feet. I throw myself into the forest, sucking up the pain of moving 'cause I have a feeling dying would hurt a whole lot more.

Starbucks, Corallis
1:00 p.m.

Dove Connelly waited while the customers in Starbucks ordered their fancy drinks and settled themselves. Then he took out the picture Charlotte Bradley had given him and showed it to the girl behind the counter.

"I'm wondering if you've seen the blond woman in here."

"Yes, sir. Kind of hard to miss her." The girl eyed the photo and then looked back at Dove.

"When was the last time?" Dove asked.

"She's here pretty much every time I am," the girl answered.

"I need you to be little more specific. I'm thinking last night. Were you here last night? Or the night before?"

"No, sir, not after six. Last time I saw her it was about noon, three or four days ago." The girl picked up a rag and started to wipe down the counter. "She was wearing the coolest jacket I ever saw. It was denim but it had fur all on the inside. Bet it cost a fortune. You don't see anything like that around here. Least not unless it's on a tourist. I don't think she was a tourist, though. I seen her too many times."

"She isn't a tourist. She lives over in Bleden Town." The girl shrugged as if to say that made sense, too.

"Marcus might have seen her since he did the night shift. He'll be here in about half an hour if you want to wait."

"Maybe you could give me his phone nu... Hold on a minute." Dove's own phone was ringing. He held a finger up while he answered, listened then held it away from his ear and asked the girl: "Is there a place I can get a fax around here?"

"Sure. The copy shop is just over there." She raised her chin. Dove checked it out. Shyly the girl slid a cup of coffee his way. Dove smiled and went back to his call.

"I got a Kopy Kat across the street, Jessica. Call them for their fax number. I'll head over right now and wait for it." Dove picked up his coffee, said his thanks and headed to the door. The girl stopped him before he made it out.

"Should I tell Marcus you'll be wanting to talk to him?"

"Yes." Dove went back to the counter. "But in case something happens and I don't make it back, here's my number."

"Okay. I'll leave it for him. That woman didn't do anything bad, did she?"

71

"Not that I know of."

"That's good. I wouldn't have thought she would. She just seemed kind of sad. Funny how you can have all that expensive stuff and look the way she did and still not be happy. Don't you think that's funny?"

"You never know," Dove answered.

It wasn't his job to think about such things but he wondered about Tessa Bradley, too. Just a picture of her charged his imagination. In real life she must have been fuel to someone's fire. The girl looked at Dove's card like she was thinking hard. Suddenly she smiled; pleased that she had remembered something that would help.

"Did you want to know when the last time I saw the man was?"

"What man?"

"The man who always watched after her. From his car," the girl said.

"What did he look like?"

"Well," she answered. "Like that."

She pointed toward Dove's breast pocket. It took him a minute to realize what she was talking about. When he did, he fished back in, took out the picture. He gave another look to Tessa Bradley smiling at the camera while her husband, Jake, had his arm around Charlotte.

The Coffee Shop, Jerome
<u>1:02 P.M.</u>

Agent Brian Drake was eating lunch when his pager went off. He looked at the number, switched it off and went back to his burger and his book. It had been a long morning of getting nowhere. The locals were a closed mouthed bunch when it came to telling tales about their druggie neighbors– Drake's current assignment – or wanting to blow the president off the face of the earth – his last assignment.

Brian figured no matter what the office wanted, it wasn't going to be anything that was likely to make a difference in his afternoon plans. Then again it might be Ashley. She was the new secretary who made no bones about the fact that she thought Agent Drake was a person of interest.

Sighing, Brian set aside his Mickey Spillane paperback, finished the last bite of his burger and phoned in. Ashley answered and told him that a local sheriff had called and needed to speak to him urgently.

Agent Drake thanked her, took the contact information and thought about suggesting dinner. Deciding to let it go a few more days just to keep her on her toes, he finished his fries leisurely, paid his bill slowly and headed out to his car. It was a fine, crisp day. A good day for a walk in the woods. But he had stuff to do and now a local sheriff had to be added to the list. He'd have to wait his turn, though. Besides, how urgent could it be in this neck of the woods?

Starbucks, Corallis
1:24 p.m.

Dove was back at Starbucks and this time he brought a grainy fax of a bad booking photo of Simon Hart, a drifter with a long and unimpressive rap sheet. He looked exactly as Charlotte Bradley described him.

"Ever see this man?"

The Starbucks girl was alone and bored when Dove returned. Her elbows were planted on the counter. She put a hand under her chin as she got a closer look at the fax.

"Oh, yeah. I saw the lady get into his car."

"Do you remember what the car looked like?"

The girl laughed, "Sure do. Mercury Mountaineer. Blue. It didn't have a front bumper."

"How can you be so sure it was a Mountaineer?"

"My brother drives one," she answered. "He keeps it a whole lot nicer than that guy. That guy treated his car like shit."

The girl put a hand to her mouth, unsure if the law minded when someone took to swearing. A young woman came in pushing a stroller. The girl adjusted her cap.

"Gotta work."

"One more question. The man watching her? Did he ever see that lady with this man?" Dove pointed to Simon Hart's picture again.

"I don't know, but he could have. See, you can look straight through the window to Main Street if you're parked on Pine." Dove watched her point to where Jake Bradley had parked then he followed the line of sight to the side of Main Street where Simon Hart would have picked up Tessa Bradley.

Corallis Sheriff's Station
1:30 p.m.

It was just one thirty but it felt to Dove like he'd been on the move for a week and running on empty to boot. Folding the fax, he wondered why Jake Bradley hadn't said anything about his wife's trips to Corallis or his knowledge of Simon Hart. There was one reason Dove didn't want to think about: Jake Bradley hired Simon Hart to harm his wife. Maybe Bradley sat in his car watching to see that he got what he paid for. But why take her to the Mountain Store? Why hurt Fritz? It didn't make sense, but neither did the fact that Jake Bradley lied by omission. Dove walked into the Corallis sheriff's station with nothing more than a heavier load.

The buxom redhead out front was in uniform and she inquired politely as to what Dove's business was before showing him into Sheriff Savick's office. The man stood up and put out his hand. He was middle aged, tough and affable in the way a man can be when he believes his muscle is the best around. He stood behind his desk.

"Sheriff Connelly? Will Savick."

One hand clasped Dove's, the other captured his forearm. Savick's grip was firm, his smile was broad and his eyes were intelligent. He was the other side of the coin from Harold Lynd who had run the police department for as long as Dove could remember. Where Harold had grown soft in his job, this man was lean to the bone. He wore his uniform casually, sleeves rolled up, shirt open at the neck. On his hip was a tooled belt with a fine silver buckle. It wasn't big; it just wasn't regulation in any jurisdiction Dove knew of. Neither was the pull of tobacco nestled between lip and gum or the impressive tattoo Dove glimpsed on his arm. The welcome, though, was regulation.

"Come on in. Sit down. Good to finally meet you."

"Nice facilities," Dove said. "Looks a little different than the last time I was in."

"The city council thinks highly of us ever since we managed to redirect the Hell's Guardians to another part of the mountain for their yearly outing. They used to roar into Corallis like they owned the place. Scared the shit out of everybody with those bikes of theirs and tattoos and such."

Savick chortled delightedly, took a seat in his fine chair and offered Dove one almost as good.

"How'd you manage to get rid of them?"

"Didn't take much talking if I'm going to be honest. I used to ride with 'em in my younger days." Savick winked and pushed his sleeve up a little higher showing off a woman impaled on an iron gate, her torso licked by flames. "Contacts are a good thing in our business. Guess that's why the city council is so obliging. Maybe they figure I'll turn on 'em if they don't keep me happy." The sheriff lowered his sleeve, mighty pleased with himself. "I'll have to stand in the next election, but I think folks know I can keep them safe. So, what can I do for you?"

Dove put the picture of the Bradleys and the fax of Simon Hart's rap sheet on the desk. Savick eyed them both.

"I had a run in with the woman. I didn't like the way she parked, she didn't like the way I asked her to move her vehicle. Somehow I don't think you made the trip to talk about parking tickets." Savick talked like Tessa Bradley hadn't impressed him and that impressed Dove.

"And this one?" Dove moved the fax closer to the man on the other side of the desk.

"Don't recall seeing him." Savick shook his head and furrowed his brow as he thought hard.

"You're sure," Dove prodded. "The girl who works at the coffee shop has seen him."

"Oh, I'm not saying he doesn't look familiar. I just can't place him. Hold on. Ginger! Mike! Get on in here!"

Savick hollered for his staff. Ginger came running. Mike was a little slower. The deputy couldn't have been more than twenty, fresh faced and regulation down to his shoe laces. They passed the picture between them.

"I've seen him around," Ginger said as she gave the fax a close look. "Over at Drop Inn. He drinks. He looks. That's about it."

"Does he work?" Dove asked. Ginger shook her head and passed the fax back to the young deputy.

"Not regular that I know of. He's been over at Jim Talbot's place helping out," Mike said. "We get a lot like him. You know, the kind of guy who works for awhile and then moves on."

"He would have been with this woman," Dove pointed at Tessa Bradley.

"If I'd seen him with that woman, I would have remembered," Mike laughed and gave the paper back to Dove.

"We probably would have arrested him just for looking at her," Savick chortled. "Is that what you want him for? Something he did to that lady?"

"Might be." Dove took the photo back. "She's gone missing from a grocery up top of the mountain. The grocer's dead. This woman's car was left at the scene and this man—" Dove held up Simon's sheet, "—his prints were in her car. Plus, I've got an eyewitness that puts the woman and Hart together up my way and one that puts them together in Corallis."

"That's a hell of a lot of intrigue for your little part of the world, Sheriff." Savick raised an eyebrow. Dove took exception to his patronizing tone but let it pass.

"I'd say it's a lot for any place," Dove noted. "I want to talk to Hart."

"You sure the lady just didn't leave her car there 'cause she went off with him? Rich women can be funny that way." Savick spit into the trash can leaving Dove to figure that passed as commentary on women in general.

Dove shook his head.

"We found her purse. A man is dead. I'll assume the worst until I know better."

"Okay, then." Will pushed away from the desk but stayed seated. "You thinking he's dangerous, Sheriff Connelly? You need us to pull out all the stops? The big guns?"

"I'm thinking I'd like to find him and talk to him. If you can give me some help, I'd appreciate it," Dove answered. The man's cavalier attitude was starting to put his teeth on edge. "Probably don't need the riot gear yet."

"I'll send Mike out with you. How's that?" Savick raised an eyebrow at his deputy. "You wouldn't mind seeing a little action, would you now Mikey?"

"I can cover it," the deputy answered tightly.

"Okay then." Savick put his hands flat on the desk like he was holding it down. "Much as I'd like to be in on this with you, we've got a lot of work that needs tending to right here. There's lots of bad things trying to make their way into our little community. Drugs, that's my bailiwick. Ask anyone. I got this town cleaned up lickety-split when I took over from Harold. Ginger, you're going to help me out with those reports, right?"

"You got it, boss." Ginger moved closer to him and picked up a stack of papers as if to prove she was up to the task. She smiled shyly at Dove. "We're writing for a grant. Sheriff Savick wants a trained drug dog."

"I'm grateful you can spare Deputy McCall." Dove got up, eager to be on his way.

"Mike, you take care of our visitor. Give us a holler and we'll come running if need be." Savick put a narrow hand out to Dove. "Sheriff. Good to meet you. Hope you find your man."

"I will," Dove answered, locking in on Savick, watching something take shape behind those eyes of his. Savick cut him off before Dove could work it out.

"Be good, Mikey." Savick dropped Dove's hand.

"Mind if I follow you out to Hart's place?" Dove asked when he and Mike McCall got outside.

"What? Oh. No, that's fine." Mike took his sunglasses out of his pocket and put them on.

"Are you okay with this? I'm not expecting any trouble, but if you're having second thoughts…"

"No. Not at all. Happy to help." Mike buttoned up his jacket. "I just don't particularly care for my new boss implying that Harold was lying down on the job. Believe me, this place was plenty clean before he got to be Sheriff."

"The man is just marking his territory. It takes a while to settle into the top job," Dove noted. Mike shot him an appreciative grin. It was a little lopsided which was good because it kept his face from being too pretty.

"Yeah. And sometimes the fit is never right. But hey, what do I know? It's not like I've got a lot of experience under this old belt."

"Maybe you won't have to worry about the real criminals with Savick around." Dove joked but it was only by half. Sometimes it was nice not to know your limitations and that's probably where Savick had Dove beat.

"Hope you're right, Sheriff. It's just that I lived on this mountain my whole life and for someone who's only been here a few years to act like he owns the place – well, it just wasn't what I was expecting. Then again, I'm probably not what he was expecting either, huh?"

Mike smiled and opened the front door of his patrol car. Dove did the same. Savick, after all, wasn't the problem. Simon Hart was and neither of them knew what to expect from him – if he was still around.

Talbot's Fixit Shop
2:06 p.m.

Corallis boasted a downtown that was not only big enough to warrant Starbucks' attention but also a SEARS's annex, a real library and two churches – Baptist and Catholic. It seemed like a small town because it was spread out over more than a few miles, its borders sketchy and far-flung. At five thousand feet above sea level and only an hour's drive from the valley, it was still too much of a town for the likes of Dove.

In fifteen years there would be no telling Corallis from the city below. Five people would build houses on the mountain, then they'd want a store close by and somebody would oblige. Another store would spring up to take the run-off. Some builder would take ten acres and put up forty houses.

Like connecting the dots, Corallis would be swallowed up by the city below and then Dove's part of the mountain would be next. Could be that Fritz's death was nothing more than a harbinger of things to come; people taking the old roads to new places, doing their worst, thinking nothing of it as they drove on. Crime was like litter tossed on the highway: once it was shoved out the window the only ones who cared were the ones close to where it landed.

Dove gave the wheel a turn. His car bumped onto an unpaved road. Most of the land had been cleared but building was spotty here. Mike hit the gas, passed an unmarked intersection then hung a right onto a dirt road. His back wheels spun out briefly before he righted himself and went on like a jackrabbit. Dove followed. Both cars kicked up a good deal of dirt like youngsters haulin' ass on a back road just for the fun of it. When Dove pulled up to the big barn-like building Mike was already out of his car, his thumb hooked into his belt, one leg cocked on the running board as he waited on Dove. Together they walked into a big old building with the name Talbot's painted on the side.

It was colder inside than out and quiet the way big wooden buildings can be. The structure had weathered a lot of seasons. The wear showed in the open knotholes, the missing slats and the slanting beams. Mike and Dove were striped by ribbons of light and shadow as they walked the length of the place. Dust sparkled in the weak sunlight or hung grey and heavy like it had given up trying to escape.

"Watch yourself."

Mike warned Dove away from a rusted scythe that lay across a crate. Dove gave it a look as he sidestepped. Talbot's place was more museum than business, a shop where broken things went to be repaired, cannibalized or buried. There were washing machines and cars, farm machinery and typewriters. Architectural stars overflowed their bins and those bins sat beside buckets of bolts, nuts and nails. There seemed to be more parts strewn about than there were machines to put them.

"Cy? Hey Cy!" Mike called.

He picked up a gear only to toss it aside. He was checking out the front end of an old Corvette when a man appeared from behind something that looked like an X-ray machine. He was huge, matching Dove in weight but out running him in height. Almost bald, unshaven and covered with dirt and grease, Cy Talbot talked to Mike as he eyed Dove.

"Don't you go touching stuff, Mike. There's a reason why you're a cop and not a mechanic."

Mike smiled easily and walked up close to Cy like he knew him well. Together they faced Dove. Introductions were made but the big man kept his hands to himself.

"Don't want to get you greased, Sheriff," he said.

"Not a problem," Dove responded.

"I know I didn't do a damn thing to be ashamed of, so what brings you out here? Got something you need fixed?" Cy asked.

"We need to talk to you about Simon Hart," Mike answered.

"That piece of trash?" Cy spit into the dirt. "I sent him packing five days ago. He swore he knew how to work an engine. Didn't know shit — not to mention he had his hand in the till."

"Do you know where he went?" Dove asked.

"Is he in big trouble?" Cy raised a bushy eyebrow as if he hoped it was true.

"Could be," Dove answered. "We want to ask him about a woman he knows."

"Didn't look like a ladies man to me." Cy spit again and this time a thick black stream of tobacco juice hit the ground. He wiped his mouth with the back of his sleeve. "Still, not for me to say. I seen pretty women go with men who look like a beetle's butt and act like a horse's ass; I seen a bashful Nellie take on a whole tavern full of outlaws. Nope. Not for me to say where women are concerned, but I never saw him with a woman and none came here looking for him."

Tired of standing still, Cy ambled off toward a lathe and picked up a piece of wood. Dove and Mike fanned out: Mike to rest up against a stack of bricks and Dove standing close enough to hear and not get in the way. Cy hit the switch and the lathe started up with a shimmy and a whine.

"Sheriff Connelly could be looking at him for murder, too, Cy." Mike raised his voice and that little tidbit made the tinker pause.

He ran his hand over the wood and flipped the switch again as he cast a glance Dove's way.

"How'd he do it?"

"Shotgun," Dove said. "That's how the man died."

"Then I'm thinking Simon's probably not the one for you. I never saw him with a gun."

"But you saw something," Dove pressed.

"I saw him pull a knife when I wasn't going to pay him for work that hadn't got done. My grandma could have done more than he did."

"Why didn't you report him? I could have taken him in for assault," Mike pointed out.

"Because nothing happened. He pulled a knife. He made noises about cutting me then he backed off. Said it didn't really matter. Said he could starve a few days 'cause he was coming in to some big money. That's what he said. Big money." Cy spit again. It hit the ground but it might as well have been directed to Simon Hart's eye. "Like I was supposed to be impressed."

"Did he say where he was getting the money?" Dove asked.

"Nope. Didn't seem we had much to talk about once that knife was showed. I just told him to get out. Least he was smart enough to do that. If he hadn't, I'd be the one you were looking at for murder. Stupid little shit."

Still grumbling, Cy disappeared behind a jumbled mess of stuff. When he came back again he handed Dove a ripped piece of paper.

"That's the address he gave me. I wasn't exactly asked to dinner while he worked here, and he didn't want to see my sorry ass after I canned him, so I can't vouch for it."

"Appreciate it. Can you tell me what he was driving?" Dove asked, handing the address off to Mike.

"Blue Mercury Mountaineer. Needed brakes."

"And a bumper?"

"Yep," Cy confirmed.

Mike and Dove exchanged glances. They had what they wanted.

"Much obliged for the help, Cy," Mike said and by the time they were outside again the lathe was turning.

"Where we going?" Dove asked.

"That's an apartment building at the end of a cul de sac. You want to take one car so we don't look like the damn army on maneuvers?"

Mike slipped his Billie club from his belt and tossed it on the seat. He ran a hand across his short hair as he rested his elbow atop the car door waiting for Dove to decide how he wanted to make the approach.

"What are we looking at? A mile?" Dove asked.

"Three, more like."

"I'll follow you. If this is a dead end I have to get back up the mountain fast as I can."

"Your call."

The doors on both cars slammed shut. The engines revved. Simultaneously they whipped the wheels and caravanned back to town to chase down a man Charlotte Bradley believed was her mother's lover, a man who might have killed Fritz. If Simon Hart was kidnapper, killer, or both Dove would know it the minute he saw him and Simon Hart would be the next dead man.

I sit quietly at the base of a tall tree. To my right is a pile of rocks, to my left a bramble bush that scraped me when I crawled behind it. In front of me is a log cabin on stilts.

The end of the day comes while I watch this place. I am wary of what's inside. I have been fooled before into thinking there was safety, affection and promise inside a place just because it looked right. Instead, I found – well, I don't want to think about what was inside that villa in Italy. I will only think about the lessons I learned there: know what you're walking into, outside can be safer than in and, sometimes, there's no safe place at all.

So, I am patient. I move my eyes slowly over the clearing around the tower. A car sits on blocks. It is old and rusted. Unusable. That can mean one of two things: whoever lives here comes and goes in another vehicle or this place is abandoned. I don't think it is abandon. There is a towel on the railing around the deck. The windows are clean. The rungs on the ladder are in order. On the other hand, it is dark now and no lights come on. I don't see a shadow moving inside. I don't hear a radio.

There is another explanation for the quiet, though. I have lived on this mountain long enough to know there are season people. They come and go with the change of weather: men who clear the roads in the winter; people who look for fires in the summer. This is near spring. That's something to consider. I just don't think about it too long.

I am freezing now that it's dark. My ear hurts something awful; my neck even worse. A minute later a hot flash rips through me. My body is breaking down. Hungry and hurt, my choices are limited. I can pass by here and move on or I can climb that ladder.

I choose to climb the ladder because out here I will not last the night I don't know which is more painful: my shoulder where I now am sure the bullet entered, or my legs which feel afire as I climb.

Not that it matters. I cannot holler or curse or cry because I must assume there is someone inside until I am positive there is not.

There are thirty-two rungs on this ladder. They are all solid. I rest on the twenty-fourth. The empty rucksack is heavy and cumbersome because I have laced my walking stick through the flap. The rusted metal of the lantern handle cuts into my left hand. I think it's bleeding. I can feel something wet on my palm. I probably should have left it all below but I couldn't bear to. I have so little that I rationalize about why I carry these things: the stick can be a weapon; the lantern still has a small bit of fuel. If whoever lives here has left provisions, I will fill up my sack.

My hands are on the lip of the deck that surrounds this place like a widow's walk. My instinct is to throw myself on it. Instead, I put the lantern up quietly and then I crawl up like a soldier. Belly first, keeping down, moving to the corner just to the side of the front door. I put my back up against the wall and pull my long legs in. My heavy breath comes white out of my mouth. I worry that the little puffs can be seen, that my labored breathing can be heard even though the door is sturdy and windows are thick.

Swallowing hard, my nostrils flare as I pull in a final breath through my nose. I shake back my hair, close my eyes for just a second then get to my knees. My hands brace against the wall and I move cautiously as I peek through the window.

Inside the space is spare but I can see the outline of furniture, a darker area that I believe is the kitchen. The left part of the room is hidden. I fall back and wait.

When nothing happens I reach for the doorknob. My hand is shaking as I close my fingers around it. Before I turn it, I pray and promise the way fearful people do. I pray that it opens; I promise God whatever he wants if the place is empty. I turn the knob, listening for a click, wondering if anyone is on the other side *watching it turn. The door is locked and that is just as well. I didn't want to know what God would have wanted if it had opened.*

Staying low I make my way around the deck only to stop short, almost undone by what I see. The forest is never ending, impenetrable, unfathomable. Tears sting the corners of my eyes. I look away and then suck it up. I might not have to go into the forest. Salvation might be at hand. I will hold onto that.

This side of the cabin is nearly all glass. The windows are set low to the deck. It will be easy to crawl through when I get one open. I don't have a helluva lot of time to do that because the cold is spreading fast — down my legs and to my fingers. I can barely feel my extremities.

My head goes up to check things out one more time. Two big chairs are silhouetted near what I assume is the fireplace. The table I saw before, a door leading to another part of the cabin. There is a lot of dark but nothing moving in there.

I wriggle out of the backpack and pull out my stick. Working fast, I wrap the bottom of my sweater over the blunt end of the stick, turn my head and swing. The glass cracks. I swing again. This time it shatters and I am quick to put my arm through the jagged hole, stretching for the latch even though I am cut by the shards. Finally, my hand is on it. With a grunt, I throw the lock and force the window.

I swing my legs through. The window is higher than it looked on the outside. I fall a few inches and my ankle crumbles, my possessions fall in behind me. There is only more cold inside. No one has turned on the heat because no one is inside who needs to be warm. Except for me. I will find the heater, a phone, food, a bed. I am safe and I can hardly believe it.

Standing up, I close the window and make a bee-line for the front door. I bang my foot on something hard near the table and step over it. Otherwise, it is smooth going. My blind-woman-hands meet the wall and flutter over it. The light switch is a little lower than it should have been but finally I find it and flip it. I am smiling as my eyes adjust to the light. I think I am home free until I turn around.

In the wing chair near the fireplace is a man looking straight at me.

Simon Hart's Apartment
3:00 p.m.

It was two-point-seven miles to the address Cy had given them. Mike parked his car across the driveway, Dove pulled his behind. It was odd to see a cul de sac at the end of the only street for miles around. A development gone bankrupt, its only legacy was three buildings clustered at the curve: an abandoned house on the left, one that might as well have been on the right and in the middle was the two story apartment building where Simon Hart lived.

The house on the right looked a lot like Talbot's shop except there was a big Husky on the porch. It raised its head to take a good long look at Dove and Mike. Neither man gave it a passing glance as they concentrated on the apartment building.

Built like a cellblock, the back of the building was to the street. The bathroom windows facing them were high, narrow and made of crackled glass. One was open. Dove saw a shampoo bottle and a blue shower curtain.

"The guy who built this must have been dyslexic. This damn thing is backward," Mike muttered.

They walked up the drive, doing a visual sweep, looking for the entrance, people, a blue Mountaineer – Simon Hart. They landed in a carport roofed in tar paper.

There was a Chevy and a boat of an old Cadillac. No blue SUV, but that didn't mean Hart wasn't around.

Dove pointed east. Mike turned on his heel and led the way down a narrow walk that cut between the carport and the side of the apartment building. Their boots crunched on loose stones; they stepped over discarded beer cans. On the wall was a lewd message to Tina. It smelled like urine in this tight space, a stench even the mountain air couldn't clear. Finally, they were in front of the building.

On the first floor were sliding glass doors and four postage stamp slabs of cement that passed for patios. On the second floor picture windows were to the left of cheap, hollow-core doors. A wrought iron railing that needed painting and a sagging staircase led up from the ground. Vain attempts to soften this place had been made with flowerpots and barbeques, cheap drapes and window stickers. Nothing could change the fact that this depot was at the end of a line few traveled.

Dove and Mike started up the stairs. No one looked out the windows, curious about the two lawmen. They heard no sounds from inside the apartments they passed. Simon Hart lived in the third unit up top. If he hadn't covered his front window with tin foil, the man would have had a spectacular view of the sunrise. The two men parted: Dove to the left of the door and Mike to the right.

"You want to do the honors?" Mike asked quietly as he drew his gun.

"Nice of you to let me have the fun." Dove drew his weapon, too.

"Least I can do for a guest." Mike grinned and put his back to the wall. Dove raised his left fist and brought it down hard on the door.

"Police. Open up!"

Nothing.

Dove pounded again and gave Mike a warning glance. Despite the cold, perspiration beaded on the young deputy's upper lip.

"Relax, he's not…"

Dove was just about to tell him to holster his gun when the door flew open. Mike pivoted, bending at the knees, arms straight, and the gun level. Dove backed up a step and did the same. He lowered his weapon first then put his hand on the barrel of Mike's gun. The last thing they wanted was to blow the head off the very small, very irritated woman in the doorway.

"What in the hell do you think you're doing?" she demanded, unimpressed and ticked off.

"We're looking for Simon Hart."

Carefully, Dove slid around her and into the apartment while Mike took the woman's arm and ushered her onto the landing to keep her out of harm's way. She shook him off and followed Dove so Mike followed her.

"You don't need all that." She waved at their weapons and sniffed in disgust. "I could take Simon down with a good right if he was here, which he isn't. Look, I'm going to be late for work if I don't get out of here so if you want to talk, do it while I find my shoes. Just put those damn guns outside or something. I hate guns."

Mike kept his weapon out while he checked the apartment just in case this woman was one heck of a liar and Simon Hart was hiding. She went down on her knees and shoved one arm under a rickety couch.

"Do you know where he is?" Dove asked, still on his guard.

"Not at the moment." Her words were muffled as her cheek mashed against her arm. Her rear end wiggled with the effort, her color rose. "Ugh. Damn, what I wouldn't give for another six inches."

Dove lifted one end of the couch high. It was heavier than it looked. She scrambled under as if she wasn't quite sure Dove would hold it and was back just as quick.

"Got 'em. Thanks." Delightedly she held up the smallest pair of tennis shoes Dove had ever seen. Sitting back on her heels, she eyed Dove appreciatively until she noted the wedding ring. "Bummer. You're taken. Bet you're handy to have around the house in all sorts of ways."

"I try."

Dove smiled. It was hard not to. By the looks of her, she had skied a few tough slopes in her life. Her hair was a mess, her nails were broken and yet she was cute and feisty as could be.

"What's your name?" Dove asked.

"K.C. What's yours, big boy?" She tied her left shoe and started in on the right.

"Dove Connelly."

"Like the bird, huh?"

"Yep. Like the bird."

K.C. double knotted the right one and stood up. She wiggled her toes to make sure she hadn't knotted the laces too tight.

"Well if that isn't a fancy-dan name for a big guy. Don't get me wrong. I like it. Jacket?" Dove pointed and she sauntered over to retrieve it. It was old, pink and reached her knees when she put it on.

"Always nice when a good looking woman pays a compliment." Dove adjusted his stance so that he could see everything she did and still keep tabs on Mike.

"That was just an observation. If I wanted to pay you a compliment I'd say your pants fit just right." K.C. laughed heartily. Dove colored when he saw Mike beaming. Done with his search, Mike lost the smile as he joined in the conversation.

"So, K.C. how long have you been with Simon?"

"I'm not *with* Simon. I just needed a place to crash and he was the best offer." K.C. tiptoed up to check her hair in the Budweiser bar mirror on the wall. There was nothing she could do to make it better but she tried anyway. "Hell, who am I kidding? He was the only offer I had and then it was 'cause I gave him a few bucks. He's behind in everything."

"We heard he was coming into some money." Mike told her.

"If I had a dollar for every time I heard that line I wouldn't be working at the Circle K. Besides, have you seen him? I mean, come on. What goose is going to lay the golden egg for him?"

"How about this woman?" Dove took out the picture of Tessa Bradley. K.C. She took a gander and pulled a face.

"Which one?" K.C. asked.

"The blonde one," Dove answered.

"Honey, if I'd seen her I'd make a play for her myself." Dove chuckled despite himself. K.C. looked darned pleased. "Thought I had you with that one, you gorgeous hunk. So, okay. I don't know nothing about nothing, so I gotta go. I work down the mountain and I hear it might rain or snow soon and my car hasn't had new tires in ten years. I really don't have anything to tell you about Simon, but if he managed to get in that one's pants then maybe he was telling the truth. Maybe he did have money coming in. Meantime, all I know is he left around two and didn't tell me where he was going."

"But you live here, right?" Mike insisted.

"For now." K.C. was getting perturbed. "Something you didn't understand about what I told you?"

"I'm just saying. You wouldn't mind if we took a look around, would you?" Mike pressed. "I mean, we have your permission, right?"

"Knock your socks off, boys." K.C. slung her big bag over her shoulder.

Just then a big wet snowflake hit the window.

"Damn. Gotta go."

A minute later K.C. was gone leaving Dove and Mike alone in Simon Hart's apartment.

I sit opposite the man in the La Z Boy. He is dead with a clean shot through the head. I'm figuring the bullet maybe went straight through to the wall because the powder burns around the neat little hole means he was shot up close. I don't know how I know that, but I do.

He is handsome and young – or he was. Tall and narrow faced. He died surprised because his dark, slope-eyes are open and startled. His nose is too small for his face but his wide lips seem to even things out some. His thick thatch of hair is neatly combed. One hand dangles over the side of the chair and the other is in his lap. He is pale. I have not touched him. I have seen death up closer than this and there is no way in hell this man has a heartbeat.

It is shock that keeps me still and dry eyed. I have been in shock before. After Italy. After Sharon. When I saw my mama the last time. I don't like to think of those times but recollections like that come back when life is shaky. Italy is strongest. It is a monster memory that refuses to stay locked down.

Peter took me there to meet a man named Ubert Yahobi, the master of all couture masters. He had chosen my face out of a thousand beautiful faces to become the next Yahobi muse. His blessing meant riches beyond my wildest imagination. After Italy, I would pick my projects like peaches. I would have money and I could claim Charlotte for my own. But Italy wasn't what I expected. I never saw what was coming. I didn't even see Ubert Yahobi up close until the third day when I left the villa where they put me up. It was there that I wandered through the gardens to a verandah overlooking the ocean. For a Texas girl like me this was like being in a movie. Who knew people lived like this? I breathed in the salt air, I was near blinded with the colors of the garden but I was not really alone.

Below me, on an outcropping of rock, were two men. The older one was dressed in sky blue: boots, jodhpurs, an open shirt showing a wrinkled chest. He was neither tall nor short just sunken under those fancy duds. His long grey hair was pulled back into a braid. He held a gun. His companion, younger, square and muscled, hunkered down as he attended to the trap. The man in blue yelled 'pull'. He raised his rifle fast. The pigeon was blown to pieces. Over and over again I watched Ubert Yahobi kill clay.

I don't know how long it took to realize Yahobi had stopped shooting. He was pointing his rifle at me and that gun had a scope. The man must have the smallest penis in town if he carried around a thing like that and used the sites like binoculars. I turned my back on him. When he wanted to work, I'd be ready. Until then, I didn't want to watch him kill anything — even clay — if he wasn't going to play fair.

My own cry pulls me away from memory. It comes out of nowhere to remind me that my choices are limited. I can waste time thinking about Italy or I can deal with this dead man in front of me. I vote for the lesser of two evils, push myself out of that chair and step around the little table between us. I lick my lips, running my tongue over the scab that has formed where the bottom one was split.

"Sorry 'bout this," I whisper.

I mean what I say. I'm sorry that he got shot for surely the shots that murdered him are what I heard outside the mine. I'm sorry he was alone when he died. I can't think of anything worse than dying alone. I'm sorry I brought him this misfortune. I'm sorry for what I have to do.

My hands go into the breast pocket on his shirt. There is nothing inside that pocket but I feel his chest. It is well muscled and rigid. He is so young. His head swivels and falls sideways so that it rests on his shoulder. I squeal and wipe my hands on my jeans. I have at it again, pushing him onto his right hip. When I have his wallet I let him fall back. He looks like a rag doll.

"Jonathan Truesdale." I read his license and then look at him. "I sure as hell wish you were still here, Jonathan Truesdale."

He is twenty-eight. There is a picture of a pretty young woman in his wallet. He has twenty dollars, which isn't much. I leave it, and go 'round to push him from the other side. His head stays where it is. I am looking into dead eyes that were probably nice when he was alive. There's nothing in his other pockets.

He is slumped in two but I leave him that way and look around. There is a desk with a radio. It is smashed. There is no phone. The forest worker is killed and I'm good as dead if my only choice is to walk through the wild below. It takes no more than that thought to double me over. I heave but nothing comes out of me. It is fear and it is hunger and cold and uncertainty and it is the fact that there is a dead man in the chair behind me. All these things make me ill.

I crash into the table with two chairs. Fall over the small footstool. Stumble into the hallway. Clutch at the wall. Spin through another door. When I fall it is onto a bed. I feel the stitching of a quilt beneath my cheek and a pillow just above my head. Then I feel nothing at all.

When I wake I am confused to be in this girlish room. I have drooled and bled on the quilt of pink and blue and spring green. Atop the bureau is a bowl and pitcher painted with flowers and a china-faced doll. I am reminded of the rich girl's house in our Texas town. She had a pink quilt and three china faced dolls. I had the feeling that God made a mistake and I was meant to live there. Even then, I think I knew I was meant to be someone else all along.

Not so today. There's no getting around that I am me. I can barely move. Perhaps I drift in and out because, when I finally set myself up, the light in the room seems different than it did when I first opened my eyes. My first thought is of my friend Sharon, gone for years and still missed. My second is of Simon and standing in the bedroom of that place he called home. My third is I have to pee.

I throw back the covers.

When I find the bathroom there is no water. Jonathan must have just arrived to open up the watchtower. They must have been waiting for him. No fire laid, no water turned on. Things just get harder. In the living room I see that Jonathan has gone from pale to chalky. He has slipped down further, his hand still drapes over the arm of the chair but it is at a strange angle. I go back, grab the quilt and toss it over him. I don't want him watching me.

This all feels like a dream.

Fifteen minutes later I have done everything I can do. I have written a note and left it on the desk, looked in every cabinet in the house and found two tins of canned meat, a can opener and crackers. I eat some of the crackers but I think I've gone too long without food. It doesn't set well. I really can't taste them so I toss them away. I will only open the tins if I am desperate. I don't want to be caught sick outside.

When I am done, I stand by the window trying to come to grips with the fact that I have to move on. Standing in front of this glass reminds me of my home in New York. I bought a co-op overlooking Central Park from a seller who had taken a bath when the dot coms failed. I, on the other hand, was making more money than ever. A beautiful woman with no particular talent, it seemed, was worth more than a smart man. That's not how it should have been, but there it was.

Sometimes I'd stand buck naked in front of that window looking out at the trees of Central park, not caring if anyone saw me. My body was my craft, after all. I'd been naked in front of half the world on the covers of magazines so what would it matter if someone across the way got an eyeful?

Once I walked in the finale of a fashion show clad only in a veil. I carried a cascading bouquet that covered just enough down south. White surgical tape covered my mouth. I was dressed as the perfect bride. There was outrage of course but not because my tits were showing. It was the tape that caused the commotion. How ridiculous things could get.

People I knew worried about clothes and nakedness and political correctness. What bull when there were other people worried about staying alive. I wonder what they would say if they knew I was one of those people now. They would probably say nothing. They have probably forgotten me and moved on to adore someone else.

I have been crying. I put the heels of my hands on my eyes and rub. I still feel the wet of those tears on my dirty cheeks as I turn, hitch my rucksack and look at the lump in the LaZboy chair that used to be Jonathan Truesdale. I am so sad and so afraid. I envy him just a little.

"So," I say. "I guess I'll be going."

Simon Hart's Apartment
3:21 P.M.

Simon Hart's apartment was dirty and near bare. Along with the couch in the living room there was a broken down recliner, a television with rabbit ears perched on a crate and carpet that was matted with food and wear. There was a suitcase on the floor. Dove flipped it open and closed it again. K.C.'s things. In one corner of the room there was a jumble of magazines; in another free weights gathering dust. Dove tipped the magazines with the toe of his boot.

"Hustler. Very classy," Mike noted as he looked on. "Guess he wasn't looking at his girlfriend in any of these."

"I don't think she did that kind of modeling."

Dove moved on, putting together a profile of a loser. The idea Tessa Bradley would jeopardize her marriage for this man was hard to believe, yet they were something to one another. If they weren't, Jake Bradley wouldn't have followed his wife, Tessa wouldn't have waited to be picked up and Charlotte wouldn't have been so damn sure these two were an item. Mike wandered away.

"This guy sure travels light," he called from the bedroom.

"It just means he can take off real quick," Dove called back.

He paused in the doorway checking out the mattress on the floor. It was littered with a worn blanket, laundry, one pillow and a rumpled sheet that shared space with a tire iron and another magazine. Absentmindedly, Mike lifted one of the shirts with the tips of his fingers and glanced at the magazine only to do a double take. He lifted the shirt higher. Mike chuckled.

"Looks like the lady was in bed with Hart after all."

Dove came into the room, looked around then stepped over to look. Under the shirt was a fashion magazine with Tessa Bradley on the front. She wore tuxedo pants. The jacket was slung over one shoulder. Instead of a shirt, the single word TESSA was scrawled across her chest in bold print. She leaned toward the camera, her chin up, her eyes straight on, her lips parted. The woman looked like she could eat you alive. It seemed like she was looking straight at Dove Connelly, daring him to find her. She had no idea how much he wanted to find her and save her. If he did, it might make up for not saving Cherie when she needed him the most.

"It's old," Dove noted. Mike looked. The issue was December 1992 and was worn as a bible in a true believer's hands.

"You think he's taken off with the real thing?" Mike asked, tipping his head to get a better look.

"Nope," Dove muttered. Mike let the shirt fall, covering the magazine again. "K.C. would have known something and she would have told us."

"She would have told you." It was a tease that embarrassed Dove.

"Doesn't matter how you get the information, just that you get it," Dove reminded him.

"I'll remember that."

Not wanting to look at Hart's dirty laundry lying over Tessa Bradley's face, Dove checked out the half-opened closet.

"Got a shotgun in here," he called. Mike came to check it out.

"I'll be damned." He whistled when he saw it. "Think it's your weapon?"

"Can't tell," Dove said without either hope or disappointment. When Mike reached for it Dove stopped him. "Let's just look. We can argue K.C.'s permission to poke around, but she's not on the lease. We'll wait for a warrant before we touch anything."

"You're the boss," Mike shrugged. "I'll check out around the kitchen."

Mike went off but Dove wasn't finished with the closet. He committed everything he could see to memory: three shirts hanging side-by-side, one pair of pants, and a hat with earflaps. What Dove didn't see was just as telling. There was no jacket. That meant Simon Hart only had one to his name and he was wearing it. He was also wearing his only pair of shoes because there weren't any others in the closet. Dove made allowances for the dark corners but would bet there was nothing of interest in them.

"Kitchen," Mike called.

Dove pushed himself up. His knees cracked. He walked out to the living room and then into the kitchen. Dishes were in the sink, the floor hadn't seen a mop in a good long while. Tossed over a stool near the refrigerator was a blue and white sweater. Dove put his hands on his hips trying to remember the exact hue of the ball of fuzz he had seen swimming in Fritz's blood, the texture of...

"No, Sheriff." Mike insisted when Dove didn't react. "I mean that. Right there."

Mike pointed. Dove looked. Beneath the sweater was a bloody silk scarf.

I am distracted. That's why I fall when my stick hits a soft patch.

I was thinking of Simon and his place and the beer he offered me. It was wrong to take it because I wasn't a beer drinking girl anymore and probably never had been. That's a big thing to come to grips with: the fact that all my life I'd pretended one thing or another so people would like me.

Anyway, that is why I fall into the leaves. They close in around me like bread dough closes around a fist. I smile because it is the first thing that's felt good in a while and because I've been in a place like this before.

Back then my soft place was a bed piled high with silks and satins, gowns and skirts and blouses. My friend Sharon, my double in beauty, was there with me. We were paid ridiculous amounts of money for our stone-faced, high stepping strolls, our posing and posturing. We were paid even more to cavort on beaches in exotic places wearing next to nothing while people took our pictures. We both thought that was crazy – amazing, but crazy.

That night – the one I'm thinking of – we were someplace hot and exotic. Our crew was asleep; we were bored. We stole away with the wardrobe, piled those fancy things on the bed and jumped in them like they were a pile of leaves. We drank tequila from the bottle and brandy from bathroom glasses. We smoked cigarettes and burned a hole in a dress that had taken twelve women three weeks to embroider. We tried to color out the mark with lipstick then I turned that lipstick on Sharon.

I fashioned her boobs into wide-open eyes, her perfect little belly button was a nose. I drew a smiley mouth further down than that. Sharon touched that mouth. She wanted a baby, she said. I had one, I answered. The spell was broken. Nothing was funny anymore.

I rolled onto my back in that pile of fancy clothes and looked at the ceiling. Sharon went to the bathroom. When she came back she dropped a scarf and it floated over my face. I watched her through a veil of lavender chiffon while she tended to her kit: a spoon, the flame, the syringe, the needle. Finally, she tugged on one end of that lavender scarf. I took hold.

I would have refused to help her if she hesitated in the slightest. She didn't so I sat up. I tied off her vein but I didn't watch the needle go in. The drugs were aging Sharon but if they gave her peace, who was I to deny her? When she was done, Sharon lay down beside me. The doctor said she died minutes after I took her in my arms but I was already asleep and didn't know it. We were so young. We thought nothing could hurt us. We were so unhappy despite our beauty and our wealth and we didn't know what to do about it.

I slept with a corpse that night. I slept with a corpse last night. And now I'm thinking I'm the next one to go. It's a pity I will die alone. My head lolls. The leaves smell good. My body doesn't seem to hurt so much. My eyes close. I miss Sharon. I should have saved her. I never should have gone with Simon. I never should have left Charlotte. I should have recognized the evil in Peter. I wonder if I did anything right in my whole entire life.

Then I hear a sound.

A shuffle.

I think it is the whimper of a child.

Crystal's Cafe, Corallis
<u>4:15 p.m.</u>

Simon Hart lounged in the last booth near the alley door at Crystal's Cafe.

Not the best seat in the house but nobody on the street could see him and he could see everyone coming through the front door. Except now he couldn't see anything 'cause a greasy old plastic menu was being shoved in front of his face.

"You ready to order yet, Mister?"

"No ma'am," he drawled, sliding his eyes over the more than ample Crystal. "I told you, I'm waitin' on someone. But if you're so all fired up to wait on me then pour up another cup of coffee, sweet cheeks. You got the pot right there."

The woman's free hand went to her hip. She had the ugliest hand he ever did see. It was doughy and dimpled. Her nails were too long and thick and square to be real. They were painted orange with a purple stripe on the pinky. She wore a bunch of cheap rings that cut hard into her fingers and a heart shaped wristwatch as big as a bagel. Her face was almost as bad as her hands. Coyote ugly for sure. She shifted her weight one way and the opposite hip rose under her pink, polyester pants. Reluctantly, she refilled his cup like she'd rather be pouring it into his lap.

"This isn't a library, you know. You can't just sit here all day and take up space without ordering something or such." Her lips pulled together tight, widening the tiny cracks around them. It looked like she was bleeding 'cause her lipstick was soaked into them.

"Yeah? Well, when the crowd comes in you be sure to let me know and I'll give up my seat in this fine establishment," Simon shot back.

"You just tell whoever's coming that they better order or you're both out of here. I'm not wasting anymore of my coffee on the likes of you."

With a 'humph' she left. Simon wagered that Crystal there would be singing a different tune if Tessa was sitting across from him. It was amazing what looks and a little money got you: respect, class, service. Any damn thing you wanted. People just fell all over themselves trying to please someone who was rich or beautiful. If you were both, they just let you walk all over them.

Who would have thought Tessa would grow up so good. Damn, but he'd be on easy street if he'd stuck by her. Life would have been rich, indeed. Luckily, it still could be. The front door of the diner was opening. Simon sat up straighter and put his two feet on the ground. He raised his hand. He called out.

"Over here."

His meal ticket had arrived.

Will Savick's Office
4:18 p.m.

"Ginger? I've got to go out, honey. You going to be okay with that paperwork on your own?"

Ginger looked up and smiled at Will Savick. She smiled as hard and sweet as she could because she thought he was something special. A lot of women didn't care for a man like Will, but Ginger wasn't a lot of women. She liked that he was just one big, long knot of muscle. She liked that he wasn't married and that, far as she knew, he wasn't seeing anyone. Even when he was a deputy, Will Savick didn't have a woman calling to find out what he was up to. On top of that, Ginger liked the mystery of him. He was a man who played everything close to the vest – sometimes he kept his own counsel behind a smile, sometimes behind a sharp word, sometimes just with a look from those narrow dark eyes of his. Ginger would just give anything to know what it was that made that man tick. If she couldn't figure that out, she'd settle for knowing just how far that ink on his arm went. She figured it went all the way up and over his shoulder and down his back and maybe even…

"Ginger! You got it covered?" Will barked.

Startled, Ginger's hand went to the buttons on her uniform shirt. She always did that when a man got testy with her. You'd think now that she was wearing a uniform she'd be a little tougher, but experience told her that when a man yelled the next thing was he got rough.

"Sure, Sheriff. I'm on it. Figure I'll be done about one if you want to go over it at lunch. I mean, if you're not eating on the road."

Savick's lips didn't even so much as twitch when she made the offer so Ginger stopped smiling. He checked his watch. His wide forehead was beetled; there was a little flush under his leathery tan. The man had spent a whole lot of time out in the sun, on the road with that biker group he used to ride with, and it showed. Funny how a man could change but still carry with him all the cuts and hits of what went on before. For Ginger that was just a little more sugar and spice on top of an already sweet thing.

"Just leave them on my desk. I'll take a look when I get back," Savick directed.

"Okay." Ginger answered brightly.

If he'd bothered to look, Savick would have seen that she was clearly disappointed. She was running out of coy ways to suggest they get together. Soon Ginger would have to ask him straight out and if he rejected her then that would hurt. Worse, what if he laughed?

Sighing, Ginger pulled the stack of paper toward her. She watched her boss walk across the street and get in his car. She didn't really wonder where he was going as much as she wondered how it would feel to give that poor leg of his a little massage or that tight little ass a good squeeze.

The Highway
4:30 p.m.

Will Savick cruised the highway like he was on vacation: window down, arm crooked, checking out the scenery. Wind and speed and cold made him feel alive the way few things did but speed wasn't something he wanted people to take notice of right then. He raised a friendly hand to everyone he passed but still he thought about the cold inside him. Sadly, it would take a hundred years to thaw his old heart. He'd been so sure the uniform, the badge, the responsibility would do it for him. Savick even thought a good woman might settle him some but women never held his interest for long. One was just like another. All except one. She was interesting as hell. Her heart was frozen, too, but he was the only one who knew it.

He reached for his tobacco tin but decided against a pinch. The turn would be coming up soon now that he had come to the road marker, a memorial for some stupid kid who took the curve too fast. Less than a tenth of a mile later Will Savick left the highway and followed the ancillary road to another fork.

He pulled the car into a grove. He looked for a hiker, a neighbor, one of those environmental whackos hoping to find something to protect. You just never knew who might be looking your way.

Satisfied he was alone, the sheriff put on his jacket. Like his belt and tattoo, it wasn't uniform issue. He turned the collar up high, went to the back door, knocked and waited. He heard a slither, a falling, a bending of things in the woods. Savick looked over his shoulder, unhappy that he was left standing so long. He knocked again and finally the door opened. The woman was as careful as he, opening the door slowly, standing back in the shadows, keeping to them even when he crossed the threshold. She closed the door with both hands then quite deliberately faced him.

"This isn't going to be as simple as we thought," he said.

Jake found me splayed out on the marble floor of a bathroom, drunk, stoned, puking my guts out into a bidet. It was supposed to be a party but I wasn't having fun. I was ultra-famous by then. Italy was behind me but the memories of it were never far away.

Sharon was gone. I was a mess. Preoccupied with the bidet, I didn't notice Jake step over me, to get to the toilet. When he turned to leave, though, I lifted my head, looked at him as best my bleary eyes could and said:

"I'm so sorry."

This, according to Jake, seemed not so much an apology as a lament that the world had come to this. He thought that was profound. It wasn't. Still, he locked the door, sat beside me on the floor and took my head into his lap. I lay with my knees pulled up, my hands folded under my cheek; the fetal position preferred by abused women and abandoned children. In a million years, I never would have imagined that, at my lowest and ugliest, I would have found someone to love me. Or maybe Jake was thinking to make me over, make me better, save me from myself.

Any which way — love or challenge or cause — I was grateful to him. I never repaid him for saving me but I can pay it forward. I heard a whimper in this forest and followed the sound. Now I have found me a beautiful, hurt thing just like Jake did when he found me.

Here in the forest is a fawn, her back leg pierced by a trap. A step this way or that and she would have gone on: unhurt, still beautiful, not knowing of her narrow escape. I plant my walking stick and hold tight as I lower myself to the ground. I don't want to scare her more than she already is.

"Okay, little lady, let me look there."

I coo at her the way I think a mama should talk to a child. I never had a chance to use that voice with Charlotte so I take my best shot now. The fawn's wide, dark eyes blink. Her front legs are bent, her chest is thrust out, her long neck is straight, her delicate head is turned my way.

She is so proud, so graceful, so delicately lovely. Her beauty brings to mind a question: would I have stopped if this were an ugly creature? Would Jake have wasted his time with me if I wasn't beautiful? The fawn stirs like she is impatient with me for wondering these things. She tries to get up and there is more blood. It's not a pretty sight anymore.

"Okay," I whisper, mostly to give me the strength to do what I must.

The fawn's eyes close slowly. She is trusting that I am not the one who set the trap and that feels like an honor. I touch the gleaming metal. Before I'm ready, the little doe's front legs beat at the earth, startling me. She will do more harm than good if she tries to go too soon and I don't want that.

Making noises of caution, I position myself as strong as I can. With my hands on either side of the trap I push and pull. I grunt. I sweat. Saving is a painful occupation. Jake must have been in a helluva lot of hurt all these years with saving me.

Finally, the trap gives. The fawn strains forward. Once, twice, three times she lunges, pawing at the ground as I do my best to give her enough space to escape. Just when I think I can't hold on any longer her front hooves find traction. She is up and gone, scampering off on three legs, pulling the broken, bleeding one behind her. The trap snaps back with a horrible sound. I fall on it, unhurt, not an ounce of strength left.

My arms are caught under my chest. I close my eyes. I want Jake. If not Jake, I want someone to find me the way I found the fawn. It is just then that I do feel someone thinking about me. It isn't Jake. This is a stronger, more determined mind reaching out to my weak one. I close my eyes tighter trying to make that person hear me back.

When the moment goes, I am so lonely I want to die. I have walked too far into the woods, the river is lost. I don't know which way to go. The light is fading. Doesn't matter. I see one thing *clearly. The fawn has come back. She stands beside me, shaking on three legs and bleeding from the fourth.*

I get up and gather her in my arms.

Crystal's Café, Corallis
<u>4:36 p.m.</u>

"Do you want a menu?"

Crystal went through her routine again, throwing her hip out, shoving a menu eye level. This time Jake was the one getting mad, shaking his head, waving her away.

"No. I don't need one. I don't want one."

"Well, then, mister, you and your friend can just get your butts outta here." Crystal made 'outta' a two-syllable word just to make sure he got her drift.

"Fine. Bring me a sandwich." Jake dismissed her but Crystal stayed put.

"What kind do you want," she snapped.

"I don't know. I don't know, for God sake. We have business to do." He dug in his pocket and came up with a handful of bills. "Buy yourself a sandwich, but leave us alone."

"Honey, are you sure? You could buy the place for this." Crystal looked over the wad of money with pleasure. Usually people just cussed her out when she got in their face.

"Keep it all. Go away." Jake buried his head in his hands then let them slide over his ears. He shut his eyes tightly like a child disappearing himself.

"High strung." Simon pulled a thumb at Jake and gave her a wink.

"I don't care if he's higher than a kite. Enjoy yourselves." She pocketed the money and took off. When she was out of earshot, Simon reached across and pulled on Jake's hands. Jake cringed and kept his face covered.

"Oh, hell. Come on, Jake. Lighten up. You see that caboose on her? That'll give you a chuckle. Take a look." Simon cackled and splayed himself over the table. He still smiled but his face darkened as he patted the Formica tabletop. "Okay, so you're not feeling particularly social. But, since you're in a generous mood, want to hand over mine? Come on. Come on."

"Shut up. Don't draw attention." Jake dropped his hands; his voice shook.

"Like the two of us sitting at the same table doesn't make people wonder? You are clueless." Simon sat back and drew one leg up on the seat. He had a toothpick in his mouth and moved it around like a joystick. "Cough it up, Jake. I did what you wanted with Tessa. Cross my heart and hope to die, I'll never be seeing her again." Playfully, Simon crossed his heart then held up the Boy Scout sign before his smile faded and that hand was out again. "Come on, I don't have all day."

"I'm not giving you anything until you tell me what I'm paying for. Is she dead? Did you kill her?"

"Whoa. Hey." Simon pushed himself back in the booth and held his hands up. Both feet were on the ground and he paused long enough to look shocked. Then he was leaning close again, whispering.

"I'm not getting into particulars about Tessa. Just give me my money, and I'm gone."

Jake put a hand to his cheek then he spread his fingers to hide his mouth. He talked through clenched teeth.

"I want to know what you did with her last night. Did you take her somewhere? Is that it? I'm not going to believe you just told her to go away. If that's all you did then she would have come home and she didn't."

"That's not my problem, man," Simon drawled. He took the toothpick out of his mouth and flipped it toward Jake. The other man flinched; his agitation was growing.

"I'm making it your problem. Either you killed her or she's somewhere waiting for you. Are you both laughing at me? Is that it? Are you running away together? I'm not giving you money so you can run away with my wife. I'm not paying you so you can get away with murder." Jake stretched his neck out. He was flushed, and his eyes were bulging. "I'm not a fool."

Simon matched him, mocked him as he put a hand to his own mouth and sneered. "You're right. You're not a fool, you're an idiot."

Jake's eyes filled with tears and his heart with fright. This man scared him because he was what Tessa wanted. How could she desire someone so base and brutal?

"I know whatever happened is horrible. You killed that grocer. Was Tessa with you when you did that? Was she there when you shot him? I know you were in that store. I know she was there. You're a murderer. You've got Tessa and..."

Simon threw himself at the table and grabbed Jake's collar.

"You shut up, little man. You shut up," he hissed. "You want people to think I know what you're talking about? 'Cause I don't know what you're talking about, got me?" He twisted the sweater around. Jake clawed at it but Simon had him tight. "I don't listen to the radio. I don't read no newspapers. I don't know anything about nobody getting killed. If I did, I sure as hell wouldn't be talking about it in a public place. Got that?"

"They're looking." Jake gurgled and Simon glanced toward the door. Those who had been looking weren't anymore. This was a mountain town. Simon's business was a curiosity but it was his own. Still, Simon relaxed his grip. He patted Jake's sweater back in place and took his seat again.

"Don't make me mad, man. Just don't. And don't talk like I know this dead guy, 'cause I don't," Simon complained.

Jake nodded slowly. The knot of Simon Hart's knuckles left an impression on his throat that would last until the end of his days. It would remind him that some people fought dirty. What Simon Hart didn't know was that a man of words could fight dirty, too. Jake used his last ounce of courage.

"The police believe Tessa has been kidnapped. I will tell them about you. I will tell them where to find you. I will tell them you wanted me to pay ransom for my wife. They will believe me because of who I am and because of who you are." Jake's voice quivered. "If you do not call me by this time tomorrow and tell me where I can find my wife, that's what I'll tell the police."

Jake stood up but Simon was a bully and he was fast. He grabbed the hem of Jake's sweater again then clutched at the older man's pants. It was an ungraceful, frightening attack.

"Let go of me," Jake swatted at Simon's hand. "Don't touch me again. Don't touch anything I own."

"Hey, you two," Crystal finally yelled. "Take it outside."

Simon laughed and let go of Jake Bradley. Jake stumbled and put his hand against the wall while Simon slid out of the booth. Simon put his arm around Jake like they were old friends but what he said wasn't friendly at all.

"You're such a pussy, Bradley. In case you forgot, Tessa belonged to me first. I touched her first. Hell, I done things…"

Jake shrugged off Simon's arm but the man stayed tight and uncomfortable as an itch in the wrong place.

"Okay. Okay. No need to go into detail. I get it. In fact, I should have been straight with you. I could have saved you some bucks because here's the thing: you can't pay to keep a woman, Jake. If Tessa wanted to be with you, then she would have gone home last night. You can believe me or not. No skin off my nose."

"I don't believe you. Tessa would have come to her senses. She's lived our life too long to give it up for a cheap apartment and a crass man. It was a chance in a million, you showing up here, but you don't have staying power. It was as easy as handing you money to make you leave. Tessa would have figured that out."

Jake inched away, trying to talk his way out of this mess, but Simon had him boxed in. Simon wiggled his fingers and leered.

"Oooh, Fate. That was something, wasn't it? Running into Tessa here? But the rest – that was between you and me. It doesn't matter how you said it, I did what you wanted me to do. And, as soon as you pay me, I'm gone the way I said I'd be. I am a man of my word."

"I'm not going to give you anything. This is out of hand. I'll let the police sort this out. If they want to prosecute me, then so be it. I need to know about...I just need to know where she is. You have until tomorrow."

Jake sidestepped Simon intending to find safety at the front of the restaurant. Simon, though, cut him off so Jake had bolted for the alley. The minute he was out the door Simon Hart was, too. He threw himself on Jake Bradley like a dog on a bitch. Jake hit the pavement hard. His breath came out in a whoosh and there was no time to catch it before Simon pulled Jake's arm behind him, high and tight.

"You self-righteous bastard." Simon pulled that arm harder still and Jake cried out. "You fucking millionaire, cartoon boy."

Simon drew back his fist and punched Jake in the face, grinding it into the pavement.

"You and Tessa all high and mighty. Money coming out your ears." Again, that fist came down, the power of it fueled by all the anger of a have-not, a lost-out, a never-would-be.

"Tessa thinking she was all better than me. Hell..." That fist drew back. "I should have killed her just for turning into what she turned into."

It came down again and Jake's teeth seemed to shatter.

"I should have done it a long time ago for all the heartache she's caused me."

Another smack and another. Worn out, Simon collapsed, falling on Jake, laying over him, sandwiching their right arms between their bodies. He rocked to his right. Jake's body pulled up and Simon searched his pant pocket only to come up empty. Simon rocked the other way and switched hands. Barely conscious, Jake rolled with him. Simon's hand went back into the pocket on the other side.

"You better have brought the money, you bastard."

Simon flipped Jake over. He was bleeding from his nose and his face was embedded with the dirt. He moaned, barely conscious.

"Damn if you ain't a sorry piece of work."

Simon grabbed Jake's jacket and ripped it open. Buttons flew. Fabric tore. Finally, Simon found what he wanted. He sat back, putting all his weight on Jake's legs as he opened the fat, white envelope.

"Well, here we go, now," Simon muttered as he took the money and tossed the envelope at Jake. "Nobody ever paid me to stay away from their wife before. Usually, they just beat the shit out of me, you stupid ass." Simon reached out and ruffled Jake's hair. It was wet with blood and Simon made a face at his fingers then wiped them on his pants. "Then again, there aren't many wives like Tessa who'd give me a second look, are there?"

Simon pushed off and stood over Jake Bradley.

"If I were you, I'd be heading home, Mr. Bradley." Simon held the envelope up. "Just in case anyone comes after me. If they do, they get this envelope and this money with your fingerprints all over it. And, for good measure, I'll tell 'em Tessa was screwing the dead, guy, too. Then they'll be looking at you real close because you are one jealous S.O.B."

Simon leaned down and gave Jake's head one more pat.

"If I go down, guess who's coming with me, Cartoon Man?"

I carry the fawn a long way. She dies. It's as simple as that. I dig a grave. It isn't much of one but it's the best I can do. I bury her beautiful little body. It is only later I realize that was wrong. I should have left her under the sky where her mother could find her.

Can't go back. Can't undo. I had the best of intentions. I always do.

I have forgotten the lantern.

I sit. I cry.

It does no good.

I knew it wouldn't.

It never has.

Simon Hart's Apartment
4:47 p.m.

"Is Judge Marston still handling things around here?" Dove asked.

"You bet." Mike nodded.

"Then I want you to go down and get a warrant. Soon as you've got it we're going to tear this place apart. Who does your forensics?"

"We send down to the valley." Mike zipped up his jacket. "Back in half an hour with that warrant."

When he was gone Dove dialed Jessica, congratulating himself for finding a couple of nails he could drive into Simon Hart's coffin. That scarf was a big deal. It had a sheen and weight that screamed expensive. No mountain woman owned a thing like that and no woman who did used it like a rag. A woman didn't...

"Sheriff Connelly's office, Jessica speaking."

"Jessica," Dove said. "Glad you're there. I'm going to be awhile yet. Have you heard from Nathan?"

"Nothing for the last couple hours. Do you want me to run him down?"

"No. I just wanted to touch base." Dove answered. "What about Cherie. You haven't heard from her, have you?"

"Matter of fact, Dove, she made a point of leaving you a message around one o'clock. She said, and I quote, tell the sheriff I've gone home to lock myself in tight and he can call me there if he has a mind to. Unquote. What did you do to her, Dove? She was in a snit for sure."

Dove chuckled. "I looked at her cross-eyed."

"Well, don't do it again, you hear? We've got enough people beside themselves around here."

Dove smiled, relieved that worry was off his plate. There was nothing to do now but wait and wonder who would walk through that door first: Mike with a warrant or Simon Hart. Mike came back first – without the warrant. The judge was out sick.

I started lying to Jake because I wanted to see Simon. How could I have lied to him? That good man who saved me?

I lied to myself, too. Somehow I convinced myself that Simon, Charlotte and me would be a family the way we were meant to be in the beginning. I tried not to think about how wrong it felt to wait in Starbucks like a call girl, how dirty I felt sitting in Simon's broken car.

I tried to overlook his old, worn clothes and ignore how sick I felt lying to the man who cared for me. I fooled myself into thinking this was love because, when I looked at my daughter, I saw Simon's face. When it came time to choose, though, I came to my senses. There was a lot to lose. The only thing to gain was the settling of my heart and that wasn't much compared to losing Jake and Charlotte.

On the upside, as Peter would have pointed out, a scandal would revitalize my career. There was news in a woman like me leaving some one like Jake for a man like Simon. But even that seemed less an opportunity and more a big, backward step.

I must have grown up some 'cause I knew Simon wasn't worth tossing away everything I had worked for. I felt a little sick that I'd wasted all those years pining for the likes of him. I will tell this to Jake. I will make him see that I have grown up and will make it up to him for my emotional transgressions. How could I think that where I came from was where I wanted to be again?

It makes me sad that I ever wanted to go backwards and it devastates me to see that I have done so again. I have come full circle in this forest. I am back at the mine. I have gotten nowhere.

I look at my watch to see how much time I have wasted. I'm an idiot. The watch is broken and I am screwed.

I crawl back inside.

This is it. I'll wait to die.

Dove's Mountain, the woods
5:00 p.m.

It was near impossible to walk a straight line in the forest but Jed Braimen did the best he could. He inched around trees, ducked under branches, and used a stick to perforate the low brush. His brother Karl liked to weave wide and it bothered Jed to no end because that's not what they were supposed to do.

"If you do that you might miss something. Nathan specifically said to stay shoulder to shoulder and walk straight," Jed called out, berating his brother.

"That only works when there's a whole lot of us and we're in an open field or on a beach or someplace flat. It doesn't work up here," Karl shot back.

"Still, we could miss something really important," Jed groused. Frustrated, he stopped and took his hat off to wipe at his brow.

Concentrating like this, knowing he was probably looking for a body, made him sweat through the cold. And he was hungry. And he didn't want to find a dead person. And it wasn't like they were looking for one of their own but he would keep that thought to himself. Cherie Connelly gave him an earful when he said it out loud and he wasn't about to say it again, even to Karl.

Jed put his hat back on and considered there were only two good things about today: he didn't have to work and he got to Fritz's store long after the body had been carted away. It was awful enough seeing all that blood. If he'd seen Fritz's dead body Jed would have had nightmares for a year.

"Think we're wasting our time?" Karl asked as he shuffled through the pine needles and the muck left wet from the night before. Half-heartedly he hit the heavy brush with his stick. Even Karl, always the optimist, was starting to think this was a wild goose chase.

"I don't know. How am I supposed to know how a kidnapper thinks?" Jed asked. "Or a killer for that matter."

Karl shrugged and took out a smoke. He leaned back against a tree, lit his cigarette, took a good drag then put his head back to rest a minute. The mists and the fogs hadn't exactly cleared; they had just slipped away down a gulley or wound themselves up high in the trees. It kind of felt like when him and Jed were kids and their mom threw a blanket over some chairs and called it a tent. It was that kind of quiet and that kind of weird cold/warm. Karl thought this was the most beautiful sort of day in the mountains. If that woman was still alive she'd have the day; if she was dead, there wasn't a better place to lie. Karl also knew, alive or dead, the forest made it near impossible to find someone who wasn't supposed to be found.

Fritz's murder was one thing. You could see what was left after the deed was done, but the woods were a sponge. Whatever happened here – good or bad – it would all be soaked up and held tight. It would take a helluva powerful person to squeeze the secrets out.

"I think we're wasting our time, Jed," Karl mused. He wasn't really making a decision; he was just throwing the idea out there. "I think we should go back and tell Nathan there's nothing here."

Jed hunkered down, still poking at the ground. Karl watched him with a lazy eye and smoked in his lazy way.

"I mean, I'm no expert or anything," Karl went on with great practicality, "but it seems to me that if whoever killed Fritz took this woman, they would have pretty much killed her right off. And, if they did that, and they were running hard, they would just dump her soon as they could. Maybe they'd put her a little ways in to give 'em some time to get away – I could see that – but I don't think you'd drag her all the way up here. I don't think they'd keep her tied up or anything. I mean, we've gone about as far as a mile."

Jed attended to his brother as Karl blew smoke through his nostrils, his eyes almost crossing as he checked out the trick. Karl was a nice looking man. Divorced twice, no kids, he had a passel of bad habits and a good head on his shoulders. Jed was a little more fanciful. Maybe it was because he was younger or maybe because he was never really happy in all this quiet. He wanted a little more excitement than his days afforded so he let his mouth run on to what he was imagining in his head.

"Unless whoever took her is a freak, Karl. I mean there was just a story about that guy in Austria who kidnapped that girl and kept her as a sex slave for like seventeen years. There's been a bunch of guys like that. Maybe whoever took her has a slave house out here. You know, a sex slave place. Whooee, what if we could find that?"

Jed twisted his head this way and that as if he expected one to materialize. Karl snorted the notion away and Jed smiled. He knew Karl would be just as excited if they found something like that. They'd be heroes. They would be on TV.

"There's been two or three we've heard of and they're always in really strange places like Austria or down in Georgia," Karl snorted.

"That doesn't mean it couldn't happen up here," Jed insisted, not ready for his brother to take the fun out of this adventure. "I mean, there are plenty of places to hide, lots of old shacks all up and down the mountain. What about the abandoned mines? We wouldn't even know anyone was up there if they were hiding in those places. That woman might be chained up right now, as we speak. Hey. Hey. Maybe she could be in some sort of coffin. I heard about that, too."

Jed shivered, so taken was he with the story he was spinning. Karl ground out his cigarette on the trunk of the tree. He picked a piece of tobacco off his tongue so that he sounded like he had a lisp when he talked.

"Yeah, I suppose. Still, I think it's a little far fetched. I could see it if she was some young thing, but she's older, you know."

"Yeah, but she's really pretty. I wouldn't kick her out of bed for eating crackers," Jed chuckled.

"You wouldn't kick any woman out of bed, crackers or not," Karl pointed out.

Jed chuckled then he and Karl laughed together because it was the truth.

"I think somebody came through here, took out Fritz just 'cause they didn't like the look of him and grabbed that woman 'cause they did like the look of her. Simple as that," Karl said this like God's own truth. "That's what I'd do if I was a murderer."

"Yeah, well you're not." Jed stood up, put his hands on his back and stretched. "I still say there's something bigger than us that's happened. We just get too settled up here, Karl. The rest of the world is pretty complicated. People do stuff we'd never even think of doing. Even for all my talk about going somewhere else, I really like it up here. It's nice except when something like this happens. I'm just happy it doesn't happen very often."

Jed picked up a stone and threw it over the tangle of undergrowth. He knew he cleared it because he heard it bounce off a rock on the other side then tic-tac-toe down an incline. He perked up. He picked up another stone and got ready to throw it.

"Hey, did you hear that?" Jed cocked his head. He held up a hand. "I didn't know there was a creek down..."

"Shhh." Karl waved Jed quiet. His head was cocked, his eyes were narrowed. "Listen."

"I heard it. That rock hit water down there." Jed whispered back as he wiped his hands on his pants. "I'm not going to fall for any of your jokes..."

"No. No. I mean it." Karl waved again, annoyed. "I heard something. Listen."

Jed searched the woods like he could see what Karl was talking about. He listened hard.

"There," Karl whispered. "There."

"Oh, my God," Jed whispered back. "I hear it. Damn straight, I hear it. That's the dog going off."

"Then let's get our rears in gear, brother. We got us something going on," Karl whooped.

"I hope it's that woman he found," Jed hollered, chasing back the way they came.

"I hope she's alive," Karl called over his shoulder as he led the way.

After I came back from Italy, I offered my mama a fortune to let Charlotte go but by that time Charlotte was mama's gravy train.

Mama threatened to tell a court of law and the newspapers that I was an unfit mother. There were records: the motel, the ambulance, the hospital. I didn't want anyone to know why I had been in the hospital — especially Charlotte — so I went away with my tail between my legs. I went away without my baby and it seemed there wasn't much sense to my life after that. I was in so much pain that I finally understood Sharon. Drugs and drink never quite cured my pain but it dulled it enough to live with it.

After I married, though, Jake managed what I couldn't. He never told me how much he paid my mama or what he threatened; he just brought my baby home. He presented Charlotte like a jewel. I reacted like I didn't care for the setting.

What did he expect? Charlotte was confused. I was ashamed about what had happened to me and about leaving her in the first place. I shouldn't have been, but who's to say I was wrong? I missed a lifetime of important things while I brooded about the past. Now I almost miss something important because of my self pity. That is the most useless emotion of all, self pity. I must leave the past behind and tend to the moment because salvation is close. There are men somewhere. I can hear them. I almost missed them because I was wrapped up in my sorrow.

Their voices are distant but distinct and it takes no more time than a mule kick for me to get myself up out of the dirt. I fall hard on my knee and howl in frustration and pain only to quiet real quick. I wait, barely breathing, hoping they heard that.

They call my name!

They must have heard me!

I move fast. My knapsack flaps against me as I hurry along. I make my way, hand-over-hand on the smooth rock wall of the tunnel. I try to run, dragging one foot behind me, as I go toward the fading light ahead.

"Hold on. Don't go."

I call out to the light and holler to those men as I shoot out of that tunnel. The smile on my face fades fast because I have taken a wrong turn and come out in a different part of the forest. Taller trees. Higher branches. There are boulders, not stones, in my way. I am on an incline like the one I fell down but brambles cover the rise like an unkempt beard. The sound of the men's voices is muffled. They seem to be farther away. The beat of my heart spikes.

"I'm here!"

I throw myself at the slope. The pain is excruciating as I climb. I slip. I scramble over the rocks and clutch at the boulders. I hear them again.

"Here! Help..."

I am caught midway between the rise and the bottom. With my left hand I hold onto a bush with thistles. The key is still in my right and I'm afraid to open it for fear it will be lost. I'm scared to go up and terrified of falling down.

"Here. Please."

I say this so small it will take God's ears to hear it. A dog yaps and barks the way the ones in my town did when they lived their life chained to a stake in a dirty yard. Those desperate dogs would snap their necks for one last chance to be free. I am that desperate. Tears stream down my face; so many tears that my hair is wet. I cry buckets.

I pull myself up a few inches. My arm is stretched almost out of the socket. My dirty hand looks awful. They are right. I am old. It is the cold. I can't see the blue of the blood in the veins running beneath the surface of my skin. I have hold of a sapling. My shoulder is blazing. My face scrapes along the dirt as I pull and pull until I am lying over the tip of the ridge. I raise my head and see that there are two of them going one way and a third further on. They are running and calling out. I am silent, so tired I don't even hear my own breath. I should. I must be gasping for it this climb has been so hard. That's okay, though. I have faith they will feel my presence because it's always been that way. But I am not the Tessa of old. The magic is lost on these men who weave in and out of the trees as they run away from me.

I cannot speak and I cannot hold on.

I am sliding, sliding, sliding down again.
I was so close to salvation. So very close.

Bernadette's House
5: 12 p.m.

"Bernadette?" Cherie called softly as she closed the back door.

The house was stuffy with neglect, most of the rooms shut off. It was strange how quickly the life got sucked out of a home – faster than it got sucked out of a person if Bernadette was any indication. Dove wouldn't be happy that Cherie was here again, but Bernadette hadn't picked up the phone during Cherie's afternoon check so here she was, straightening things as she went.

In the living room, Bernadette was curled so tight under her covers Cherie almost missed her. The coming storm made the twilight even darker so Cherie navigated carefully around all the equipment: the IV stand near the chair that was close to the fireplace, the hospital bed cranked up at the feet to ease the pain in Bernadette's legs when she managed to climb in. There were monitors and beepers and testers and machines that Cherie would have to figure out how to work now that Fritz was gone. The place was Bernadette's own private hospital.

"Hi." Bernadette's voice was muffled.

"You scared me," Cherie whispered. Smiling, she knelt by the couch so that she was nose-to-nose with her friend. "I thought you were asleep."

"Resting." She licked her dry lips. "Why you here?"

"I was worried," Cherie put one hand on Bernadette's head and lay her cheek on the sofa. They stayed like that, the two women looking at one another until, slowly, Bernadette's eyes closed.

"Did you eat?" Cherie asked. "Just shake your head. Yes or No."

"Soup," she answered instead.

"You sound like you have wool in your mouth."

Cherie sat up, poured some water from the carafe and held it to Bernadette's lips. The sick woman made an effort but Cherie doubted much got through. Putting aside the cup, she took the baby out of her carrier, lifted the edge of Bernadette's quilt and eased the infant under.

"Here, you go. I know you have a cuddle or two left in you. Hang on to her and I'll pick up a little."

"No." Bernadette's eyes opened, she tried to object.

"Yes," Cherie insisted. "Then I'll get your pills and leave you alone. Unless you've changed your mind since this morning?"

"No," Bernadette whispered and put her lips to the baby's head.

With the baby cared for, Cherie went about her chores: changing the laundry, putting Fritz's thread-bare robe on the back of the door, washing down the sink, counting out Bernadette's morphine pills — then counting the rest to make sure Bernadette wasn't taking more than she should.

Back in the living room Cherie tackled the mail stacked up on the dining room table. Before she could get to sorting it, Bernadette jerked and moaned. Cherie rushed to the couch. In one fluid movement she took the baby and set her down on the rug before tending to her friend. Bernadette's cheek was ice cold so Cherie turned up the thermostat before checking the hearth.

Bernadette had made a half-hearted attempt to start a fire but she had only managed to burn a bunch of paper. Junk mail, newspapers and bills of lading from the store were crumpled inside the fireplace. Poor Bernadette didn't care what she burned, it seemed. Cherie made two trips to the woodpile then stacked the wood on the hearth. She stuffed the paper and kindling between the logs, checked the flue, and lit the fire. She stoked it until it caught.

Sitting in its warmth, she watched her baby play as Bernadette struggled with whatever was happening inside her head. Maybe her brain was like the fire, blazing one minute, burning low the next, crackling and popping with memories of Fritz alive, exploding with the realization that Fritz was dead. Cherie could not cry right now. There was too much to do. It was only nature taking its course: the baby at the beginning of her life, Bernadette at the end and Cherie in the middle to see that the circle was complete. The baby cooed. The room was cozy. Bernadette had stopped her thrashing and moaning so Cherie scooped up a dish near the chair.

"She didn't eat more than a few spoonfuls." Cherie talked softly to her daughter as she passed. "Sit tight. We're almost done."

In the kitchen the floor needed a sweep and a wash but today wasn't the day. The sink was dirty with gooey black stuff and a beer bottle sat near empty on the counter. One Cherie washed down the drain, the other she tossed. Putting some applesauce in a dish, she went back to the living room, set it on the table and took Bernadette's cold hands between her own.

"Hey, what have you been doing?" she said, holding up her friend's dirty fingers. Bernadette opened her eyes, lips parted. It was hard to watch her struggle with the simplest thing so Cherie laughed away the question. "Don't worry, it was rhetorical. I have your pills. Want to take them now?"

Bernadette struggled up. Cherie handed her the first one and then the water. Bernadette choked on the second and it took another three minutes for her to get it down. Cherie chatted, trying to make this all seem normal.

"I see you had a visitor."

Bernadette shook her head.

"No?" Cherie said. "Then you've taken to drinking, huh?"

Bernadette's eyelids fluttered.

"Fritz," she whispered and lay down again. Slowly she pulled the quilt over her shoulder.

Sighing, Cherie tucked Bernadette in and picked up the baby. Poor Fritz had quit drinking years ago. Pity he had taken it up again. Not that he didn't have cause. Still, it didn't matter now so Cherie started for the chair near the fireplace. Bernadette stopped her.

"Go home," she mumbled.

"I'll stay awhile..."

"Dove..." Bernadette insisted.

Cherie smiled sadly. The widow was sending the wife back to her man. What a lonely, lovely thing for her to do even though they both knew Dove wouldn't stop looking for whoever killed Fritz until long into the night.

"Okay, I won't fight you." Cherie bent down, put her cheek against Bernadette's. She let herself out not knowing the last thing the sick woman wanted was for Dove to come looking for his wife.

Outside Simon Hart's Apartment
6:00 p.m.

Michael McCall applied to the police academy before the ink was dry on his high school diploma. It was pretty much that or the army since there was no money for college and no great passion gripped him.

In six weeks he learned that he was a good negotiator, a patient student, a great runner, had a decent brain, a high moral standard and was a pretty good shot. Mike also learned that he wasn't exactly a coward, he just didn't share his classmates' desire to mix it up and that limited his employment opportunities.

His first interview was with old Harold Lynd, sheriff in Corallis for a hundred years. It was more like two hours of drinking coffee and listening to stories of a career gone slow. Harold warned Mike that if he was a hot dog he could just walk right out the door 'cause he already had one of those by the name of Will Savick. All the while, Ginger fussed in the outer office, singing along softly with the radio every time a love ballad came on. Mike felt like he was home.

The only glitch was Savick. He was smooth, glad-handing everyone, greasing the skids for Harold's ride out of town. Mike didn't care for the man but, while Harold was around, there was no trouble. Then Harold had a stroke, Savick took over and things changed.

Not that Mike had been called upon to do anything out of the ordinary; not that Corallis had changed really. It was Savick whose edge got sharper. He kept a tight reign on Mike and Ginger yet his own business was his own. Savick was casual, rolling up his sleeves, chewing on that smokeless tobacco even in the office, laughing like a good old boy one minute and bad-mouthing people the next. None of it was wrong but all of it made the deputy antsy and uncomfortable.

Still, Mike reasoned, all this may just be the difference between a complacent old man and a young one who wanted to swim big in this little pond. And, if what was happening now came down on the right side for the law, Mike McCall had little doubt it would be Savick taking the praise for catching a fish like Simon Hart.

"Round left!" Dove bellowed. "Left!"

Mike bolted around the side of the garage, pumping his arms, raising those legs. He was just in time to see Simon Hart dodge right again and head across the street. Once he got there, Dove was bound to lose him. This was Mike's place and, now that he was putting everything together, it was feeling pretty good. Not like when Hart walked in on them. The way Mike acted had been just plain pitiful.

The whole thing took a second and a half: Hart's eyes bugged out, Dove's narrowed to pinpoints, Mike's mouth fell open. Hart turned on a dime and took the outside steps two at a time as he ran. Wiry, he flipped himself over the railing before he got to the bottom. Tripping, falling, scrambling he sprinted off before Dove could catch him or Mike got his speed up. Still, Mike joined in with a whoop. Younger than Dove and faster, he caught up in no time and the chase was on.

All the while Mike heard music in his head. It sounded like someone pickin' a banjo. Dove and Hart went this way and that way. Mike zigged and zagged then he saw Simon Hart make a mistake.

"Dove! Go that way. That way!"

Mike screamed at the top of his lungs and jumped up a little. He threw his arm toward a tight stand of trees a couple of times to make sure Dove understood. To his credit Dove changed direction seamlessly. If Hart was going where Mike thought he was going, Dove would cut him off easy. Mike would pull up the rear. Slam, bam, they'd have their man.

Giving it all he had, Mike dashed into the street, dodging a truck whose driver was none too happy with the scare and flipped the deputy off to prove it. Mike barely noticed as he rolled around and over the hood. He hit the shoulder of the road running. Dove and Simon were nowhere to be seen but Mike sure could hear them. Just past the brush and trees there was a hell of a fight going on. It wasn't Dove doing the yelling so Mike wasn't at all surprised when he burst through and saw the sheriff holding onto a slightly bloody Simon Hart. Still winded, Mike bent from the waist and put his hands on his knees to catch his breath. He raised his eyes to Dove.

"You alright?" Dove asked.

"Yeah, thanks."

Mike straightened. He drew the back of his hand across his nose. It was cold, his cheeks were hot and he fought the urge to laugh from the sheer joy of getting their man.

"Take care of this."

Dove shoved Hart toward Mike who caught him, cuffed him and pointed him in the right direction. Dove picked up his hat and straightened his jacket. He dusted off the knees of his pants, gave Simon Hart a good long look.

"Nice work, McCall."

"My pleasure, sheriff," Mike answered.

He pushed Simon Hart ahead of him so the man couldn't see him grinning.

I've decided it's time to let go of Italy now. I won't go to my grave giving Ubert Yahobi the upper hand. Basically, the guy made dresses. He was never a god. To make him irrelevant I have to look the whole matter of Italy straight on and make my peace. It would be easier if someone was there to hold my hand but I am alone, not even my little fawn is there to comfort me. So, I do what I have to.

Italy was a long time ago and yet it feels as if it happened yesterday.

Ubert Yahobi.

The great designer's face was pulled tight but no surgeon could make it stay put. His skin fell in folds, drooping around the eyes and cascading around his mouth. It had been sanded and peeled to sheen. His grey hair was dry and dull. He looked like he was made of wax.

He spoke softly, his words muffled by a faint rumble as if he didn't trust himself to speak. He didn't touch me as we began our work. Instead, he invited me to raise my chin, turn my head, spread my arms, and stand in front of him so that he might see the perfect contours of my face and body.

I won't lie, I was excited by all this, and it wasn't just about money. For the first time, I felt powerful and validated. Peter set me on this road, Yahobi was at the end of it. Because I had been chosen, I would become rich. That meant I would build the next road I walked down and I would say where it ended. I would finally control my life.

Seamstresses stitched 'round the clock, waking me when fittings were necessary. Peter set up his equipment. Assistants manicured the locations. Make-up artists studied my face, stylists twisted my hair, fried it, fluffed it. Yahobi's people from New York poured over layouts and media schedules and discussed launch strategy. I ate lobster from crystal that had belonged to a queen. We shot from sunrise to sunset. I wore clothes that felt like my skin. My work was great art. I had a gift and I gave it to Ubert Yahobi.

Peter was gone by the eighth day.

I was invited to stay on to rest.

On the tenth day Ubert Yahobi and the big man came to my bedroom. It was time for me to say thank you to Ubert Yahobi for all he had done for me. The big man was there to see that I thanked him properly. He took my arm. He held it above my head. I was half asleep until I felt something cold on my wrist. With that, I woke up pretty darn fast. I'll never forget how cold and heavy that thing was.

I am cold all over now. I blink. I have been so lost in thought I felt myself transported to Italy. But I am not at Yahobi's villa; I am lying on the banks of a river. I get up only to sink knee deep in mud. To reach solid ground I Frankenstein step through the muck.

While I do, I try to remember how I got here but I can't. Maybe I lost my mind, blacking out once those men ran away. Maybe I wandered through the forest shell-shocked. Either way, here I am.

Dirty and scared. When I hit solid ground and turn around, I see there is a watermelon-wedge of a boat just waiting for me on the other side of this river.

I don't have the words to describe what I feel. Relief is solid, hope springs eternal. I want to shout out that I am saved but there is no one to hear. Besides, I'm not really saved. The boat is on the other side of the river.

Since I can't walk on water like Jesus, I look for another way – shallow water, a bridge, anything. Upstream the trees shade the river and I can't see clearly. Downstream is a bend that cuts off my view. I could walk for miles and never find a place to cross. In front of me the water is calm and deep. There is nothing to do but swim for it.

I open my pack and take out the food tins. When I do, I see the piece of paper inside, the one I couldn't read in the mine. It says: Giant Sail. I shake my head and look again. It says: Giant Sale. It's an advertisement, yellowed from age. Wishful thinking gives me a sorely needed chuckle. I toss it away, sling my backpack over my shoulders and pull the straps tight. My wound starts to bleed. I can see red seeping across my sweater like a Rorschach test.

Bracing myself, I hold my stick out and Frankenstein step back through the mud before I lose my nerve. The water is so cold it burns. I want to turn back. Instead, I plunge in and get it over with. My stick is buoyant. It won't hold me up but it makes me feel secure. I bob gently in the river but, sadly, the surface of that water was deceptive. There is a current and it locks onto me. A moment later I understand that this current is not at the bottom of the river – it is the river. I am swept along, washed at an angle toward the boat but still not close enough to grab on.

Suddenly the swift water becomes dangerous. I am slammed against a rock, thrown up and crashed down. The water pulls me under. My rucksack catches on a branch and I am caught with it. Even empty, the weight of it is enormous. I fight against the odds *and listen to the underwater sounds: bubbles, my swallowed scream, fish talking. I swear I hear fish talking.*

Then I am up again and breathing. Gasping. Gulping. Under again but the rucksack is gone and I'm free. My left arm breaks the surface. I reach for the boat. My fingernails scrape old wood.

Under. Holding my breath. Above me the water roils. I twist and turn. The fishes come closer. Their fish lips purse. Their little heads shake with dismay. They blow me kisses. Blow me on my way. So sorry. But there is no time to say good-bye. In fact, for me, time has run out.

My watch is gone.

Denny's Parking Lot, Williamsberg
<u>6:12 p.m.</u>

Brian Drake sat in his car and thought about his choices. He could drive all the way back to the field office with nada since the big drug informants he'd been sent to meet turned out to be nothing but a bunch of old hippies growing their own weed, or he could stop in Corallis and see if Dove Connelly was still there. It would be easier if he just waited for Connelly to return his call. On the other hand, if he went to Corallis Brian Drake could chat up the redhead in the local Sheriff's office, the one who wore her uniform so very well. If Connelly was there like he said he would be then it would be the old two birds with one stone scenario even though the only bird he was really interested in was the redhead. It was a no-brainer. Before Brian got the government-issue car fired up, he dialed the field office. He told them that he was going to track down something promising in Corallis — no need for them to know the something promising went by the name of Ginger.

Dying thoughts should be comforting. Mine aren't.

The cold thing Yahobi's man put on my wrist was a manacle made of gold. The other end of the chain was locked around the bedpost. I thought it was a joke. When I figured out it wasn't, I fought like a wild cat.

I called for Peter even though he was gone. I swore a blue streak. I threatened. Yahobi was not put off. He watched it all without expression.

Underneath his silken robe he became horribly aroused. This old, disgusting stud could have had any woman for the asking but Yahobi, it seemed, found sport in the taking. My helplessness, my beauty, the fact that, for most men, I was unattainable made me attractive but what made me irresistible was my fear.

The big man stepped back.

Yahobi opened his robe.

I screamed. He hit me in the stomach so my face wouldn't be marred. Still, I fought. Silently, breathlessly. I fought then like I fight now. The two incidents are one and, as I drown, I hear the rattle of that gold chain. I hear the bedpost crack because I pulled so hard. I heard another crack that day and it didn't sound like wood. Before I could look, Ubert Yahobi hit me again.

Then Ubert Yahobi raped me.

Sheriff's Office, Corallis
6:24 p.m.

"Look at this. Look!" Dove grabbed Simon's wrist and waved the man's own hand in front of his face. "You have blood on your hands. We got a scarf with blood on it. There's blood on your pants and we have a fair idea of who that blood belongs to. We have a whole lot of money that we know you didn't make working at Cy Talbot's. So, if you want to save any part of your sorry ass, I suggest you start talking."

Releasing Simon's wrist, Dove twisted around and propped himself up on Savick's desk. His expression was so black that Mike McCall expected Simon Hart to turn into a pillar of salt. But Hart wasn't looking at Dove. He was rubbing his wrists like he'd been bound with barbed wire and his eyes still kind of wiggled like he couldn't quite get them settled in his head.

"I ain't got nothing to tell you about nothing," he growled.

"You sure about that?" Mike spoke up to just feel useful.

It wasn't like Connelly needed him unless it was to keep the sheriff from killing Simon Hart. Mike had seen losers. He had seen men with a lot of hate in them. He had seen cowards and bullies. He had seen men down on their luck and men up on it and men who still gambled even though they had never had any luck to begin with. He had just never seen all that wrapped into one man before. Simon Hart was that odd mix of great potential and a train wreck.

"I couldn't get my window open this morning in my apartment. Scraped up my knuckles trying to open it. Cut myself when it finally gave." Hart cut his eyes to Dove. "Damn, my head hurts. I'm going to sue your butt. That was police brutality. That's what it was."

"The windows were closed in your apartment. It's too cold to have them open." Dove paid Hart's complaint no mind. Mike tried to remember if the windows were opened or closed. He had his answer a second later.

"Then it was my car," Simon shot back.

"Then we'll find that out. We impounded it for tests," Dove replied smoothly.

"My car? You bastard." Simon made a move and Mike clamped down on his shoulder. Even Hart could figure out the math. Two against one were not good odds.

"We're having it tested for blood right now. We'll let you know what we find on that window." Dove raised an eyebrow then leaned forward and looked at Hart's knuckles again. "Looks to me like you were trying to keep someone in line. Maybe it was Tessa Bradley."

"Who?"

"The woman who disappeared last night. Six one. Blonde hair. Blue eyes. Dressed real well. People noticed a woman like that with a guy like you."

Dove reached behind him to a paper bag. He opened it.

"She was probably wearing this."

Like a magician on stage, he pulled the bloody scarf from the bag showing just enough of it to tease. Hart registered just enough fear to please Dove.

141

"Oh, sure. Tessa. Yeah. I saw her last night. We're old friends." Hart tossed his head and his long hair creeped into the collar of his shirt. He flipped it out again.

"How long have you known her?"

"All my lousy life," he shot back only to note their skepticism. "Come on. We grew up together in Texas. Small world, huh? It's funny us running into each other again. We were just catching up. No law against that."

"Where were you doing this catching up?" Dove asked.

"Here. There." Simon shrugged.

"The Mountain Store?" Dove asked.

"Never heard of it."

Dove looked at Mike. The deputy went to Savick's desk, picked up a manila envelope, reached in and handed Dove a piece of paper. Dove, in turn, held it up for Simon Hart.

"We found this in your apartment. It's a receipt from Fritz's Mountain Store for a six-pack and cigarettes. It's dated last night."

"You have a warrant to search my place?" Hart demanded, his bravado lasting only until Dove leaned close and gave him a fierce look.

"Don't push me," Dove warned.

"Okay, I saw Tessa last night. She brought me a little present. Look for yourself. Camels. That's what I smoke. She told me she stopped for them and that's probably the place she stopped."

"What does she smoke?"

"I don't know. Some long cigarette. Something." Hart's brow pulled together. Thinking was hard. "We had coffee and I remember her saying she was almost out. No law against smoking yet, is there?"

Dove remained expressionless. The butts in Tessa's car matched: One Camel Filter, two Marlboro Lights 100.

"Not yet, but the law doesn't look kindly on murder. The owner of that store was killed last night. We found a shotgun in your apartment..."

Hart blanched. His head swiveled between Mike and Dove while he weighed his choices: tell a lie, the truth or confront with outrage. Hart chose wrong.

"You had no right. No right at all to go looking around my place," Hart shouted. "You show me the warrant. You show me..."

"No need. Your roommate gave us permission to look all we wanted," Mike answered.

"My what?" Hart started out of his chair, incensed, indignant only to deflate a second later. Still, he struggled, trying to work his way out of the mess. "Damn bitch. K.C. ain't my roommate. She couldn't give you permission."

"That's why the deputy there called for a warrant. We're going to be headed back there to tear your place apart, Hart." Dove made his voice real low and thoughtful. "I'm thinking it was that gun in your closet that killed the grocer. And I'm thinking whoever killed the grocer knows what happened to Tessa Bradley.
And–" Dove was almost whispering now. "If Tessa Bradley is dead then you're looking real good for a double homicide unless you can show us otherwise."

"Tessa took off last night. I swear. I cut my hand on the car. She gave me that scarf and I wrapped it around. See?" he held up his hand and sure enough there was a cut. Not long, not deep but it would have bled some. "I brought her to my place. Things didn't go the way I thought so I took her back to her car. She took off somewhere around twelve or twelve-thirty. I don't know nothing after that."

Like a cornered rat, Hart looked for a way out as he tried to convince either lawman he was telling the truth.

"And I wouldn't hurt Tessa. We got history. Way back when we had something big. Even I didn't know how big until I saw her again. Pure happenstance, I swear. "And she came after me. I was minding my own business and she came after me. Hell, I'd have to be made of stone not to want a piece of that action when it shows up on my doorstep."

Hart talked fast, scared because he knew what they were thinking. A woman like Tessa coming after him sounded crazy. Simon sniffed.

"You got a Kleenex or something. My nose is starting to bleed again."

"Suck it up." Dove pushed off the desk. "You think I'm going to believe that woman was in the store alone and killed the grocer?"

Hart wiped the back of his sleeve across his nose, checked out the damage and talked to the sleeve.

"Damn straight. I didn't do anything to the fat bastard."

"How did you know what the grocer looked like if you've never been in there?" Dove asked.

"Okay, I've been in there." Hart's eyes cut away from Dove as he realized his mistake. "But not yesterday and if he got offed then he probably deserved it. The way he looked at me when I was in there the week before, like I was scum. Like I wasn't worthy to walk behind Tessa much less be in the same place with her. You ask me, he was jealous. Fat boy probably couldn't get any of his own so…well…the dick head…"

Simon never knew what hit him. Dove's attack was so swift and smooth Mike wasn't even sure it had happened. But when Dove walked out of the office there was fresh blood gushing out of Simon Hart's nose so Mike figured he hadn't imagined anything.

Mike tossed the whole box of tissue at Hart and followed along after Dove.

Dove was in the bathroom soaping his hands so hard it seemed he wanted to wash them right off the ends of his arms.

"You okay, Sheriff Connelly?" Mike stuck his head through the door.

"Been better."

Dove yanked a paper towel out of the holder and listened. Simon Hart had stopped howling and was screaming bloody murder about owning Dove, suing the state, the city and anyone else he could think of. They heard a thump and a crash. The man was throwing around Savick's furniture.

"Take a lesson, McCall." Dove said.

"What would that be, Sheriff?"

"Don't do anything like that unless you really mean it." Dove wadded up the paper towel and tossed it in the trash.

"I'll remember that," Mike answered.

"So what do you think about him?" Dove leaned back against the wall between the front office and the cells.

"He's low and he's stupid. If he was smart, he would have told us he was home asleep last night and alone. Least of all, he'd be waiting on a lawyer before admitting he knew Mrs. Bradley. It's the murder I'm not sure about."

Mike moved over and put his shoulder up against the doorjamb as he listened.

"Yeah, I know." Dove's disappointment was palpable. "I'm thinking to take that shotgun with me. It was in clear sight. We can get around it if you'll sign off on the paperwork."

"Sure. I'll do it."

Mike answered without hesitation. Dove was appreciative and not above asking for more favors as Mike went to Ginger's desk in search of a release. Another crack was heard in the office. The men paused and Ginger shrieked then they got back to business.

"Do you think you could check on any friends Hart had around here who can verify when he was with Tessa Bradley?" Dove went on. "Also check with any of the neighbors who might have seen him coming and going. I'm especially interested if they saw a man with Hart on a regular basis. What he looked like, how he dressed. And I'm going to need…"

"You're needing an awful lot from my deputy, Sheriff."

Mike looked up and Dove looked over his shoulder. The grin on Will Savick's face wasn't exactly neighborly. Neither man had heard him come in and Ginger was looking ashamed that she hadn't given warning. Savick kept his hand on the knob like he was ready to help Dove out the door.

"Don't get me wrong, Connelly, we're happy to help keep your problems out of Corallis. Better nip it all in the bud, right?"

"That's what I was thinking," Dove agreed.

"Good. Then we're all on the same page." Savick raised his chin toward Mike. "You go on ahead with what you were doing McCall."

It was that very minute the prisoner chose to raise his voice to high heaven again. Savick looked toward his office.

"Simon Hart," Mike ventured. "The man Sheriff Connelly was looking for."

"Well, we'll be happy to take care of that too because it seems you're one popular man, Sheriff Connelly." Savick pulled the door wider. "The FBI is working late and they're looking for you."

Outside the Sheriff's Office, Corallis
6:48 p.m.

"Hi there. Sheriff Connelly? Agent Drake, FBI."

The man who offered his hand to Dove was young, tall and solid. His hair was short, his eyes hazel behind sensible glasses. He carried himself soft and spoke slow. Even standing in the early evening dark Dove knew the package was deceptive. Drake was deliberate. Those eyes checked Dove out top to bottom, committed the details to memory, read the background scene with as much relish as a steamy novel.

"Nice to meet you." Dove shook Drake's hand then opened the door." Hope you don't mind talking out here on the street. It's a little crowded in there."

Drake glanced through the front office window, checked on Ginger and Mike who were getting an earful from Savick, then smiled back at Dove.

"Not at all. I understand you've all had your hands full today. Too bad there's going to be some overtime," Drake answered good-naturedly.

"For you, too. I appreciate you tracking me down," Dove said. "We could have handled it over the phone."

"We could have, but when you didn't return my call it was just as easy to head over here," Drake said affably. "What can I do for you?"

Agent Drake crossed his arms and dialed up to deep concern as he listened. Three minutes later the agent had the basics of the crime and the Bradley connection. It took less than a second for Drake to react.

"I guess I could have saved a trip after all. Jake Bradley's a nut case."

"I must admit, his wife's disappearance does put a spin on things, but there must be some explanation other than those letters of his."

Brian Drake and Dove ambled up and down the sidewalk with their heads bent. They ignored the few people who hurried by. On the third pass, Dove leaned up against the hood of his car. Drake stuck his hands in his pockets.

"The New York Office transferred Jake Bradley's file to us when he moved out here. We did everything but stick our heads up our rears trying to figure out who was sending those letters. I mean, Bradley is high profile. We didn't want to be caught with our pants down and we sure as heck didn't want to find him gutted and strung up on some pine tree.

"But there was nothing to go on. Not a fingerprint, no matches in handwriting analysis or syntax to political stalkers on the rolls. We did saliva tests on the glue. Nothing. I'll tell you, it had us plenty worried because we're a field office and this was a big responsibility. Still, we pulled out all the stops because it would be a real feather in our cap if we could have wrapped that up for him and beat out New York."

"So why'd you take him off the hot list?" Dove asked.

Brian chuckled. He popped a piece of gum out of its wrapper and offered Dove some along with the punch line. Dove shook his head and listened.

"Turns out that the last three letters – the ones from the West Coast – those were printed out by Jake Bradley himself. I'm assuming they were written by him and mailed by him, too."

"Damn," Dove muttered.

"The guy wants attention," Brian went on. "If he's saying his wife's disappearance has something to do with those letters, then I'd look under his bed. Maybe he packed her away himself. He was pretty good at keeping us on our toes, I'll tell you. It took us a year to figure out what he was doing."

"How come you didn't prosecute?"

"Oh, right," Drake chortled. "Like we're going to blow the whistle on a guy who goes to dinner at the White House? We handled it quietly. We told Mr. Bradley to cease and desist his little letter writing campaign and never darken our doorstep again – which he hasn't until I got a call from you."

"What about the other letters? The ones from New York?" Dove pressed.

"Couldn't tell you." Drake shrugged as he looked back toward the office. Ginger was pursing her lips, looking into a hand mirror.

"You mean, you can't tell me or you won't?" Dove called Drake's attention back to the matter at hand.

"I mean, I can't. I doubt anyone in New York could either. They didn't trace to Bradley but, then again, they couldn't be traced to anyone else. It was a draw in New York. After what happened out here we decided to archive copies and give him the originals."

"Did he ever give you an explanation for why he wrote those three himself?" Dove asked.

"Nope. Bradley never admitted he had done it. Talk about denial," Brian chuckled. "The guy is a master. You'd think he'd have enough attention without that kind of crap. I mean he's a celebrity in certain circles."

"When was the last time you talked to him?" Dove asked.

"I don't know, over a year ago. I can look it up if you want. The guy's got balls giving you my name. He had to know I'd tell you the truth."

"He's not thinking straight..." Dove held up a hand, the radio inside his car was squawking, "Hold on a sec."

Dove reached inside the car and pulled the handset out.

"Yeah, Jessica."

"Nathan needs you back here now," came the response. "They found something."

"Who found her?"

It was a man who asked that and a man who ripped the shirt from my chest in that Texas motel.

"The maid," some one else answered. "Don't usually see this at the Holiday Inn."

A tube was stuck down my throat. I was barely conscious but I remember the tube because it hurt like hell. The two men worked as if they had known one another a long while, as if I was just another day at the office.

"Do we know what she's on?" Man number two again.

"Vicodin and then she had some..."

I lost the rest of what he was saying. I wanted to tell them I wasn't 'on' anything but there was a tube down my throat. I couldn't tell them this was a mistake. I couldn't tell them to call my mama because that's who I was afraid of.

They talked above me, reading my vital signs, mentioning I was a good looking woman, asking if someone got my purse. The rest was lost to the sound of the siren. They said it was lucky I wasn't dead. I didn't know it then, but they were wrong.

When I got better my mama came to the hospital. Instead of asking how I was, she told me she was keeping Charlotte. She said I was a drug addict, not fit to raise a hog. If I told her about Italy she would have said I was a whore. If I told her I took those pills to help me forget Italy she would have called me a coward. So I stayed quiet.

I left there alive but without my heart. Back in New York I worked and took the pills to kill the pain but I was careful never to take too many. I missed Charlotte. I met Jake. It was a tradeoff. I didn't do bad; I just didn't get that old brass ring. See what I mean about beauty? It isn't all it's cracked up to be. It doesn't always win the prize.

I'm choking on that tube that has been put down my throat once again. That's what I think about as I panic. I can't breathe. I am dying and I don't mean to. I don't want to die in Texas.

"Come on. Wake up, honey. Wake up," someone says. It doesn't sound like the ambulance men.

Maybe there's still a chance for me.

Maybe I'm not in Texas.

Dove's House
6:48 p.m.

The dog Dove owned was big, sleek and black. His ears had been docked, his tail, too. Cherie called him a beast and watched him with caution; the dog eyed her coolly. No matter how they felt about one another, she and the beast had an understanding: if he did his job, she would do hers. Her job, at the moment, was to feed him.

It was early-dark and not cold enough for perfect snow. Instead, what fell on her came in fat plops like gelatinized rain. A particularly large one fell on Cherie's head. She shook it off.

"It's going to have to be the end of the world before I let you in that house with that baby so you might as well get in your own place over there." Cherie scooped up the last of the dog's poop and dumped it where the garden would grow in spring. "Dove worked real hard making that house for you. You better appreciate it. 'Course then, Dove got you because of me and I don't exactly appreciate you, now do I? No reason you should appreciate that old dog house, I suppose."

Cherie opened another bin and dug inside with a scoop. She turned around and held it above the dog's dish. They stayed like that, staring one another down. The beast didn't move so Cherie wiggled her ears and grinned. He stayed still as a post. Sighing, she waterfalled the food into his dish.

"I swear you have no sense of humor. Least you could do was beg for it."

Cherie tossed the scoop back in the bin, closed it and pulled her jacket tighter. She squinted against the wet snow that was falling in earnest and wished Dove would come home. She didn't like him out when the roads were slick even though he had the best car the town could afford. Then she put that lie aside. This worry of hers had nothing to do with slick roads and everything to do with the kind of police business he was on.

In all the years they had been married, there was only one time Dove needed to hunt down someone dangerous. That hunt had changed him, made him scared of the ugliness deep down inside himself. The man she married wasn't vengeful nor was he violent. He was a just man until then – until now. This murder and the woman's disappearance had resurrected the monster inside Dove. He was itching to get his hands on whoever did this and God help them all when he did.

Feeling the beast's gaze, Cherie realized how tired she was. Deciding she was done for the day, she chained the dog. It was a good, long, humane length. The only thing she asked of Dove was that the beast not be allowed to run free at night. She didn't want him killing some poor helpless animal or, heaven forbid, an innocent person. If someone evil wasn't scared off by the beast's bark then the security system would alert Jessica and help would be on the way.

Dove, on the other hand, would rather have the dog kill anything that moved. Yet, in this, as in most things important to Cherie, Dove gave in. She affixed the chain and went back inside. The big black dog watched her go, waited until he heard the door lock and, only then did he begin to eat.

Dove's Mountain, the Forest
7:03 p.m.

Dove followed Nathan, picking his way into the forest, up the rises, around the rocks in the dead dark. The flashlights shivered with their movement and both of them kept a keen eye out so as not to disturb Nathan's evidence markers. Dove counted twelve small flags — three orange, five yellow and four blue — that had been stuck into the ground at various intervals along the route.

The snow drifted through the trees, the flakes dry and light. They lay atop the pine boughs, sprinkling the green like sugar atop cookies. The weather service predicted three inches before morning and that's why the frantic call for Dove's return went out.

"Almost there."

Nathan threw that over his shoulder just as Tim, the Braimen brothers and Aaron Green came into view. Coleman lanterns were set out. Some of the men had flashlights. Aaron had his hound on a tight leash. Nathan reminded Dove to do the same with himself so the sheriff took the last steps with extra care, going where Nathan pointed. The young man positioned himself and now they formed a ring around the blue plastic tarp staked high to the ground. It tented over a patch of earth about seven feet by five feet – big enough to cover a body or a grave. Given the solemnity of the group, Dove figured he might be looking at the latter.

Suddenly, a wind snapped through the trees. The dog whined and danced, Aaron pulled him back. The man was no less upset than the dog but he was silent and looked sickly. Jed Braimen looked like someone had just hit him upside the head with a two by four and his brother Karl was holding an unlit cigarette and staring at the tarp like he could see through it.

"You're not going to believe it, Dove," Karl said. "I don't even know if I can look at it again."

"Then you best go somewhere else, Karl, because this needs to be taken care of before the weather starts. So go on home now, nobody will think the worse of you," Tim said, having no patience for the weak at heart.

"No, I'll stay. I want to see it through." Karl looked to his brother for support and got it in spades. One without the other wouldn't have stood their ground but the two of them together were brave enough.

"Show Dove what you've got, Nathan." The doctor took the light and held it up high so the golden circle widened.

The young man nodded. He wore a stocking cap over his hairnet. He hunkered down and put evidence bags to the side. On top of those he placed a big spoon, tweezers, tongs. Finally Nathan lifted the edge of the tarp with both hands as if it was a girl's skirt and this was his first time.

When he had rolled it up just far enough, those big eyes of his turned on Dove.

"You better come on down here," he said. "Try and keep your own light steady."

Balancing on the balls of his feet to keep from disturbing this scene anymore than he already had, Dove did as Nathan directed.

"Jed," Nathan called softly. "I want you take this and hold it at a forty-five degree angle. We've got to keep as much moisture off it as possible but Dove's still got to see."

When Nathan's hands were free, he took a pen from his pocket and pointed. It took a minute for Dove to understand what he was looking at.

"Sweet Jesus," Dove breathed, finally processing what he was seeing.

"Yes, indeed. Amazing what human beings can to do to one another," Tim concurred.

Karl crossed his hands low and bowed his head. Jed hid behind the tarp he was holding up. The dog strained toward the patch on the ground where a human eyeball was nestled in a bed of pine needles.

"Wake up, girl! Haven't got all day!"

I cough.

My lungs are on fire and there is something in my throat. It is unlike anything I have ever tasted. At least it isn't a tube to pump my stomach. Someone flips me over onto my side and whacks my back like I was a rug hung out to air. They hit me hard. I'm alive. I'm grateful and pissed.

"Sto..."

Instead of telling whoever this is to stop, I cough some more. Water comes out of my mouth. I probably spit up a few fish, too, from the feel of it. My eyes are closed and there are sparkles behind them. They make my head spin and hurt.

Another whack right in the middle of my back.

I gag. I gasp. I gasp again and then it's over. My chest rises and falls. I breathe more easily as I lay on the ground. A rock sticks into my shoulder. I squint into the overcast. It hasn't taken long to save me. It isn't night yet. In fact, it seems like the slow twilight of a summer's day. When I find the strength, I flop onto my back. My chest rises so gently that I almost can't feel it. My hair is plastered to my cheek, my clothes cling to my body and an old woman sits beside me.

Her hair is a ball of frizz. There is a child's barrette holding it back at the top of her head. Her shoulders are narrow, her hips are wide. She wears a sweater and a blouse, pants and a dress and an apron over that. I think she is angry with me. It's in her eyes like the fury I saw in Charlotte's the day Simon drove me home. Charlotte didn't know there wasn't anything to be angry about. I should have told her. This woman doesn't have anything to be angry about either.

"Did you pull me out of the river?"

Maybe I don't actually say this because the frizzy-haired woman gives no sign that she has heard me. I close my eyes, moving in and out of consciousness. Each time I open my eyes she is still there. I wonder how such a tiny old thing managed to drag me out of the water. More often than not, things go black. Sickness and exhaustion force me to rest.

Finally, I am awake for good. The woman is shaking me, telling me we have to go. She leans over me the way the men who pumped my stomach did. I see every wrinkle. She wasn't a beauty in her day. This is the face of a tough cookie. I struggle to my elbows and glance

157

at the river. It is calm and beautiful here. The river is emerald green as if the bottom is lined with velvet.

"Did you pull me out by yourself?" I ask again.

"Yah."

"What's your name?"

"Don't matter. You have to come the rest of the way on your own."

She stands over me. I know what bothers me. She has an accent.

"I doubt you could carry me," I say, wishing that weren't the case. I would love for her to carry me.

"I could if I had to," she answers sourly.

I won't make her prove it. I get to my feet and look for my things.

"I had a stick. I had a backpack."

"Not no more." She starts to walk away. She pauses. She turns. "You coming? I already wasted too much time looking out for you. Didn't expect you to come through the back door. Good thing I was down here when I was. Might have missed you."

My head pulls up. This is a piece of news.

"How come you were expecting me?"

"Heard on the radio you were missing," The woman answers. "You're trouble. I don't like trouble. That's the talk. Trouble."

"You've got a radio?"

"Yah, I got a radio. Sometimes it works. I'm going, now. Come if you want." She goes a few steps then calls over her shoulder, "My name is Marta."

Marta doesn't seem the type for second chances. I hurry up behind her as she picks her way up a path of rocks that have been laid like steps through the forest.

"You know who I am then. You know I need to get home."

"Yah," she answers without looking at me. Catching up, I put my hand on her arm and try to make her look. She pauses but her eyes don't meet mine.

"Thank you — for saving me."

"You ain't saved." She grouses, moving away. "Dumb if you don't know that."

I ignore her comment and pepper her with questions. Not the least of which is:

"You've got a phone, right? You do have a phone?" I ask.

She doesn't.

Dove's Mountain, the Forest
7:03 p.m.

"Is it hers?" Dove peered at the thing because that's all it was to him — an 'it', a thing, perhaps evidence of the crime.

"Maybe if I'd seen it within the first hour of excision, Dove, but not now. It's been out too long. The film forms on the cornea fast and that woman has an unusually light blue iris. And, see the way it's torn? We'll only see a part of the iris. No, sir, Dove, this old doctor's going to have to take it with me to figure out if it's the same color as Mrs. Bradley's eyes. The same blood type and all. You see, it's a process, Dove..."

Dove gave a nod and cut him off.

"Nathan? Have you got anything different?"

Nathan shook his head, "No, sir. I couldn't tell either."

Dove's gaze swept past each man. They all murmured, none venturing a guess and no one relishing the idea of looking at it close. Aaron spoke up to say it had taken him a good long time to even figure out what he had found when the dog went wild. He was lucky he hadn't squished the damn thing.

"I already took pictures, Dove," Nathan offered. "But I'm not sure they'll turn out the way I hope. When you give the say so, I'll send it down with Tim. We'll mark it off all proper. I picked up the pine needles for blood samples. I saw some strands of hair before it got too dark, Dove, but I really need to get the magnifier out here, kind of inch over everything as soon as possible."

"What color were the hair strands?" Dove asked.

"One was light and long. I won't know if they came from a man or woman for a while. And there's this."

Nathan pointed again with his pen. Dove strained to see. It was almost buried but Nathan had found a ply of yarn. It looked like a thread from a fringe, the kind of thing a woman would add to one she knitted herself. There was no doubt that it was blue but the color ruled out it being from the one in Simon Hart's place. Dove stood up. His knees ached. The day had been too long and it wasn't over yet.

"Jed. Karl. Can you two stay and do whatever Nathan needs?" Dove asked in a tone that seemed to say this wasn't a request at all.

The two men looked at one another, each wanting to have an excuse but neither coming up with anything. In the end, they agreed.

"Aaron, you and your hound go back home unless there's somewhere else he wants to take us," Dove directed.

"I don't think so, Dove. He backtracked that way," Aaron nodded up and toward the west. "Then he caught this and that was it. I tried to get him going back, but he wouldn't budge."

"This is real good," Dove assured him. "Tim, soon as you know what this is, I want you to call Nathan. See if you can find a blood trail when it's light."

"Not a problem, Dove." Tim was on his knees, a small jar in his left hand and the spoon in his other. "Must, say, I've never seen anything like it. Whoever did this – I mean if it is that woman's eye – must have hated her something awful. This was an angry crime. Nothing but destruction of a beautiful face. That's what it was. Jealousy. They must have wanted to ruin that beautiful face. That beautiful..."

Slowly Dove turned and looked at Tim. That proverbial light bulb had just gone off in his head and was shining with a thousand watts. Could it be this was simply a bid to ruin Tessa Bradley's face? Could Fritz's ugly death have been all about beauty and specifically Tessa Bradley's beauty?

Dove didn't hear the rest of Tim's muttering and mumblings. He was already walking back through the snow. His footsteps were sure, his heart was hardening, his mind was warring as he tried to keep his anger in check.

In the last few hours he had been sent down two roads that led nowhere. Now that the outrage was fresh again another road was opening up. The next place he had to go was Bleden Town. God help the people there if Fritz died because someone didn't like how Tessa Bradley looked.

The Bradley's Lodge
8:32 p.m.

"What are you doing? What are you doing? Stop it!"

Charlotte Bradley screamed and clutched at Dove Connelly but nothing she could do or say could stop him. It took only the shrug of a shoulder, the flick of an elbow to send her reeling away. Still she came at the big man.

Fairly blind with rage by the time he reached the Bradley's lodge. Dove stampeded through the door the minute Charlotte opened it. He went up the stairs to Jake Bradley's office. It was empty. Dove slammed the door, turned on his heel and pounded back down stairs.

"I told you, he's not here," Charlotte screamed from the bottom of the stairs. "I'll have you arrested. I swear I will. I'll call the FBI."

"Yeah, you just do that." Dove pushed past her.

"What do you want? Why aren't you out looking for my mother?" Charlotte ran beside him, reaching out but not daring to touch him. "If you'll just tell me what you want, I can help."

"I want the man who murdered my friend, and right now I'm thinking I know who probably had a hand in that," Dove snapped.

Dove went through the living room to the opposite wing of the house. He threw open the doors: Charlotte's bedroom, a guest room, a room with exercise equipment. Then he hit a locked door. Charlotte threw herself in front of it, arms spread.

"You're crazy," she screamed. "Tell me what you want. I'll tell my father. I promise. Just give me a minute! Just one minute!"

Charlotte's face was white with fear and blotched red with hysteria. She was beautiful but not as beautiful as her mother and, in an instant, Tim's observation rang true. A crime of jealousy, he called it.

"How much did you hate your mother?" Dove demanded.

"What? What are you talking about?" Charlotte lost her voice. The question came out as a shocked whisper.

"I want to know why you hate your mother," Dove demanded. "Is it because she's more beautiful than you? Because she got the attention and you didn't?"

"That's absurd." Charlotte sputtered but Dove had hit a nerve. He'd torture her with it if it meant getting to the truth.

"Did you hate her enough to want to ruin her face? Did you think that would keep her home? Or did you want to make her so ugly he wouldn't want her. Did my friend die because you wanted Jake Bradley for yourself?"

"Oh, God. You're sick. You're out of your mind. He's the only father I have ever known."

Charlotte spun away putting her back against the locked door and one hand across her stomach. She did look sick but Dove didn't care. He put his hand on her shoulder and set her aside. Swiftly, smoothly, he raised his booted foot and stomped the door while Charlotte screamed.

"Stop. You can't do that. Stop it. Jake, run."

Once, twice more he kicked. With a huge crack, the door shattered and splintered. Dove put his shoulder into it and pushed through into Jake Bradley's bedroom.

There, in a room unlike any Dove had ever seen, was Jake Bradley. He was curled into a ball atop an aquamarine duvet. The headboard was dark blue suede. Three steps led to the platform where a bed – bigger than a king size – rested. There were pillows everywhere: round and narrow, square and lush. At the foot was a coverlet that looked like mink.

This was not a bed where husband and wife rested or made love. This was an altar to a goddess.

Behind the bed, the wall was made of glass making the forest look like an extension of the bedroom. The opposite wall was dominated by a portrait of Tessa Bradley. Though it was drawn with minimal strokes of black paint on white canvas the effect was amazing. There wasn't a picture in the house that was more beautiful than this.

If the bed was the altar and this room was Tessa's cathedral then the penitent was lying on the bed curled into a fetal position.

With a roar, Dove Connelly went at Jake Bradley hard, pulling him up by the shoulders, ignoring the blood and bruising on the man's face. Dove's voice boomed through this sacred space.

"Did you put a hit out on your wife because she was beautiful? Is that why my friend is dead?"

Dove's House
8:29 p.m.

Cherie hummed as she rocked her daughter and fed her from her breast. When the baby's rosy lips slipped away, Cherie buttoned up and kissed her child's silky hair. The poor little thing was done in from such a busy day. Surely she would wake up in the middle of the night and realize she hadn't quite finished dinner. Ah well. The way of the world; the way of mothers and babies.

Gently, Cherie raised the baby to her shoulder and got up. She didn't bother with the bedroom lights, preferring the soft glow cast by the fire to guide her. It was as if the entire world had stopped to consider what had gone on that day. More than one family, Cherie was sure, was saying an extra prayer for Fritz and Bernadette. She hoped they might remember Dove in those prayers, too. A few might even be thinking about the missing woman. It didn't matter if she was rich or a celebrity, she was on the mountain alone. Cherie didn't know anyone who wasn't respectful of that danger. The baby gave a quiet little burp and Cherie smiled. Life went on.

Seeing well enough for what she needed to do, Cherie changed the baby's diaper, put her to bed and covered her up. The girl fussed for a moment so Cherie put a hand on her back and waited until she settled down. While she did that, she looked out the window and watched the night. She cherished times like this. She had a home, a man who loved her, a fire crackling in the hearth. She was just thinking there was more good about her life than bad when something outside the window startled her.

Cherie shook her head. She blinked her eyes, and straightened her shoulders. Perhaps she had been dreaming even while she was awake. Maybe this was a flashback and she had been in the grip of a mini-nightmare. But that wasn't it at all.

There were people on her property.

Here.

Now.

Two of them darted past the window.

The minute she acknowledged that they were out there, two things happened: the beast erupted like a volcano and Cherie Connelly remembered she had forgotten to set the alarms.

Stepping back from the bedroom window, thankful there were no lights to silhouette her, Cherie kept her back to the walls as she slid into the living room. The dog was crazed. Even inside, she could hear the yank and clank of the chain as the animal tried to free itself in an effort to protect the house. Not for a second did it stop its growl and bark. It served to remind her that she should have listened to Dove. They should have let the animal loose. After all, it wasn't just her that needed protecting, it was the baby.

The good thing was that the chained dog gave Cherie perspective. If those men were trying to come in the front, the dog would have eaten them by now. That meant they were going 'round back and that meant Cherie had a chance.

Dropping to the floor, she crawled to the closet where her father's things were stored. Sweat beaded on her brow. She whispered encouragement to herself even as she listened for any change in the dog's attention. Slowly, she opened the closet door. There was no way the people outside could hear the slight squeak of the hinge but if they paused by the kitchen they might see the shadow as the door swung open. Assuming they had not, Cherie took what she needed. It was heavy and cumbersome but she knew exactly what to do with it.

Scurrying back against the wall, she put her legs out straight and let the weapon rest on her lap. She wiped her forehead, took a deep breath and set it. There was a click and another. She paused, listening for any sign that they were trying to come in the house. When she heard nothing but the dog barking, Cherie lay her head back against the wall and blew a breath to settle her stomach. Swallowing deeply, she knew it was now or never. Getting to her feet but staying low, she stole through the house again, opened the front door and eased herself outside and into the cold.

The beast paid her no mind, focused as he was on the back of the house. He was lathered to frenzy as he danced and pulled and tried to free himself from the chain. The sound of him, the look of the black devil dog who was darker than the night, terrified her. Unsure if she could control the dog, Cherie left him on the chain and crept around the house, sure-footed on this familiar territory. When she got to where she wanted to be, Cherie Connelly set herself solid and gave fair warning:

"If you're looking for trouble, you've found it."

The two men by the back door whirled around, exclaiming once in surprise then again in horror as they looked at the slight woman holding steady to her father's loaded crossbow.

The Bradley Lodge
8:32 p.m.

Charlotte threw wood on the fire. It was no easy task. A man could walk into that fireplace and the wood was not cut into short pieces but long, substantial logs. Still, she didn't ask for help. She seemed to take comfort in the physical challenge of stoking the fire, taking her anger out on it.

A wounded Jake sat in a big chair near the cavernous fireplace, his chin propped up on his upturned palm, his unblinking eyes staring at the flames. The light from the fire danced over his damaged face and showed him for what he was: a small, aging, broken man.

Dove sat on the couch. His hat was beside him, his feet were spread and his elbows were on his knees. His head was in his hands. When Charlotte left the room he didn't move. He didn't look at Jake Bradley. The two men needed time in their corners before they got back into the ring. When Charlotte returned she had a cup of tea for Jake and a stiff drink for Dove. Jake ignored the tea. Dove shot the whiskey. Charlotte sat on the hearth.

"I didn't know about Jake writing those letters," Charlotte said, opening the dialogue. "I didn't know he knew about that man in town. If I had, I would have stopped him from going. I couldn't believe what happened to him. I just didn't know."

Dove raised his head, he sat up straighter but he kept his hands on his thighs. He looked at Charlotte without sympathy. The clock was running and the time for nonsense was long gone.

"I'm not interested in what you knew; I'm interested in what he did and why. Either he talks or I'm taking him into custody. He can sleep in my jail until he tells me the truth."

"Don't be ridiculous. He can barely move. He couldn't go anywhere if he wanted to," Charlotte scoffed.

"You can drive. You're used to moving fast when you take those pictures in all those places you go to," Dove reminded her. He would cut her no slack. "From what I've seen around here, taking off would suit you just fine. It's pretty clear you think a whole lot more of him than you do your mother."

"What I feel is none of your business and I wouldn't help Jake run," Charlotte answered evenly. "Do you think you're the only upstanding human being on this mountain? Whatever Jake did, whatever my mother did, none of it is criminal. If it was, I'd be the first to tell you."

"I don't know," Dove pressed. "You two are pretty close, and I'd say that's a little unusual for a stepfather and a stepdaughter. I think you have some explaining to do on that score, don't you?"

"How dare you? How dare you? Get your mind out of the gutter and bring charges against the man who did that." Charlotte rose and pointed at Jake Bradley. She took a step toward him but her outrage was directed at Dove. "Look at him. Beaten to a pulp. If anyone did anything to my mother it's that man in town. That horrible excuse for a human bein…"

"His name is Simon Hart and it's my fault about Tessa," Jake muttered.

It was the first time he'd spoken since Dove dragged him into this room and shoved him into that chair. Only the Taser jolt of the *feel* kept Dove from finishing the job Simon Hart started. It came out of nowhere. It came from Tessa Bradley and it brought Dove to his senses just as he raised his fist to her husband. She was alive. She was reaching out to him. She didn't want Jake Bradley hurt.

"Did you have her killed?" Dove turned his dark eyes on Jake Bradley, that sad excuse for a man.

Jake sighed. "No, I didn't pay to have her killed. I love my wife. I was paying Simon Hart to end whatever was between them and to leave her alone."

There was a butterfly bandage on a cut above his eye, the scrapes and contusions on the right side of his face had been cleaned and salved. He seemed exhausted deep down to his soul. Not only didn't he care what happened to him, it seemed he didn't care what happened to Tessa. He was pathetic.

"Jake," Charlotte pleaded, "You don't have to tell him anything. You're not in court. There is no subpoena or whatever it is they'd have to get to make you talk."

"You're wrong, Charlotte. I do have to talk because I've been a fool." He sighed again and considered his hands. They weren't interesting enough to hold his attention so he raised his eyes to Charlotte. "I only did what I did because I love you and your mother so much."

"People kill for love," Dove reminded him.

"They kill for lust and I never lusted after Tessa. We had something deeper than that." Jake moved himself in the chair but it hurt and he settled back in awkwardly. "I loved her because she was courageous and loyal. Do you know she was only sixteen when Charlotte was born? A child having a child. And Tessa wouldn't give her up."

"Oh, God, Jake, don't make that something noble." Charlotte was disgusted. "Tessa left me with her parents while she flitted off to New York. That wasn't courageous, it was selfish. She lived the good life and I lived with alcoholics who tortured me with their..."

"Your grandparents," Jake said, warning her to silence with a surprisingly sharp voice. "Your grandparents were horrible people. They wanted Tessa to abort you, did you know that? Oh, yes, they did. Your mother wouldn't listen, not even when they threatened to put her out.

"Then they saw all the money your mother sent back for you after she started modeling and decided it wasn't so bad looking after you. They extorted money from your mother and threatened to drag her to court if she wouldn't give you up."

"I don't want to hear it." Charlotte shook her head again but Jake knew it was time she understood Tessa.

"You're alive because your mother stood up to them. She tried to get you back. Things happened you don't know about Charlotte. Ugly, terrible things happened to your mother. It's a miracle Tessa survived at all."

"Simon Hart said he was from the same town as Mrs. Bradley," Dove broke in. "What do you know about their history?"

"I know all about Simon Hart," Jake answered sadly. "I know he is the man Tessa loved and I know he is Charlotte's father."

Marta's place is a trailer.

My mama hated trailers because temporary people lived in them. People you couldn't count on. She said that's why they called 'em mobile homes. They could take off in the middle of the night and nobody would be the wiser. If Marta's place was ever mobile, it isn't now. It is rooted like a tree and I have got to believe I can count on her. I believe I am wiser after all I've been through.

Three little dirty dogs come up to greet us. They are mops of matted hair; white and brown. Marta bends and kisses each of them in turn and they raise their little faces to her. They lick her back and come to me next, sniffing and jumping; light little feet pawing at my legs. I push them down. Marta goes up the three steps and opens the screen door. It flops back on her and she catches it with her rear.

"Do you live here alone?" I venture.

I can't keep the hope from my voice but she doesn't acknowledge it in the same way she doesn't acknowledge that I nearly drowned to death.

"You were expecting some prince, yah?"

She answers sarcastically but I'm not cowed. The men who tried to kill me had accents. They could be inside this trailer. I need an answer and I'm going to get it. I splay my feet. I put my hands on my hips. I am not as steady as I would like. My clothes are damp and uncomfortable. I do not look formidable but I am trying.

"Well, do you?"

"Yah," she says quietly as if finally understanding my fear. "All alone. Now you're here."

"How long have you lived here?" I am relaxing but still not moving. I will soon but I want to be sure this is safe.

"I think maybe fifty years — sixty." She looks at me again and waves a hand as if ask what's a year or two?

"How did you get here?"

I turn my head and take in my surroundings. There is a rutted, overgrown road. I really am curious but she isn't interested in giving me her history.

"What do you care? I am here when you needed me. That's the trick."

I guess I don't really need to know how she got here except the information might give me clue as to how I can get out. She points to the trailer and says, "In there."

I hesitate for just a second. Common sense tells me those two men would have put a bullet in me and Marta by now if they were around. We would have died the way Jonathan did: surprised, fast, clean. I am exhausted so I stop worrying and go up the steps. Behind me the little dogs romp. They haven't a care in the world.

Inside, the metal house is freezing. There is some furniture and a lot of junk: boxes, tools, magazines stacked everywhere. I wonder how the postman gets them here.

A cat darts through to the kitchen. Marta points to a bathroom that is no bigger than a closet. This place feels weird, like the witch's cottage in some fairytale. If I was Gretel coming out of the forest then this place should have been made of cookies and candy. Pity I'm not Gretel.

Marta prods me.

"You stink. You've been in the river."

I laugh aloud. All of this is absurd. I won't even know how to tell this story when I get home. I stink! Good lord, I don't think the woman has taken a whiff of her surroundings. So I do, fully intending to point out that all these old things have a stench of their own. To my surprise, they don't. I smell pine. I smell warm food and yet nothing is cooking.

"Do you have hot water?"

"Yah. Yah. There's towels. They don't match. Nothing fancy." She flips her hand. That means 'Go. Go on. Don't bother me'.

So I go. I close the bathroom door and lean back against it. My chin is on my chest, my eyes are closed and I start to shake. At first I think I am laughing because Marta and her house in the forest are absurdly funny. I couldn't have dreamed this up. Then I realize I'm shaking from exhaustion and fear and relief. I never thought this would all end and now I see the end is near. So close. I am lucky.

Slowly, I sink to the floor, shivering and shuddering, unable to control myself. I pull my legs up. Those high skinny heels of my boots are planted on the ground and my arms hang limp at my sides. I put my forehead on my knees and sob. That's all. I do not cry.

Not yet.

The Bradley's Lodge
8:57 p.m.

"Jake?" Charlotte whispered but he stayed silent. The next time she spoke it was to whimper. "Jake? Him? That man? She couldn't..."

Still Jake Bradley said nothing. His voice was lost, his shame overwhelming. Instinctively, Dove started to get up to help but Charlotte Bradley flinched, keeping him away with a glance. She was more her mother's daughter than she knew. Her body trembled but she managed to stand. When she walked by Dove it was without a look. Her head was held up high, her arms were rigid by her side.

When Charlotte was gone, there was nothing but the sound of the fire. The men didn't look at one another. Both of their thoughts had followed Charlotte. Finally, Jake broke the silence.

"I'm sorry she had to find out that way but it would have come out sooner or later. It couldn't be helped."

Jake watched the doorway as if he expected Charlotte to come back. Dove knew he would be disappointed. That woman was zeroed in on herself and her disappointment. Jake touched his cheek gently as if he needed a reminder of why they were there and what they had been talking about.

"So, Simon Hart. You can imagine what it felt like to see him. It was such a cruel joke. Almost like I delivered her to him. Oh, don't look so surprised, Sheriff," Jake said with a sad little laugh. "I always knew I was second. Tessa was very honest about that. That is one thing I love so much about her. That incredible honesty. She thought her first love was a misunderstood, country boy. She almost had me believing it, too. Then I saw him. I talked to him. Poor Tessa. The only person she couldn't be honest with was herself. The only person she didn't see clearly was him."

Jake shook his head slowly. There was a small, gentle smile on his lips as he recalled this one failing of the woman he adored.

"The memory of this man gave her a reason to keep living and all I gave her was everything else. Why would I pay someone to kill her now when I've known about him all these years and lived with that knowledge?"

"Because he was real now and she was with him." Dove stated the obvious. Love made men do strange things and he had no doubt that Jake loved Tessa Bradley to a fault.

"It would have been smarter to have him killed instead of creating the kind of elaborate scheme that you're suggesting." Jake shifted again, every move bringing more pain. "It's a good thing I don't write fiction. The reader would figure out instantly that I am not a devious thinker."

"But you're a smart man. Maybe the plan was simpler than I've been thinking," Dove suggested. "Maybe your wife was the one who was supposed to be killed and the grocer got hit by mistake."

"Don't be ridiculous," Jake scoffed. "I wouldn't jeopardize myself like that. I'd be found out, sent to prison. I don't have that kind of passion in me. Besides, ten thousand dollars was all it cost to make Simon Hart disappear. You've seen the money. It would kill Tessa to know how cheap her price tag really was." Jake sighed then looked at Dove as if he pitied the effort he was putting in to trying to figure this all out. "If everything had gone as planned, Tessa would have assumed Hart just drifted away like he had before. That's all there was to it."

"What about faking those letters? What about that stalker?" Dove asked.

"That was just my way of trying to protect this family from the big, bad, evil world, Sheriff." Jake laughed ruefully. He touched his eyes then looked at his fingertips to see if those were actually tears on them. "Oh, make no mistake, that person is real. Those letters scared us to death when they started coming. But then they stopped and the FBI lost interest. I had to do something to keep them interested."

"According to the FBI, moving did the trick," Dove reminded him. "Why bother with the charade?"

"Do you think a threat like that ever goes away?" Jake snapped. "That kind of person would resurface when I least expected it. When that happened I wouldn't just get a letter. Maybe he would put a knife in my stomach or he might slash Tessa's face. He might find Charlotte out in the middle of nowhere. God knows what he would do to her. If the letters kept coming, my file would still be active. I did everything I could think of to keep us safe and now..." Jake buried his face in his hands "...now Tessa is gone. I can't even imagine what Charlotte is feeling."

Jake Bradley's shoulders heaved under his thick grey sweater and, as if on cue, Charlotte returned. She had come in so quietly Dove hadn't noticed. Pale and unsteady, she walked up behind Jake and slid her hands on to his shoulders. She seemed torn, unsure if she was there to give comfort or take it. Dove was surprised. He had assumed there was no room in that woman's heart for anyone but herself. It was good to see he had been wrong. He got up to leave. He slid his hat off the couch and held it in both hands. Dove had a few more questions.

"Why didn't you tell me about Hart? Why were you still paying him when your wife was already missing?"

"Please, Sheriff." Jake Bradley begged Dove not to be stupid. "It should be obvious. I didn't want anyone to know Tessa had associated with a man like that. She still had a name to protect. Can you imagine the embarrassment?"

"Too bad you didn't think about protecting your wife. Did you ever think we might have found her if you'd come clean from the start? Did you ever think she might die while you were protecting her 'name'?" Disgusted, Dove didn't wait for an answer. With a shake of his head, he walked to the door. "Don't either of you leave town."

"What are you, John Wayne?" Charlotte muttered.

"Don't," he reiterated, turning and pinning her with a look that kept her quiet.

In the foyer, Dove reached for the door handle, a sweep of brass that reminded him of the small of Cherie's back. Dove touched it and thought of all the women caught up in this: Tessa Bradley, Cherie, Bernadette, Charlotte. He let his hand slide down the curve, depressed the button that opened the latch and walked through the door. Before it closed, he turned to look at Charlotte Bradley.

At least Charlotte had one thing in common with her mother: she looked lost.

Before Dove could begin to think what to do next, his phone rang and he didn't have to think twice about his next step.

He needed to get home.

"Girl. I hear you, girl."

Marta knocks on the door. She wants in but I want to be alone. She can't help what's wrong with me. I am crying now over my wasted my life. I did as I was told instead of choosing the way I wanted to live it. How awful to have lived forty-six years and never really chosen anything. Sadly, the good things were happenstance as much as the bad. Charlotte being my child, Jake saving me — those things simply happened in the same way that Simon seduced me and Ubert Yahobi abused me.

I cry because I don't know if Jake and Charlotte will want me this way: stripped down to my bare bones, self aware, beaten and battered but still kicking. I can't even pretend to be what I was in New York. Even my face will be different now. I'll carry this time of my life stamped on it. I can already feel that my face has changed. I don't mind but I'm not sure about them and that worries me. For the first time in my life, I realize how deeply important my husband and my daughter are to me.

I can be honest now. What Jake showed me was love in its truest form. He asked so little from me. In return, for next to nothing, he gave me safety and understanding even when I drifted because I wanted Simon. Jake was a good man who stood by my side.

Charlotte? She was always important but I wonder now if I didn't pay that concept lip service. I told myself she was important because I gave birth to her. Now I see that there is a deeper connection between us. I realize that, until now, I carried Charlotte in my mind. Because of all this, I now carry her in my heart.

I pull my body small. I am already small inside where it counts. I am humbled even though I don't think I was ever arrogant. All my life, I have been afraid people would discover the truth and the truth is, I'm not that special. It was the old brass ring problem every step of the way. It hung out there, tempting not me but the people who believed I could snatch it for them. I reached for it every time because I wanted to please each and every person who was important to me. When I gave them the prize, I was left with nothing. I should have known all along that my looks didn't make me special; my beauty was not a reason to be loved. I wasn't that special.

But now I will be.

Now I will choose my life.

"Girl. I hear you, girl."

Marta's voice drops. I feel her weight on the other side of the door. She has settled herself on the cold floor. That can't be good for her, but I think this is good for me. I like her there – close but with the door between us.

"Girl. I hear you."

She means she understands. I say I hear her back and then cry some more as it becomes dark.

Outside Dove's House
9:35 p.m.

Cherie was chopping wood when Dove careened off the road and into the drive. She hadn't turned on the

179

floodlights, preferring to use her father's old lamp instead. The steady flame, the small pool of illumination and rhythmic sound of the falling ax calmed her. The lamp sat on a stump near the woodpile and cast just enough light for her to see.

"Cherie! Cherie! Where are you?" Dove's car had barely come to a stop before he threw himself out of the car.

He 'rounded the house at a full run. The beast rose to its feet. He was off his chain, his back to Cherie, watching the path. When the dog made a move Cherie twirled, ax in hand. Seeing Dove, she snapped the dog back to his place. Dove was the only one he broke command for but tonight Cherie didn't want to give the beast any leeway. The dog did as she commanded and Cherie relaxed. She buried the ax in the stump. The lantern shook and Cherie walked toward her husband.

"Took you long enough."

"I would have been here sooner except the gas pedal wouldn't go down any more."

Dove met her half way. Cherie tried to smile. She tried so hard to be in control but it took no more than him arriving for her to show Dove a different face. Cherie fell into his arms knowing she wasn't as strong as she thought.

"You okay?" Dove asked as he held her back to look into her face. She nodded.

"I am. I don't mind telling you this, gave me a fright."

Her hands were flat on his chest. Dove's own ran from her shoulders down her back as if to make sure she was all there. He pulled her close and hugged her hard again. When she raised her face to his, Dove was finally convinced that she was shaken, not broken.

"The alarm?"

"Don't ask," Cherie shook her head and slipped out of his embrace. "I don't want you picking at me. Now that you're here, I'm feeling a little bit like an idiot. I probably should have just sent them on out of here."

"Where are they?" Dove looked over his shoulder to the house. Cherie put her fingers to his chin and turned it so that he was looking past her.

"You're kidding?" Dove laughed.

Cherie stepped back. She picked up the lantern and snapped for the dog once more. The beast stood like a champion and followed his mistress. Dove followed behind, taking note of the crossbow leaning against the side of the stump. They walked twenty yards to the old garage out back. Handing back the lantern, Cherie dug in her pocket, found the key to the padlock, worked it and grunted as she pushed up the heavy old door.

Inside, near frozen to death if you could believe them, were two men huddled together on a stack of broken down cardboard boxes. Their eyes widened with relief at the sight of Dove's uniform. Their exclamations of gratitude that they were saved were mixed with outrage that Dove hadn't come sooner. All that crying out was cut short by Cherie.

"This man says he knows Tessa Bradley." Cherie pointed to the older one. That was enough for the man to square his shoulders. Suddenly his concern turned to arrogance. He preened like a peacock.

"That's not true," he sniffed, "I said I *made* Tessa Bradley."

Inside Dove's House
9:52 p.m.

"Coffee?"

Cherie held up the pot. Peter Wolfson held out his cup. When Cherie didn't pour he looked at her peevishly. She looked back expectantly. She raised an eyebrow and it took Peter a minute to realize what she wanted.

"Thank you." Reluctantly he put the house rules into practice.

"Mr. Reilly?"

Cherie held the pot up toward the other man. He nodded, murmuring his thanks right away. Shy to begin with, this experience had left him nearly mute. Holding the mug in both hands, he buried himself in the corner of the dining room away from the table where Dove Connelly sat eating a sandwich while Peter Wolfson glared at him.

"Look, there's nothing nefarious going on here." Wolfson's eyes flicked to Cherie as she settled herself next to her husband. Dove pulled out her chair and settled her. Patience taxed, Peter rolled his eyes "That means evil, Sheriff."

"I know what it means." Dove picked up his glass of milk and took a long drink.

"Well, then?" Peter waited but still Dove was silent, seemingly more interested in his food than the matters at hand. That annoyed Peter to no end. "Look, Jake called me at an ungodly hour this morning with the horrible news about Tessa. I caught the first plane out. It's as simple as that."

"Then why didn't you go to the Bradley's house if you were in such a hurry to help out?" Dove asked.

"Jake and I aren't exactly old friends," Peter admitted. "He – well – he thinks I exploited Tessa. Evidence to the contrary, of course. Jake Bradley wouldn't have looked twice at Tessa in her natural state. He should be thanking me. I was the one who saw her potential. Me. No one else."

Peter threw his shoulders back and waited for Cherie and Dove to be awestruck by the visionary that he was. Not that he needed their admiration; his self-adulation was quite satisfying.

"I discovered her. I taught her to walk. I taught her to move. I had to educate her about everything – designers, fashion, jewelry, make-up. Grant it, she was a quick study, but then I took it to another level. Did Jake tell you she became Ulbert Yahobi's muse because of me? Did he?" Peter shook his head in dismay; not realizing his audience had no idea what he was talking about. "But, of course, Jake didn't tell you that. No credit for me."

"That's all well and good, Mr. Wolfson, but I'm wondering why you're here now? And I'm wondering, if there's no love-loss between you and Bradley, why would he call you?"

Peter perked up; delighted Dove was showing some interest.

"Well, Jake called because he thought Tessa might be with me. I had to wheedle the story out of him. As to why I'm here? I am here on assignment for Vanity Fair Magazine. They recognize that what has happened to Tessa is momentous. Mr. Reilly," Peter motioned to the man in the corner, "is a most respected writer. He will do the text to go with my pictures. He will write the story of Tessa's unfortunate situation. It has everything. A small town, a celebrity husband, an estranged daughter, a beautiful woman who vanished. Mr. Reilly will barely have to work. The whole story will be written for him."

Dove's eye cut to Mr. Reilly who cringed under the attention.

"But we don't know anything yet." Dove tossed his napkin aside. He had no appetite and it wasn't the food that had taken it away.

"Sheriff, please. We're men – and a lady – of the world." The photographer's hands opened in a papal gesture. "We know what we're talking about."

Peter's eyes sparked. There was greed in them. Wolfson might well be rich but Dove could see he wasn't important anymore. He was hungry for recognition and he'd eat anything put in front of him to satisfy that hunger- even Tessa Bradley's carcass.

"Why don't you spell it out for me," Dove suggested, wanting to hear it all from the great man himself.

Cherie put down her coffee mug and gave him her full attention, too. Mr. Reilly had the decency to be embarrassed. Peter Wolfson was oblivious.

"Alright. Here it is. I called the editor-in-chief of Vanity Fair myself. I haven't worked for them for a while but I knew she would take my call. I had no fear. I took the risk of upsetting her at such an early hour because this is important.

"Well, by the time I was finished telling her about Tessa I had sold a three-part deal." Peter's hands molded three spaces on the table as if Dove needed a visual to understand. "The old pictures of Tessa before she hit big.

The ones at the height of her career and now this. Whatever *this* turns out to be, naturally, it will be brilliant. They'll have to double the print run. New York will talk about nothing else."

Wolfson tossed his hair back showing off the diamonds in both ears. Cherie thought the jewelry looked ridiculous and she knew Dove had heard just about enough. Wolfson, though, wouldn't give up.

"Trying to go through Jake and Charlotte would be a waste of time. They don't want the publicity. I have a job to do, same as you. If I enlist your cooperation, Jake and Charlotte will see that I am handling this situation in a respectful manner and they will talk to me. Or, if not me, at least they would give their perspective to Mr. Reilly. Once the law has weighed in, of course," he shot a smile Dove's way. "And that is why we are here. We just wanted to present ourselves to you before we began."

"Really?" Dove muttered.

"Yes, really." Peter's face fell. He rolled his eyes, he tugged on the collar of his leather jacket, he sighed deeply, exhausted by trying to make nice. "Don't get all evangelical, Sheriff. You'd do well to listen to me and align yourself because it's going to get a whole lot worse."

"I don't see how," Dove answered.

He and Peter Wolfson squared off. The photographer wanted what he wanted and he wasn't going to let Dove stop him.

"There's an avalanche of media headed to your little mountain. People who never met Tessa are going to be clumping all over this place looking for something quick and sensational. I adored Tessa despite our differences.

She would want me to tell this story, and all I'm asking for is a little cooperation."

Peter sat back and inspected his nails. He glanced over at Mr. Reilly who looked like he'd rather been in hell than in this room. Peter sniffed, assuming Mr. Reilly was on board.

"God knows she never did me any favors. Tessa blackballed me, wouldn't let me shoot her after she hit it big with Yahobi. But I don't hold a grudge. I'll be fair to her and to you." Peter's eyes fluttered. He pulled the last trick out of his hat. "You won't have to worry about how you're portrayed in the least. Sheriff, you are colorful. You're all American. I'd even like to put a picture of Mrs. Connelly and her crossbow in the article. Vanity Fair would pay handsomely for that, of course."

"Are you kidding?" Dove raised a brow. Cherie bit her tongue to keep from laughing.

"No. No, of course not," Peter enthused. "She would look lovely: a mountain woman protecting her own. Very Ralph Lauren. In fact, I could send Ralph the pictures. The freckles. The freshness. Mrs. Connelly would add so much. And you, Sheriff," Wolfson's fingers created a square for the photographers keen eye to consider how Dove would look in his photograph. "Glorious. So raw. So manly. All I want is an exclusive. You talk to me, and only me, and I'll make sure you are feted."

Cherie snorted but one look from Dove quieted her. Dove pushed aside his plate and crossed his arms on the table. He spoke softly.

"Mister, you turn your camera on anything that's mine and I'll break it over your head," Dove said evenly. "And now I'm going to tell you what I know. First, you're not here to tell the story of that woman's life, you want a picture of her body. You're just praying she's dead."

"I can't believe you would say..." Peter began to object.

"Don't interrupt me." Dove raised one finger to silence the man. "Second, since I can't kick you back to New York, I'm going to order you away from the crime scene and I'd say that is just about every inch of my mountain."

"It's a free country, Sheriff. I could have my lawyer get..."

"You can have your lawyer kiss my ass," Dove assured him. "This is my investigation and you will respect it. You will respect me and my wife. Most of all you will respect Mrs. Bradley. Is that understood?"

To Dove's great surprise, Peter Wolfson threw his head back. He laughed so long and so hard it worried Cherie. Mr. Reilly was intrigued. He reached for his notebook only to change his mind when Dove looked his way. Finally, Peter's laugh boiled down to a chuckle and then a hiccup and then he was wiping his eyes with his fingertips.

"Respect Tessa? Oh, yes, I have a lot of respect for Tessa but not in the way you think. Believe me, Sheriff, you don't have to protect that little flower. That woman is hard as nails. Once she made it, she threw me over like that," he snapped his fingers. "After all I did for her she hung me out to dry. Me, Peter Wolfson."

The residue of Peter's laughter was laced with bitterness. His face looked hard and old.

"I misjudged Tessa's intelligence. I should have been able to take her down the same way I built her up. But you weren't talking about that kind of respect, were you, Sheriff? You were talking about sympathy for Tessa. Well, that's not going to happen, either. She owes me and if taking a picture of her dead body is the only way she can pay me back then I won't have a problem pocketing the proceeds. You don't scare me. You don't particularly impress me, either." Peter stood up. Reilly followed suit. "I'll work around you. It will make this all so much more fun."

"Then I'd say we have something in common 'cause I'm not particularly impressed by you either, Mr. Wolfson. Only difference between us is I won't work around you, I'll walk right over you."

The two men sized each other up for what seemed a long while. It was Wolfson who looked away first.

"Well, Reilly, I suppose we won't be getting a statement tonight."

Cherie got up, too, and saw them to the door, not so much out of courtesy, as to make sure the photographer didn't touch anything. If he did, she'd have to scrub it down good.

"Your husband's making a mistake, Mrs. Connelly." Peter said as he put on his coat and buttoned it up.

"I don't think so, Mr. Wolfson."

She opened the door. Peter walked out. Mr. Reilly went after him only to come hurrying back at Peter Wolfson's direction. Mr. Reilly ducked his head as if he could dodge the snowflakes.

"Hey. Sorry. We forgot to ask, where is there a good hotel?"

"New York," Cherie answered as she shut the door.

I am on a bathroom floor again just like I was all those years ago at that party. Jake isn't here to help me so I'll have to pick myself up. The only way to make things right is to lighten the load I carry. Admitting what happened in Italy will help considerably.

What Ubert Yahobi did to me was a crime. I'm not to blame. The crack I heard as I struggled against my chain was not the bedpost but my own arm breaking. It snapped in three places — that's how hard I fought. I would have gnawed it off if that meant getting away from that man. I had only been with Simon. I was not as experienced as people liked to believe. Loving Simon and keeping Charlotte were the only times I ever really made a choice and Yahobi desecrated those decisions.

Eventually, I was sent on my way with enough pills to keep an army sedated. When I got home the campaign for Yahobi's line was breaking and I was news. My arm, according to the interviews Peter gave, was broken in a water skiing accident. He showed me the newspapers; he showed me the spreads in Vogue and Bazaar and W.

Since he didn't ask what really happened, I figure he knew. I also figured I wasn't the first woman he'd delivered up to that horrid man and that was vile. I stayed real quiet that day Peter came to preen in his expensive shirt and his too-big diamond earring. He was such a little man. No, he was a pimp. That's what I was thinking while he roamed around my house telling me how lucky I was that he had discovered me and that Yahobi had chosen me and how now we — WE — were going to be the hottest thing in New York for years.

When he stopped for a breath, worn out from planning how to make even more money off my back, I realized I wanted Peter to suffer as I had suffered. I wanted him to lose something so important that he would mourn it forever. Instead of wasting my breath on him, I picked up the phone and called my agency and told them what I wanted.

"I never want to be photographed by Peter Wolfson again," I said calmly. I watched Peter as I had this conversation.

He seemed confused, as if he thought I was joking. To prove I wasn't, I called *Vogue* and told them the same thing. I went down the list: *Bazaar, Elle, W.* No one in their right mind would book Peter after that and he knew it. He was done in the fashion business. I hoped he wouldn't even find work photographing weddings. He tried to stop me. He grabbed me and I shook him off. I turned those hard cold, model eyes on him and he backed away but he was mad.

What came out of his mouth was dirtier than a cesspool so I backhanded the bastard. It was a shame I forgot about my cast. The glass in my home was so thick he bounced off instead of going through it. I broke his jaw. It was the best I could do.

I guess I made more good choices than I thought. Ruining Peter was a damn good one. When I get home I will tell Charlotte about Yahobi. Then I will tell her about Peter and she will see that I stood up and it wasn't all for myself. There are other things to tell but that will be a good start.

I wipe my eyes. I've had enough of crying; I've given enough of my sadness and hope to men who didn't deserve it. I open the bathroom door. Marta is still there, sitting on the floor. The cat is in her lap.

"Do you think you could help me get my boots off?" I ask.

She nods. I haven't felt this strong in a long, long time.

Dove's Bedroom
12:30 a.m.

They didn't say much after the two men left. Cherie cleaned up the kitchen; Dove checked in with Jessica and asked her to call everyone to a meeting at the store first thing in the morning. Then he stood by the window and watched the snow. He had a lot of work to do but every piece of this puzzle seemed like sky – each piece of the mystery was bright and indistinguishable from the next. He had no idea how to put it together to find Tessa Bradley and the person who killed Fritz.

Cherie moved about easily in the silence knowing she could be of little help. What she didn't know was that Dove was also counting his blessings. He was blessed to live outside of Peter Wolfson's world, lucky to be married to a woman like Cherie, happy not to be Jake Bradley. Dove was also taking note of his own failings. He couldn't channel the *feel* and that kept Tessa Bradley just out of his reach. Time and the weather were making matters worse.

When it was very late, Dove stripped and climbed into bed beside his wife. He pulled her to him, feeling the softness of her flannel nightshirt against his skin and the bareness of her legs and the silkiness of her hair as it spread out over the pillow. He pulled her closer still and breathed her in but even Cherie couldn't calm his worries. There was too much of the outside world atop the mountain. There was Tessa Bradley's face in his mind's eye.

Dove Connelly turned away from his wife as if he had just betrayed her. He got out of bed again, wrapped himself in a robe and passed by the bassinette without a second glance. In the living room he looked out the window and wondered how anyone survived this dark, cold world.

My boots are expensive so they have no zippers and heels that are good for walking on nothing more treacherous than marble floors in a New York hotel. Marta shakes her head at such ridiculous footwear. She cups the heel, looks up at me as if to say 'hold on', then she yanks hard. She is strong but she is an old woman. It takes more than one try to get those boots off because the leather shrank in the river water.

It hurts like hell when the first one comes off. Heck, it hurts like hell when the second one comes off. Marta works so hard her barrette slips and hangs over her forehead like a little plastic red bow of a bindi. She massages my right foot and then the left. Finally, she peels the socks away and I see that my feet are still pretty. There is some swelling but no frostbite. I am lucky.

Pushing my feet off her lap, Marta walks backwards on her knees. She motions to my jeans. I unzip them, wriggle out of them as she pulls on the legs. She sets them aside atop a cracked toilette. My sweater is next. I lift my arms like I'm five years old. It doesn't come off as easily as the boots. It sticks at my shoulder where I was shot. Marta picks at the scab like she is undoing a poorly stitched seam. She looks close when my sweater is finally off but I'm the one who really touches the wound. My fingers touch around it then go in it. I have a hole in my body and I can feel bone. It won't heal well. There will be a scar. I don't think I will have it fixed no matter what anyone says.

"It seems so long ago." I say this as if I am commenting on someone else's misfortune.

"Yah. You shouldn't be here," Marta comments.

I think that is a strange thing to say. Does she mean a woman like me shouldn't be in this situation, or does she mean that I should be dead because of my wound? I don't ask. She doesn't tell.

Marta turns on the shower and leaves. I drop my drawers. I am naked in a little bathroom in the middle of the forest in a mobile home that my mama would have spit at. I'm in heaven. I glance at the mirror but it's old. I only see a little bit of my face; really only half of my face. It's me and it isn't. I don't fret about it as I step into the shower and shiver.

Marta lied. The water isn't even warm. In fact it's cold. Bracing. Like the river.

I pull back. My head hits the wall hard.

I cry out and curse and laugh all at the same time.

Marta hollers at me but the sound of her voice is lost in the rush of freezing water that cascades down the back of my head.

Day Two:
Fritz's Mountain Cabin
<u>6:30 a.m.</u>

They were all waiting in Fritz's Mountain Store when Dove arrived. Tim was dressed exactly the same as the day before. Nathan was there sans hairnet and wearing a Green Day t-shirt under his heavy jacket. Jessica had her hair pulled back and hadn't bothered with the fancy eyeliner she normally favored. She looked more worn out than he'd ever seen her and for good reason.

"I was up most of the night calling people who were none to happy to hear from me – even after I told them what I wanted." She handed him a list of New York phone numbers and names.

"That could have waited 'till the morning, Jessica."

Dove looked at her notes. They were thorough and unhelpful. The New Yorkers didn't know anything about Tessa Bradley's life on the West Coast and, worse, they didn't seem to care.

"Yeah, well, I couldn't sleep anyway." Jessica smiled a little. "I kept wondering if she was okay after what the boys found up there."

"That information was supposed to be held back. We've got press up here now. More will be coming. I want you all to treat this serious from here on out because they're wily. They are going to try to wheedle stuff out of you and turn it around to what they want to be true." Dove included all of them in his admonishment.

"Sorry, Dove," Jessica said. "I'll get hold of everyone and tell them before I call those local numbers. There's a whole lot of calls to that phone in Corallis."

"Good, we'll cross Hart's records and coordinate the times with Mrs. Bradley's calls." Dove pointed at the doctor. "Tim, you have anything?"

"I do, indeed." Tim cleared his throat. "In regards to the item that was found yesterday evening, Dove, it did not come from Mrs. Bradley. It is from a brown-eyed person. Hence, I have preserved the specimen for better minds than my own who should be able to determine who it belongs to and exactly how long it was out in the woods. Sadly, Mrs. Bradley is still out in the woods."

No one was cheered as they considered how harsh the night had been. For Dove, that only meant there was no time to waste.

"Give the hospitals a call, Tim. Find out if anyone came in with an eye injury. Let's start around one a.m. yesterday. After that, call doctors in Bleden Town and Corallis. Bleden Town first. Then hit the pharmacies."

"Yes sir, Dove."

"Nathan? Your turn."

"I've laid everything out, Dove." He pointed to the molds of tire tracks and footprints. "I could identify the tracks of four cars. One had pulled over in the rough so I only got a partial. It's going to be tough matching it up to tire model and then make and model of the car, but it can be done."

"Work on the most obvious first," Dove directed.

"Well, the most obvious was an SUV – the one that pulled out fast. I don't think it's the Mountaineer you're looking for Dove. This one should be a Chevy. Heavy like the trucks but not necessarily a truck. I'm trying to match up the taillights Paddy drew for me. I'm hoping to have something solid on that this afternoon."

"Good man."

They all moved over a few paces to stand in front of the next row of molds.

"These are the footprints. We've got Mrs. Bradley wearing fancy shoes. High, narrow heels and really pointed toes like Barbie Doll shoes except bigger. Size ten and a half."

"Jessica. Call the Bradley house and ask one of them to check through her shoes and see if they can identify which pair is missing."

"She's a model, Dove. She'll have a hundred pair." Jessica objected as she made her note. "No man's going to know what's missing."

"I don't care if she owns the store. Ask them to look."
Dove gave Nathan the nod to continue.

"Mrs. Bradley walked into the store with an even step.
Her footprints don't come out again so that says to me
she was being carried. There's no drag marks or anything
and the car that drove away was parked real close to the
verandah out there."

Nathan's head clicked up with each piece of
information as if he was mentally checking off a list.

"Okay, okay. So, this next one is of a man's shoe with
a waffle print sole. Pretty new; kind of small. Eight and a
half. I did a quick search last night of the major
manufacturers but didn't find an exact match. All it told
me was that there are plenty of places that make a waffle
print. What might save us on this one is that the heel on
this shoe has a matching pattern to the ball of the foot.
That's kind of different."

Nathan took a deep breath.

"This man goes out the driver's side door and directly
to the back door in a little arc. He returns from the back
door with an even gait but right at the corner of the store
he starts to run. He runs. He stops. Then he runs again to
the driver's side and gets in the car."

"Like he was surprised or excited because he was
seeing something he didn't expect," Dove mused.

"Like Mrs. Bradley was being carried out of the store
by someone else," Nathan suggested. Tim nodded. Jessica
murmured.

Nathan licked his lips and pointed to the third mold.

"She was probably being carried by this one. He went
in back but I found a partial in the blood just near the
front counter. It looks like he walked through the store,

saw Mrs. Bradley and got her there. Maybe she heard the shot or saw them moving. I don't think she could see Fritz from right inside the door."

Nathan cleared his throat.

"This is only a guess, of course. Anyway, this shows work boots. Size ten. I'm going to also assume, if he had Mrs. Bradley, she was struggling because it seems he was having trouble keeping on his feet."

"I'd be fighting like hell if it was me," Jessica added her two cents.

"How tall is that Simon person you picked up yesterday?" Tim asked.

"Five ten, maybe a little taller, but he's not heavy. A woman of that size would be his match," Dove answered, pocketing the pictures of the mold that Nathan handed him. "I'll take these pictures back and check his boots. The deputy over there has the warrant. Anything else?"

"Actually, yes." Nathan pushed back his hair. "You know the partial on the tires that were over on the shoulder parked under the tree? Well, there were some footprints, too. A pretty standard work shoe. Size eleven and a half, but whoever was wearing them wasn't as heavy as man number two."

"Could it have been someone who was at the store earlier?" Jessica suggested. "I mean people did stop at the store for things."

"True," Nathan answered. "But remember the day had been wet. There was a lot of mist, the snow on the ground had been melting and was starting to refreeze. Fritz was killed after midnight. If it was after midnight, there was cold moist ground. It was a perfect situation for prints. I'm pretty confident there wasn't a whole lot of extra traffic. Not that there had been a lot of traffic lately anyway."

Fritz's friends considered the tough time Fritz had of late. They all did their part, buying everything they could eat and store from him but nothing they did would have been enough to make the kind of ends meet that Fritz was holding.

"Go ahead, Nathan," Dove directed.

"There's something wrong with this guy's right leg. His foot rolls. He limps."

"Is that it?" Dove asked.

Nathan shook his head. "The guy with the limp? He didn't go into the store. He walked about half way, stood there, then went back to his car."

"An eyewitness?" Tim speculated. "Maybe somebody out there is too scared to come forward."

"Could very well be," Dove mused, envisioning the men who had been in the store that night.

Dove was sinking into this information like quicksand with no *feel* to let him know if there was a bottom to this pit. Was it a gang? Two drifters and an eyewitness? Three kids out for fun? Or was man number three, as Jessica suggests, a patron who had nothing to do with what went on in here? Maybe that person was come and gone before it went down. Maybe he even saw Tessa Bradley walk into the store, admiring her before driving off.

Or, could those tracks have been made by Jake Bradley who watched to make sure things went the way he planned? He had followed his wife to Corallis. He had kept silent about Simon Hart. There was the problem with those letters. All of it made Dove consider a few things he hadn't put on the *notice*. Did Jake Bradley limp?

What kind of shoes did he wear? Perhaps Dove was drawn back to the man again and again because he had proved himself a liar.

"Alright. Let's go to work. Jessica, you get on with those phone records and start tracking down shoe manufacturers that make waffle soles." Dove slapped Tim on the back and looked at everyone in turn. "I'll be in Corallis if you've got an emergency. They can only hold Hart for forty-eight hours."

Nathan said, "I'll clean up the back room, Dove. Then Bernadette can come down and tell us if anything is missing – on the off chance this was a robbery. Then I'm going back up the mountain to where we found the eye."

"Okay, we've all got our jobs to do."

Dove pocketed the pictures, got in his car and started to turn the wheel South toward Corallis.

Dove's Mountain, The Forest
7:35 a.m.

Peter Wolfson slapped at something on his neck. It was too cold for bugs to be out but he swore they were gnawing at him anyway.

Nature was so vile. Give him a studio gig any day, especially when one had to pee. Peter hated doing it outdoors like some day laborer. He would have held it if he could but, at his age, the old plumbing wasn't exactly working properly. He would see his doctor as soon as he got home. Until then, one of these trees would be given the honor of bearing witness to his toilette.

Heaving a deep sigh, Peter looked down the road on the off chance he would see Mr. Reilly heading his way earlier than they planned. If Reilly was having the same trouble getting these yokels to cooperate, he might come searching for Peter. Sadly, the road remained empty. Peter put his big camera bag beside it as a flag in case the shy Mr. Reilly was about. After that, he went in search of a sufficiently private place in which to do his business.

He was twenty-yards in when he stopped behind a particularly large trunked tree and unzipped his pants. Trying to relax, trying not to notice how the cold had shriveled him – for certainly it was the cold that played this cruel joke – his mind wandered to the morning's work. He was actually satisfied with much of what he had. They were all rather mundane shots but every one necessary for a story like this.

He had pictures of the roads Tessa drove, the forest that she had called home for these last few years. He had taken background photos of quaint cabins and rough people. He would have snapped wildlife if he had seen any. He would have shot a river if he'd found one...

Ah, it was coming. Peter's shoulders sagged in relief. As the golden shower began he heard something else. He heard a footfall behind him.

"Just in time for the show, Reilly," Peter quipped only to see that it wasn't Reilly at all who had found him peeing in the forest.

"I didn't sleep with Simon."
"You loved him, ya?"
"I thought I did. When I was a girl."

"Girls hope for love." Marta sighs at the futility of that.

"Yes," I say, wondering if she was ever such a girl

"Did you get it? Love?" Marta asked.

"Yes, but not from him"

This is the truth. Jake gave me love. I almost threw it away. I'm glad I didn't.

"Were you cruel to the man who loved you?"

I think about this as we snap beans. They pop and I drop them into a pot of water. The answer to her question is no. I didn't use Jake's love against him. I curled into him at night. I pushed his hair back when I passed his chair. I put an extra log on the fire when he was cold. In New York we were equals. Famous, each in our own way. People wanted things from us and we went home with each other wanting so little of them.

I wanted to tell Jake I had seen Simon. I didn't. I didn't ever want to hurt him but I probably did one way or another. I wanted to tell Charlotte that I wasn't having an affair but if I did that then I would have to tell her that Simon was her father. Deep inside I knew that would hurt Jake because she loved him better than me. It would change things between them.

"No, I wasn't cruel to the one who loved me. I protected him." I snap a bean. Into the pot it goes. There are a thousand of them. I don't know how we will eat them all.

"What about your daughter?"

"I did my best. I never told her about Simon or about being raped or about my mother. I let Jake have her. That was the best thing I did." Another bean snaps. "Will I be able to go home soon?"

"You can walk?" Marta raises an eyebrow.

"Yes," I say.

"I'll take you to the road. Tomorrow. There might be a storm."

"Either way, I'm going tomorrow."

"Yah. You will go tomorrow. It's time."
It is settled. I reach for another bean. I am smiling.

Sheriff's Office, Corallis
7:45 a.m.

"Hey, Ginger."

"Hey, Sheriff Connelly."

Ginger stood up so fast she almost knocked her coffee off the desk. Today she wore her uniform shirt with a red pencil skirt and high heels. She looked great but the get-up didn't seem too practical when she tripped in those heels, flustered and impatient with herself. Still, there was something sweet about the line she straddled.

"Quiet last night?" Dove asked.

"I suppose," she answered, her eyes lighting everywhere but on Dove. "I went home after you left."

Dove smiled at her and looked toward Savick's office. "Is he in?"

"No, I'm sorry. He didn't know you were coming. I mean, well, he didn't know what time you were maybe coming. I guess he didn't think. He's had a lot on his mind lately."

"Not to worry. I'm really here to see Hart." Dove headed for the door that led to their two-cell lock up.

"Sheriff Connelly?" Ginger called tentatively.

"Don't worry, I'll wake him real gentle if he's sleeping in," Dove assured her.

"No, it's not that." She pulled her lips tight, biting hard on whatever bullet she was chewing. It didn't take more than a second for her to crack. She threw up her hands.

"He's not there. Sheriff Savick sent him home. He said that he really didn't have enough to hold him on or...or something like that. Mike told me this morning." Ginger made sure the desk was between her and Dove but there was no need to worry. Dove wasn't the kind to take out his anger on her.

"Where is Mike?"

"Gone over to talk to the senior citizens. It's their weekly breakfast. The sheriff told Mike he'd square it with you about Mr. Hart. Mike was supposed to butt out."

"Did Mike leave anything for me? I'd asked him to check on Hart's phone bill." Dove's tone was even but not enough to fool Ginger that he wasn't one angry man.

With her eye on Dove, Ginger hurried to Mike's desk and rifled through the papers on top. Her ample chest lifted up in relief when she found it.

"He did. I knew he was working on it. Here. Here you go. Oh, and the search warrant. He picked it up late yesterday."

"Thanks." Dove took it, glanced at it and pocketed it. "Where can I find Savick?"

"I don't know, Sheriff. Honest, I don't. Something's been going down and he just hasn't told me about it. I'd tell you if I knew."

"Sure. Not your problem." Dove set his lips tight and went to the door. Ginger stopped him.

"Sheriff? Mike took Hart home. He told him not to leave town until things were settled. Mike was trying to help."

"He's a good man," Dove assured her.

Ginger shrugged a little, colored some. It was as if she knew the truth of that but couldn't help herself for wanting someone not quite as good.

Dove tipped his hat and took his leave. He could feel Ginger's eyes on his back as he stood on the sidewalk watching the town wake up. There was some traffic. A school bus rolled on by. The coffee shop was open, the flower shop wasn't and Simon Hart was about to have a visitor. He just didn't know it.

Simon Hart's Apartment
8:37 a.m.

Dove pounded on the door again. He would keep pounding until his fist went through it or it opened.

"Time to get up, Hart." Dove raised his hand but before he could make any more noise the woman in the apartment below hollered up at him.

"For God's sake, shut up! All that noise. Scuffling around last night, making all that racket today. Just shut up!"

Dove looked over the railing. He couldn't see her but he knew she was still there. He held out his ID on the off chance she'd look up.

"Sheriff," he called.

"I don't care if you're an Archangel and this is the end of the world," she hollered back. "Shut up!"

The sliding door screeched, slammed and locked. He hadn't seen a hair on the woman's head, but he did see a head of hair he recognized. The face under it was turned up and K.C. was beaming at him. Her tennis shoes were still double knotted and she looked tired.

"Couldn't stay away from me, huh, big boy?" Her grin could have lit up Alaska in the twenty-four-hour dark.

"You had a long night," Dove said.

"That shift at the Circle K ain't no walk in the park but it pays time and a half. Before you know it, I'll have a place of my own. Then we can stop meeting like this, and I'll entertain you proper."

She talked all the way up the stairs and down the second floor landing until she ended up in front of Dove. She didn't stop as she passed him, nor did she stop when she stood in front of the door to the apartment she shared with Simon Hart.

"That'll be hard to resist, K.C., but I'll do my best."

"I bet your missus is just the prettiest, nicest thing in the world and you wouldn't have eyes for Pamela Anderson if she paraded naked right in front of you," K.C. said wistfully.

"I think there's some truth to that, K.C.," he agreed.

"Yeah. Figured." She laughed wearily. "If you're not here to get in my hot little pants, what are you up to?"

"I want to talk to Hart. He's not answering."

"I thought you already did that." She dug in her huge bag, pulled out three partial packs of cigarettes and handed them to Dove along with a brush, a Kleenex, a wad of grocery coupons and a pack of gum. She dived in again to look for her keys. "He called me, you know. He wanted me to bail him out. I told him if I'd already paid him for this place and if I left him in jail I'd at least have the bathroom to myself. Not to mention I wasn't going to do anything to screw up this job."

"Is that really what you told him?" Dove asked. K.C. pulled a face as she held up her keys and offered her open purse so he could dump everything back in.

"Nope. I told him I didn't have fifty bucks much less five hundred to bail him out. Guess someone else came through if you're here."

"I'll have to find out who that friend is." Dove saw no need to tell her that Savick just got tired of babysitting. "Now, are you going to let me in?"

"Okay, but you have to promise to take him somewhere else if you're going to yell. I'd really like to have a nice long shower and get to sleep."

"I'll convince him to take a walk with me," Dove assured her.

"In that case, mi casa es su casa even though it's really Simon's casa," KC laughed. She had the key in the lock and K.C. was pushing the door open when Dove put a hand on her shoulder. He dug his fingers in hard.

"Ow! Hey! I don't like to play rough," she chided, snapping her head around to glare at him. One look at his face, though, quieted her.

"Stay still," Dove commanded.

K.C. stepped back. Dove's hand slid off her shoulder and fell to his side. His black eyes were hooded yet K.C. could see the shine of them just below the lashes. His body went rigid as the *feel* cascaded out that door. It was the *feel* of desperation, the *feel* of determination – this was the *feel* of violence.

"Hey, big boy," K.C. whispered. She touched his hand and Dove suddenly realized he was holding tight to his gun. He had no memory of drawing it from his holster. Dove blinked at her and then he was himself again.

"Against the wall," he said softly.

She planted herself fresco-flat against the stucco and whispered: "Want me to go for help?"

Dove wasn't listening. The *feel* engulfed him, wrapped its arms around him and pulled him into Simon Hart's apartment.

It is the silence that wakes me. Or the dark. Or the cold that has turned freezing. Whatever it is, I shoot awake, tangled in a blanket. My face is damp with perspiration. My hair is still wet. I think it's wet from the river then I remember I have had a shower. But that was hours ago.

It might be that I woke because of my dream. It was not a pleasant one. It frightened me in a much different way than I have been frightened for the last hours — or is it days?

I dreamt of the last time I saw my mother.

I had expected to meet her on home ground, collect my daughter and be on my way. I had practiced what I would tell her. I would thank her for taking care of Charlotte but I would be firm that it was now my turn to be mother to my little girl. I would still give my mama her money. I had more than enough for all of us, but I would have Charlotte. That was the plan.

But my flight was late. Charlotte was asleep. I checked into the Holiday Inn intending to get her the next morning. Alone in the night, I got the shakes. I feared seeing my mama. I feared my money would run out and Charlotte would starve. Italy came back to haunt me. Sharon was dead, Peter was out of my life, Jake wasn't a cornerstone yet. I was alone and my arm hurt. I was ashamed about what happened to me. All these things came into play but what I feared most was my mother.

207

I have no idea why she didn't like me. I tried very hard to be a good daughter. When I was a teenager I assumed she was ashamed to have a gangly ugly daughter. She used to tell me I'd never amount to anything and when I did I think she was more surprised than anyone. Then I thought she was jealous of my success. Then I thought she was so unhappy with the way her life turned out. She had been married to one man who drank and left her — my father — and married to another who didn't want to marry her in the first place. Then I stopped trying to figure out why she didn't like me and started wondering why I feared her.

That proved one too many thoughts for me that night. I needed to rest; I needed to be ready for the next day and I wanted to sleep without dreaming.

I thought I only took enough pills to get me through the night. Instead, I took enough to kill me. A maid found me. The ambulance came. The paramedics put a tube down my throat and my mama said it was a pity I hadn't died.

She called me a whore, a slut and a drug addict and said she'd tell everyone all about me if I tried to take Charlotte away. She said she would go to court and have a judge make an order giving her Charlotte and making me pay child support forever and ever.

I believed her the way I had believed her my whole life. Instead of standing up the way I had stood up to Peter, I put my tail between my legs. I believed she was better for Charlotte than me. Looking back I can see how wrong that was. My mama never once said she loved Charlotte. I should have paid more attention. Instead, I went away and left my daughter with that woman. It was the most cowardly thing I had ever done.

That's why I wake up fearful. That's why I wake up ashamed. That's why I wake up thinking I'm in a hospital in Texas and my mama will be walking through the door any minute to tell me I'm worthless.

I'm not in a hospital. This is Marta's house. I have been sleeping on her old couch but she is not asleep. She is huddled in the corner of the trailer. The three little dogs are curled up near her. The cat is on a bookcase across the room. Marta's back is to me and she is working hard at something. I hear a rhythmic ripping and crumpling of paper. I hear a rumbling outside. The storm is trying to come. I hear a vicious wind outside the window that dies down suddenly.

Then there is silence again. It has been this way since the beginning: a rush of noise, a whimper, a whisper, silence.

I throw off the blanket. My feet are still tender so I put them down gently. They are warm because Marta gave me socks to wear. She also gave me a pair of pants that belonged to a very short person, a blouse and a sweater. I look like Marta except for my hair. Only Marta's hair can look the way it does.

"Marta?" I call softly.

She doesn't hear me. My eyes adjust. When I get up, one of the dogs raises its head then puts it down on its paws again. That Marta notices. She puts out her wrinkled hand and lets it rest between the dog's ears. She hesitates as if she knows I'm up but isn't sure she wants to acknowledge me. She makes a decision and bends to her chore once more. I know I should respect her desire to be alone but I need to be with her, I need someone to look at me and acknowledge I'm there. The space between us isn't big but I tiptoe across it anyway. For a minute I stand above her and watch what she's doing. I hope she'll glance my way, invite me to sit on the floor with her. She doesn't look up but I look down and see what she is doing. She is ripping pages out of the magazines that are stacked against the wall. She crumples them, sticks the paper ball in a hole in the wall and then rips another page out.

A poor man's insulation. This is how she will stay warm until summer.

Crossing my legs, I lower myself down and sit beside her to help. I want to help. It's the least I can do. I reach for a magazine. Our eyes meet. I smile but Marta looks away. I want to tell her there's no shame in poverty. Some of us come from it, some go back to it. There is poverty of place and poverty of spirit. That is just a fact of life and you deal with it.

I pluck a magazine off the stack and open it to a random page. My fingers grasp it. I am ready to rip it out but then I glance down and lose my breath. Poverty is not what Marta is nervous about.

She looks at me. We look at each other. She wonders what I will say now that I know.

Bernadette's House
<u>9:00 a.m.</u>

The afternoon broke beautiful for the few minutes it took Cherie Connelly to walk up the path to Bernadette's place. Golden sunlight pierced the grey clouds and filtered through the trees. It swept over the newly fallen snow making it sparkle like silver. The air was crisp and clear. There was smoke coming from the chimney so Cherie knew Bernadette had been well enough to get up and add some wood to the fire. Perhaps she had even eaten something.

Cherie moved the ceramic frog that sat beside the porch and took the key from under his green butt. The lock clicked just as the hole in the heavens closed up. By the time Cherie unlocked the door to Bernadette's house, the outside was as gloomy as the inside.

"Bernadette?" Cherie called softly. The baby on her back gurgled. Bernadette didn't hear either of them because she wasn't in the living room.

The quilt was rumpled on the couch, the pillow was cold. The fire was burning but it was mostly embers. The hospital bed hadn't been slept in. The I.V. was still full and the bedroom door was closed. This was Bernadette's sign that she needed her privacy.

"Well, we'll put a few more things in order then, shall we?"

Cherie took her daughter out of the carrier and set her on the floor near the dining room table. With a coo and a tickle, she gave the baby the stress ball Bernadette used to exercise her fingers. Sure that she would be entertained for a bit, Cherie went to the mail drop.

There were notes of condolence neighbors had pushed through the slot, a few pieces of junk mail and two bills. Cherie put the notes on the mantle and added wood to the fire while she was there. She puttered about, folding the quilt and plumping the pillows all the while wondering how they were going to manage Fritz's funeral. She would ask the mortician in Corallis if he could see his way to donating the casket. Marlene White did beautiful stonework. Perhaps she could build something to mark Fritz's place. Cherie would make the food for the reception after the church service. In fact, she would suggest that the church host a fundraiser. Bernadette was going to need more than just to settle Fritz's funeral. There would be food and heat and house repairs. There would be gas for the car and, soon, Cherie imagined Bernadette would need a nurse.

The baby squealed. She had lost the ball and was too little to understand where it had gone so Cherie chased after it. She took a minute to admire the gorgeous creature she had born then settled herself at the table Bernadette used as a desk. It was to be expected that she hadn't look at the mail from yesterday, but Cherie was surprised to see that mail from a week – or weeks – before had not been touched.

Cherie ripped open the ends of the envelopes and blew inside each one. She threw away the junk mail and stacked the bills neatly after casually perusing them. There was a second notice on the electrical bill. The gas bill was past due also. She would talk to Dove about paying them for Bernadette until they figured out how their friend was going to manage. They would probably have to close the store. It would be a drain if Bernadette had to hire someone to keep it open and Cherie couldn't imagine anyone wanting to be in the place where Fritz had died.

Cherie blew into the next envelope and put the contents aside. She did the same with the next before realizing three were from Bernadette's insurance company. Curious, she picked them up and read them over twice to make sure she understood what was written. She flipped through the stack of mail on the table one more time. There was a fourth letter and all of them gave Cherie Connelly a shock.

"We've got to go. Gotta go."

She whispered to herself as she scooped up her daughter. Knowing she shouldn't, Cherie pocketed the letters with her other: one premium notice, two warnings and a final notice of cancellation.

Oh, God.

Cherie buried her nose in the warm crook of her baby's shoulder as she tried to get control of her emotions. This was worse than anything she could have imagined. Quickly, Cherie slipped the baby into the carrier pouch wanting nothing more than to...

"What are you doing?"

Cherie twirled. She hadn't even heard the bedroom door open and now here was Bernadette standing behind her, angry, glaring. Bernadette was definitely unhappy to see Cherie Connelly in her house.

Sheriff's Office, Corallis
9:40 a.m.

The door of the Corallis Sheriff's station blew open like it had been bombed then slammed shut behind Dove Connelly. Ginger shot out of her chair. Mike hollered but neither had time to try to keep Dove from Savick's office. When Dove flung open the door, the man cursed and reached for his weapon. Dove was faster than his counterpart. He was at Savick's desk, pushing up against it and throwing a duffle bag on top of it.

"You damn bastard. What in the hell were you thinking? What in the hell were you thinking?" Dove picked up the edge of the desk and brought it down hard. The duffle bag flew toward Savick who put out his hands to catch it even though he still had hold of his gun.

"What the fu..." Savick hollered. "Just hold on. Hold on."

"Put it away before I use it on you." Dove reached over the desk and grabbed Savick's wrist. The man's hand tightened on his weapon like he couldn't wait to use it. Dove Connelly stared him down before throwing that arm aside. Savick held tight to the weapon.

"Mike!" Savick called out. He wanted back up but Dove had other ideas. He was at the door in two strides.

"Stay put, Mike. This isn't for you." Dove swung his arm, slammed the door then turned back to Savick.

"You best settle down, Connelly."

The gun was leveled at Dove. Savick's lip was pushed out where his plug of tobacco had been stashed at the gum. Tobacco juice ran from the side of his mouth and he wiped it away. There was no doubt that Dove and his outrage made Savick nervous but Dove didn't care. He was sure the man didn't have the guts to pull the trigger.

"Hart is dead. I found the body and I found the syringe. He's an O.D."

"Then he's dead," Savick drawled, unimpressed. "Nothing I can do about it."

"Put it away or I swear I'll take it away," Dove ordered, indicating Savick's weapon.

Savick hesitated then tossed it in the desk drawer. His rage used up, Dove lay back against the door for a second then made his way to the chair. Savick gave the cuffs of his shirt another turn.

"He was a coward, Connelly. He was scared shitless even though you had us holding him on nothing. Say good riddance. Go tell the widow you got your man."

"And what do I tell Tessa Bradley's family?" Dove asked.

"I don't know, and I don't care. What did you want me to do when Hart started making noises about a lawyer? You had nothing."

"I had a scarf with blood all over it," Dove said. "He admitted it belonged to Tessa Bradley."

"And he said it was his blood on it," Savick snapped back. "Test it. Check it out. Then come back to me."

"I have a shotgun," Dove insisted. "I found it in his closet."

"And no ballistics. Hell, we just got a warrant for Hart's place. That was an illegal search if it wasn't sitting on the kitchen counter," Savick drawled. "That will be thrown out before you see the inside of a courtroom."

"You have the connection to a missing woman and the receipt from the Mountain Store. You had enough to hold him."

"That woman is probably waiting on him somewhere."

Savick pushed his hair back even though it was slicked into place good. His eyes met Dove's and there was hatred in them and Dove couldn't understand why. A woman was missing, a man dead. They should be working together but Savick was still throwing up roadblocks, relishing his role as Devil's advocate.

"And Hart could have stopped in that store any time during that day. Besides, he wasn't going anywhere. We impounded his car for God's sake. Do you think he was going to walk out of here?"

Savick chewed. He spat. He stared Dove Connelly down with those flat, dark eyes of his. This was his office. He would call the shots no matter what. He was feeling better now, more comfortable with Dove's silence. He smiled a little and stored that plug of tobacco while he spoke.

"I was covering *my* butt, Connelly, because I didn't think I had anything to speak of to hold him. I watch out for *my* town and *my* deputy. Corallis doesn't need to get sued for false arrest or something worse."

"Assaulting an officer. You could have held him on that," Dove said, knowing there was nothing he could say that would convince Savick he should have acted differently.

"And I didn't," came the answer. That didn't satisfy Dove.

"Why? What was so important that you couldn't hold him long enough for us to do a good search?" He heard the plea in his voice but he didn't care. The man couldn't be this heartless. Then Dove found out he was wrong.

"Not a damn thing." Savick answered with a sick pleasure. "I just don't like anyone coming into my place of business ordering my deputy around, telling me what to do, using my resources. I looked at what you had, I talked to Hart and I made the decision. Next time bring something with legs or take him with you. That's all you had to do, sheriff. Take the man with you."

Dove pushed up off the chair and grabbed the duffle that had been shoved to the edge of the desk. The anger was back. There was no reasoning with Savick. He was despicable. Dove put the bag in front of the man, slid back the zipper, pulled out a pair of shoes. He slammed them on the desk. Peas of dried mud scattered over Savick's paperwork. Dove pulled the photographs Nathan had taken out of his jacket pocket. He snapped those down next to the shoes.

"These are pictures of print molds taken at the crime scene. These are shoes taken from the duffle bag found on the bed in Simon Hart's apartment. If you weren't so worried about your ego, we would have been able to find out who Hart's accomplice was. Now we don't have anything."

"Lordy, lordy. Aren't you just going to make the front page of the New York Times, Connelly? You're a regular Sherlock Holmes." Savick chuckled and laced his hands behind his head. He looked ugly when he smiled. "If you ask me this is as simple as Hart not wanting to go back to prison. He's already been behind bars half his life. He was a three-striker then some. He offed himself. Coward's way out."

Dove listened but he didn't really need to hear what Savick had to say to know he was a small man who created big problems. While Savick talked, Dove walked to the door, opened it and called to Ginger.

"Do you have an evidence release form, please?"

"Yes, sir," Ginger called back.

"Bring it here."

Ginger scurried in, paperwork in hand. She stood in the doorway looking at Savick for direction. Mike joined her, hovering behind, watching what was going down. Dove took the release and put it down in front of Savick.

"Sign it. I'm taking this duffle with me. I want the shotgun. I've got the scarf. I want you to write it all down. Put the time there and the date." Dove pointed to the paper.

"Why should I?"

"Because, if you don't, I'm going to see that the feds look at you for obstruction of justice. I'll tell them I have proof Tessa Bradley has been taken over state lines and that means it's a federal case. Do you want them looking at you that close or do you want to last long enough to get to that next election?"

A cloud passed over Savick's brow. His eyes flicked toward his secretary and deputy. He colored, embarrassed to be put in this position in front of the people who worked for him. He reached for his pen and scribbled on the paper but Dove wasn't done. "And you better damn well go over that apartment with a magnifying glass because I'm going to subpoena your book, you got that?"

"You're pushing it, Connelly." Savick slid the release toward Dove. "And we're professional here. We don't get emotionally involved and we don't go off half cocked."

Dove picked up the duffle and hefted it to his side. There was a lot he wanted to talk about but nothing he could say to Savick with civility. He spoke to Mike on the way out.

"You got a body to take care of, Mike. K.C.'s waiting downstairs from Hart's place. She's in apartment 1A. She was with me and identified Hart and she said she'd answer any questions she can. Send me the report tomorrow."

Dove walked out the front door. Everyone looked after him: Ginger with awe, Mike with admiration and Savick with something past loathing.

Marta tears the paper, crinkles the pages and stuffs them into the hole in the wall with a rhythm that is somehow comforting. I go more slowly, looking at every single page before I wad it up. In these magazines are pictures of me and friends I have almost forgotten. There is Amy who was only fifteen when she hit the runway. Gordana who came from Russia I think. She was a hard woman. Never spoke to anyone. I wonder what happened to them. I know they all went on with their lives but what did those lives come to? I doubt any of them came to this. That makes me smile. Wouldn't they be surprised to see me like this? I am surprised to see them here with me. It is like a homecoming.

Mostly, though, I look at me. I am there, too, the way I used to be. It is like looking at a year book.

1979. Harper's Bazaar. A full face spread about beautiful skin. My eyes are closed. The photographer lit my face so that my skin looks as pure as fresh cream. I look so content, so otherworldly. The photographer told me to think about a lover. I thought about Simon.

I don't anymore.

1982. Vogue. The cover. My lips are drawn back, my teeth are bared and my eyes half-mast. The clothes I wear are no-nonsense. I am supposed to be a woman completely in charge of my life and my work. I look directly into the camera. Don't touch. Don't come near me. I am angry. I am poison. Peter took that picture.

Peter brought out the worst in me.

1980.People Magazine. Paparazzi catch me at Michael's in Los Angeles. The food was delicious and always served in portions that models appreciated – an expensive bite and no more. Charlotte is with me. A rare visit on my turf. We are smiling at each other. We are happy. She didn't know about Italy or anything. She is looking at me the way a daughter who loves her mama does. That window was only open a short time. I flew through it and some photographer was there to take a picture before I had my wings clipped.

It wasn't all bad, this life of mine but that part is over. I crumple the Vogue picture and the Bazaar picture and put myself away where I will do some good. I keep the picture of me and Charlotte. I'm sure Marta won't mind.

The trailer gets warm. I cut my eyes to my ancient hostess. We are done stuffing all the holes in her trailer. Rain falls. The wind *whips. The cat hasn't stirred and the little dogs have curled up again. They look like a furry little donut, a circle of fluff and black noses. I stand up, put my hands at the small of my back and stretch. I am pleased with the work in a way I never was in New York. My life has been a carnival ride. I think I had been a little sick with the thrill of it even before Jake brought me west. I just didn't want to admit it because I was afraid. What else did I know? What good was I? Was there a 'me' inside the body and behind the face? I have answers now.*

I have learned from the first go 'round; I will make the second better.

"I'm done, Marta."

I whisper because it is night and the dogs sleep. Marta nods but she doesn't seem tired the way I would think an old person would be. I see that there is one more picture of me. I bend down, crumple it up and push it tight into the wall without looking at it. I go back to the couch, close my eyes and sleep without dreaming.

The Road to Dove's Mountain
11:00 a.m.

Dove couldn't get comfortable as he drove. He shifted and he moved and he ran his free hand through his long, black hair and cocked his other arm on the open window as he kept his hand on the wheel. The frigid air funneling through the car didn't clear his mind.

"Damn!"

He hit the steering wheel then grasped it with both hands as he shifted his body and pressed harder on the gas pedal. The big car shot forward and he took the hairpin turn faster and tighter than he should. When the back wheels spun out on the shoulder, kicking some rock and getting to closer to the sheer drop than Dove liked, he eased off.

It wouldn't do to kill himself before things were settled. It wasn't just Fritz's death and Tessa Bradley's disappearance; it wasn't Will Savick's apathy and arrogance or Simon Hart's idiocy. It wasn't that a bloodsucker like Peter Wolfson had landed on Dove's mountain. What ailed Dove's soul was deeper and more personal. It was Cherie and the baby and the man who had changed their lives so horribly. But it was Will Savick who brought out Dove's hatred and anger again.

Sick with the burning in his gut, Dove Connelly pulled over, yanked on the emergency brake and dropped his head atop his hands as he held on to the steering wheel. There was a pounding inside his brain, he couldn't catch his breath and that effort was bringing tears to his eyes. Those tears were always there, just under the surface but they weren't always so hard to keep down. Damn if he'd let them go. Damn if he didn't hate Savick. He hated not being able to help a woman in trouble – his own or Jake Bradley's or Fritz's woman. Easing himself back against the seat, Dove eyed the miles and miles of forest.

"Where are you?" he muttered.

If Tessa Bradley had a voice, Dove didn't know how to listen for it. He didn't wait long for her to answer. Instead, he twirled the wheel and rolled out of the turnout. He kept his eyes on the road and locked down all that inside misery again.

By the time Dove reached the outskirts of his jurisdiction, the *notice* was riding with him and he saw something out of place. On the side of the road was a big, fancy, black leather bag. You didn't see that everyday. Then again, in the last twenty-four hours nothing had been like every other day.

Curious, Dove pulled over and picked it up. It was heavy and padded. If this were a city, Dove would have called the bomb squad. Since this was his mountain, he opened it. Inside were cameras and lenses. One was digital, one was film. In the outside pockets there were filters, film, memory cards, money and a card identifying this as Peter Wolfson's property. Dove chuckled and looked around. If Wolfson could lose his camera then it was a sure bet he had lost himself in the woods, too.

"Wolfson!" Dove called. "Hey, Peter Wolfson!"

Dove walked a circle and got nothing back for his efforts except air.

Shouldering the bag, he went back to the car. The day was getting on and he had better things to do than chase down a man looking to make some money on the back of grief. Tossing the camera in the back, he drove off knowing Wolfson would come complaining the minute he found it missing. Ten minutes later he was home. Wolfson's bag was in the corner and the contents of Simon Hart's duffle bag were on the long table Dove used as a desk.

Three shirts, a pair of pants, a CD player as old as the clothes, four pairs of tighty whiteys, two undershirts, a pair of socks that had seen better days and those shoes. Dove considered his haul. The clothes were old but the shoes seemed nearly new. The clothes were thrift store and yet the shoes were stylish. Where had this duffle been when Dove looked in the closet? What shoes was Simon Hart wearing as he settled himself out on that bed to die?

Even the posture of death was a bothersome thing – spread eagle on the bed instead of curled into a ball or relaxed against a wall.

Dove sat forward and rested his elbows on his knees. He clasped his hands and looked some more. There was nothing personal in the bag: not a toothbrush or hairbrush or stick of deodorant. Fine. Hart wasn't into grooming. He was running. He wasn't thinking so he grabbed whatever was close. But then he took the time to shoot up? Heroin? He would have been out of it, unable to walk much less drive – even if Savick had released his car. Maybe Tessa Bradley was alive and well and had planned on picking Hart up and driving away. But that made no sense either. Hart would have turned her over to Dove just to get the sheriff off his back. Or she would have come forward to save her lover.

Dove twirled in his chair and looked out the window toward the forest. Wouldn't Hart put his stash in the bag? Drugs cost money. Paraphernalia cost. Savick did point out that Hart was an idiot. Still...

Dove twirled again and on a second pass he picked up the phone and dialed. Holding it to his shoulder, listening to the ring, he pulled on the tongue of one of the shoes. Mike McCall answered his phone on the third ring and Cherie walked into the room at the same time. Dove mouthed to Cherie to hold up a minute.

"Mike? Dove Connelly. I need you to do something for me. Yeah, I need you to go down to the morgue."

Dove Connelly's House
12:30 p.m.

"I don't know what to do with this, Dove. I mean, I didn't ask her about these letters because what if she doesn't know? I didn't want to be the one to tell her. What does it mean if Bernadette doesn't know?"

Cherie spread out the letters she had taken from Bernadette's house just as Dove had spread out Simon Hart's belongings and tried to figure out the mystery of it.

"She was so angry with me for even being in the house. I've never seen her like that. It was all I could do to pretend nothing was wrong."

"Bernadette's not herself," Dove said. "Even when Fritz was alive, she was private."

"This was more than just her being private, Dove. This was intense. It was like she didn't even know me; like I was an intruder. I should have showed her these letters but how could I?"

Cherie pointed to the last one then she picked it up and looked at it as if she still couldn't believe what it said.

"This says that Fritz and Bernadette haven't had insurance coverage for over a year. How have they been paying for all those doctors and the equipment and the medicine? Her medicine alone is hundreds of dollars a month, Dove."

Dove took the letter out of her hand and put it back on the pile.

"Maybe the state is picking up the bill. Didn't Bernadette tell you that some of the medicine is experimental? Maybe it's a trial? Maybe they pay her."

"Not for everything, Dove," Cherie fretted. "Not for over a year already. Fritz would have told you. He always told you hopeful news."

"Then I don't know. You should have asked Bernadette about it."

Dove gathered up the letters and folded them again. He handed them back to his wife. There were bigger things to attend to, more serious questions to consider.

"She wouldn't have told me the truth and I think I know why. Dove, we need to find out if Fritz had life insurance." Cherie fussed, the fingers of one hand picked at the other. She couldn't bring herself to look at her husband when she added: "If he did, I think maybe he killed himself so Bernadette could have the money for her medicine. And, Dove?" Cherie's voice caught. "I think Bernadette knew he was going to do it."

"No. Impossible. Would never happen." Dove dismissed the speculation but Cherie persisted.

"Dove, think about it. Think about the way Bernadette took the news of Fritz's death. She was so stoic, like it was no surprise."

Cherie hunkered down beside her husband's chair and put her hands on the arm. She insisted Dove pay attention to her but he pulled Simon Hart's duffle toward him again. Cherie blinked. He had never done this. Never ignored her; never put her aside. The baby yes, but not her. She stood up and put her hands on the bag. She wasn't going to let this go but she would give an inch.

"Okay. Okay. Maybe Fritz didn't kill himself, but there could be something else. Maybe Fritz was doing something illegal."

Dove pulled back on the duffle but Cherie persisted. He'd been looking away from the truth of what had happened to them all those months ago but she wasn't going to let him look away from the truth of Fritz.

"Dove, remember I told you that Bernadette was using store receipts for kindling? I thought they were old but maybe they weren't. Maybe she was trying to cover something up. Could it be that Fritz had been doing something illegal? Maybe Fritz had something he didn't want us to see and Bernadette was trying to get rid of it? Her hands were dirty, Dove. She'd been digging, or moving something. She was exhausted like she was working hard and…"

"Okay." Dove threw his hands up. He turned on her fast and set his feet hard on the ground. Cherie stood up. "I'm listening. You want to talk bad about Fritz, woman, then talk. What do you think he was doing? What do you think Bernadette was doing?"

Cherie threw up her hands, too, and wailed.

"I don't know. I don't even want to think about it. All I know is Bernadette was everything to Fritz. He never thought of himself. He would have given his life for her. He would have taken his own life for her."

"And Tessa Bradley?"

"I don't know that either," Cherie replied miserably.

"And all those footprints?" Dove demanded.

"I don't know."

"The three cars?" Dove went on.

"I don't know. I don't know!" Cherie wailed. "Maybe Fritz hired someone to do it to him. That could have happened."

"Where would Fritz have found someone like that?" Dove asked.

"This man, Hart? Maybe him? He'd been in the store. Maybe Mrs. Bradley was there and...and..." Cherie paced, near tears with frustration. "I don't know, Dove. I just know that this is scary because it's Bernadette and Fritz and all they would have had to do was come to us — to this community — and we would have found a way to help. Wouldn't we?"

Dove got to his feet and put his arms around his wife. He was sorry he was short with her and sorry for the situation that had brought them to this moment. This was as much about their personal nightmares as Fritz and Bernadette's but Dove couldn't bring himself to talk about that. Maybe Fritz had found someone to do the deed, but that wasn't for Cherie's ears.

"Everyone would have helped if we had known how bad things were."

Dove said, agreeing with her but also understanding the need to keep something shameful private. But kill himself? Dove refused to believe Fritz would do that. He kissed Cherie's head. She snuggled closer to him, taking what little comfort he had to offer. Her arms tightened around him and, just then, the phone rang. Reluctantly, Dove let his wife go and picked up the receiver.

"Sheriff Connelly."

Cherie put her hands to her face and spread her fingers. The color was coming into her cheeks and she was composed by the time Dove finished the call.

"That was the deputy over in Corallis. I asked him to find out what size shoe Simon Hart wore. It wasn't a size ten and a half and that's what these are."

Both of them looked at the shoes on the desk.

"That's weird," Cherie said.

"Almost as weird as the fact that K.C. told Mike that Hart didn't do drugs. He had a heart problem. Hard drugs would have killed him the first time he used any of them. She saw him turn them down."

"What does it mean?" Cherie breathed.

"It means that someone wanted us to think these are Hart's shoes and that he had been at the store when Fritz got shot. Someone wanted us to think Hart was running but he wasn't going anywhere." Dove picked up the shoes and put them back into the bag. "Somebody didn't want Simon Hart talking to me and that means I'm not the only one with a murder on my hands. Savick's got one, too."

"Lord, Dove, what's happening here?" Cherie asked softly.

"I don't know but I think McCall does. He's coming over when he can get free."

"What can I do to help?"

Dove smiled. Cherie was back. No fussing, just a clear eyed understanding that there were things to be done to solve the problem – all the problems. Dove reached to the floor and put Peter Wolfson's camera bag on the table.

"Why don't you to see what that photographer's been up to before he comes back for this."

"Okay." Cherie hitched the heavy bag. "I'll work in the other room so you can have some quiet while you look over Hart's things."

The phone rang again and this time it was Nathan calling. He needed Dove at the Mountain Store and he needed him there fast. Dove kissed Cherie quick.

"I've got to go." Dove grabbed his jacket. "Nathan's found something at the store."

"Let me get the baby dressed. Let us come with you," Cherie begged. "Wait just a minute."

"No, you stay here. Nathan needs me to come now," Dove reiterated.

"I need you now. There's a storm coming. I don't want to be here alone when it breaks."

Cherie moved close and touched his arm. She wasn't as calm as he had thought. Dove reassured her.

"I'll be back before then."

"I don't know, Dove. I've got the feel…"

Dove looked down at his wife's upturned face. He understood that because the *feel* was with him, too. He didn't have Cherie's foreboding, though. It was Tessa Bradley he sensed. She was like a fog rolling in off the high mountains. He could see it coming but it was far enough away that he couldn't feel the moisture and the chill. But the idea of her was filling him so full with hope that he had to keep moving forward. Her face was all he could see even though it was Cherie standing in front of him.

"Dove, please. Let me come with you," she begged.

"You stay put. That's how you can help me." Dove held her away. "This is what I want you to do. Call Mike McCall over in Corallis. Talk only to him. Tell him to meet me at the Mountain Store. Check what's on that camera. I'll be back before you finish all that. I'll be back before the storm comes. Just promise me you'll stay put."

"I promise. I'll wait for you, Dove."

He smiled and so did she. As he left the house, Cherie put her arms around herself as if she were cold. She knew it wasn't like her to be this skittish, she knew Dove didn't know what to do with this new part of her, but there it was. Her nerves were standing on end and she knew something big was coming.

Going to the window, Cherie saw Dove's car disappear down the road yet she kept looking still. The trees bent in the wind. The sky roiled with black clouds like the bottom side of hell. The beast was chained. He sat on the ground, his ears pricked, his face pointing toward the higher peaks as if he, too, was waiting for something. Cherie looked at the road a second longer. She didn't expect Dove to turn around and come back but she would have liked to see him once more, for just a minute.

Finally, turning from the window, Cherie wondered if Bernadette had felt this frightened when Fritz walked out the door the night he died.

Dove Connelly's House
2:00 p.m.

Cherie fed the baby carrots: homegrown, cooked and pureed. Now she was in her playpen, cooing at a purple teddy bear while her mother scrolled through the digital pictures she had downloaded from Peter Wolfson's camera. It wasn't difficult to track the photographer's day.

Cherie reached for her tea. It was hot and pungent and did nothing to warm her as she looked closely at a picture of Fritz's Mountain Store. Wolfson had used some kind of filter and a wide angled lens. The result was that the store looked like the last building standing in the whole of

California. There was a wisp of fog curling around the sign like a phantom, the grounds around seemed hard and dry. The surrounding forest was dark and ominous.

In the next picture Nathan was posed with his tongs and hairnet. He looked like an idiot as, she was sure, Wolfson intended. A hick kid aspiring to a crime fighting forensic technician. She was sure Wolfson didn't have to work hard to get Nathan to pose. Not because Nathan was flattered but because he was so sweet he would want to be accommodating. Cherie had the urge to delete it. The camera was not objective. It saw things not as they were but as the photographer wished them to be. Peter Wolfson wanted every New Yorker to cross themselves when they saw the place where Tessa Bradley ended up. He wanted them to be appalled at the people who held her fate in their hands.

Tapping the cursor, she pulled up the next picture, sat back and wrapped her hands around her cup of tea. Despite the thunder and the wind that shook the tree branches against the window, Cherie was beginning to relax. The baby was quiet, the phone hadn't rung with bad news from the store, the beast was now inside and sleeping and Cherie had a purpose.

The next picture was better. It was a beautiful photo of the woods. Sun streamed through the lacey bows of the evergreens. The ground was dappled with light. This was taken mid-morning, perhaps. A lovely time. There was no point of view, no real focal point, no...

Cherie sat up so fast the tea sloshed out of her cup. The baby, quiet in her little indoor seat, squealed. Cherie paid no attention to either as she positioned the cross hairs on the top right hand quadrant of the screen. She tapped enter. She tapped again and once more, too, until she had enlarged the portion of the photograph that had caught her eye.

Fingers shaking, she hit the print button and made a copy of the cropped photo. While the printer whirred, Cherie Connelly dressed her baby warm then put her in the playpen. When that was done, Cherie whipped the picture out of the printer and looked at it once more to make sure she was not mistaken.

She was not.

Wolfson had pointed his camera at the woods where Bernadette's cabin was nestled. Cherie doubted he was even aware of what he caught in his frame: the cabin, Bernadette at the door and three men ringing her. One man had long, dark hair. One was unidentifiable behind the collar of his jacket. But the third – the third – it made her sick to look at that man. He had a white gauze bandage where his eye should have been.

Cherie Connelly pocketed the picture, grabbed the baby and ran for her car.

I stand under the metal awning, out of the rain, feeding the little dogs while I wait on Marta. The clothes I came in are dry. Marta wanted me to wear the ones she gave me but I wanted to wear my own. Dirty and torn they will be a testament to what I have been through. I will never get rid of them. Sadly, they will be wet again soon enough. My feet are back in my boots and they are so tight I can't even feel my feet. When I get home, I will never put these on again. I will probably never put on a pair of high heels again. I will become a mountain woman and be happy in the beautiful home Jake built for me.

When Marta comes out, she hands me a little rain bonnet. It is pleated and opens up to a silly little thing but I am touched she thought of it.

"The ladies in the town where I grew up used to wear these."

"They're good for keeping your hair dry. A lady should keep her hair dry."

This is funny coming from Marta. Her hair is a mess, so are her clothes. Then I think about what she said. A lady should keep her hair dry. Maybe Marta is more than that. Maybe Marta considers herself a person. I am a person, too, so I pocket the little piece of plastic. As Marta goes, so go I.

She hands me a bag.

"I found it by the river."

Inside is my watch.

"Marta."

I have no words to thank her. She doesn't want to hear them anyway. She is already walking away. I put my watch on and catch up with her. We don't talk but I think she's sorry to see me go because she stops suddenly. She turns around. She reaches up to me and cups my face. She looks deeply into my eyes and, as I return the favor, I see something wonderful in hers.

In the depths of her pale blue eyes is peace. Nothing more or less. Achievable. The lesson is simple and has been in front of me my whole life I just didn't know how to read it. Live. Grow. Expect little. Give much. Appreciate what you have. Admit mistakes. Move on.

Marta doesn't have to tell me all these things because I see the lesson in her eyes, I feel it in her touch and in the generosity of spirit that pulled me back from the brink of death. I promise to come back and see her. I will bring her things I think she needs. She says she doesn't want things. She says it in a way that thanks me for thinking of her. I think I could be happy if I stayed with Marta but she doesn't want me. She says this isn't where I should be. She says I won't be back.

We walk on through the silent woods, Marta leading. I glimpse the river now and again. At the road, Marta offers to wait with me but I can tell she wants to get back to where she belongs. She is the same as me. I do want to get back to where I belong. I tell her to go. She tells me it's Tuesday and there will be trucks headed across the pass. There will be cars. There will be an airplane that will stop for me. There will be fairies and there will be frogs.

I laugh. She is a funny old woman.

I ask how far I am from home.

Marta is sure it isn't far.

I believe her.

Fritz's Mountain Store
2:10 p.m.

"I want you to stand just inside here, Dove."

Nathan arranged Dove just so then he back-stepped across the concrete floor. Dove watched him but couldn't help noticing other things. Like how different the store looked. The blood stains had dried brown. Fritz's body was gone. Powder dusted every surface where Nathan had lifted prints. The store also looked the same. Paperwork that Fritz would never tend to was still on the desk. The little toys Fritz loved still sat waiting for him to wind them up or squeeze them or click a switch. There was the cow, his favorite toy. It started to walk as soon as you lifted its tail. There was a hammer and a screwdriver.

Dove felt nothing when he looked at all this. Fritz was a concept now, the crime a puzzle and the picture taking shape was starting to look ugly.

"Okay, Dove." Nathan called to him, wanting his attention. The young man crossed his arms high and tight over his skinny chest. "I can tell you now for sure that Fritz didn't commit suicide. I mapped all the blood spatter. See all those little strings? They show the trajectory of the shot. Fritz was kneeling. Someone shot him from above. He blew backward and out flat because the shot was so close to him, but someone else definitely pulled the trigger. It was an execution, Dove."

"Okay, Nathan," Dove said evenly, grateful to know.

Nathan dropped his hands and marched in place a few times. He was nervous. There was more and Dove waited for it.

"Okay. So I did that and then I was going to measure the stains to see if I could approximate how much blood had been lost. I figured this would tell us if he bled out. If Tim found out Fritz didn't die right away from the gunshot – you know, like the shot didn't sever any major arteries right away or take Fritz's brain out – then we might have to prove he bled to death."

Nathan sniffed and pushed his hair out of his eyes.

"So, I wanted to see where the blood went and I started moving things. This big stain here?" He pointed to the ground. "You can see the floor isn't level so it flowed right under all these boxes."

Nathan followed along his own narration. Moving with mincing steps, pointing and posturing.

"Since I needed to see how far the stain went, I moved those boxes. I took the top two off and then went for this one. When I moved it the bottom fell out 'cause the blood had softened it. Well, Dove, this is what I found."

Nathan lifted the box slightly. Dove walked into the room and bent down to see better. Nathan got down on one knee and shook his head. This was a sad treasure, indeed.

"Fritz had about three hundred of these back here. Inhalers, Dove. There might be more somewhere else. Then there's the other kind, the pills. He's got just about everything you'd need here. I guess it's pretty clear what Fritz was doing here Dove. Dove?"

Nathan looked up just in time to see the screen door slamming behind Dove Connelly as he went to find somewhere he could breathe.

The Road to Dove's Mountain
<u>2:30 p.m.</u>

Mike McCall was fairly proud of himself. He had looked Ginger in the eye and told her he was going to check on a problem at the old bridge just south of town. It looked like there was a crack in one of the pilings. Not many people used that bridge but those people on the other side of Peyton Gulley would need it if the spring runoff took out the main road again.

Ginger said *'that's good of you to check on that'* but didn't even give him a suspicious look. When that worked, Mike went straight to Sheriff Savick's office, knocked softly, listened for the bark and opened the door. Savick was on the phone, still pissed about Dove Connelly and not too happy that Mike was bothering him. Mike started in with same spiel and received a *'get the hell out of here'* for his efforts.

Mike walked out of the office, cool as a cucumber, got into his car and drove north, away from Peyton Gulley. A mile out of town, Mike McCall's heart started to pound something awful. Never in his wildest imagination did he think he'd be involved in something like this. Now that he was, he couldn't believe he was putting himself in the thick of it — by choice, no less. Maybe he was a lawman after all.

He passed a truck loaded with big logs. He passed a car going way too fast but he let it go. He didn't want to slow himself down. He needed to get to Sheriff Connelly as soon as possible. Then Mike didn't have a choice. There was a problem he couldn't ignore. Up ahead, waving his arms, was a man in a bright green jacket, his RV pulled half off the road.

"Damn." Mike cut across the dividing line and rolled to a stop behind the RV. The waving man pounded on the patrol car window before Mike had even turned off the engine.

"My wife! She's not breathing. You've got to help us."

The Road to Dove's Mountain
<u>2:42 p.m.</u>

Will Savick barely glanced at the ambulance on the side of the road. He didn't look in his rear view mirror out of curiosity and, therefore, he didn't see Mike McCall's patrol car behind the RV. Mike McCall didn't see Will Savick drive by because he was in the back of the ambulance taking a report from Mr. Greg Jones regarding the time and duration of his wife's attack of – whatever made his wife sick. After talking to Mr. Greg Jones, Mike had the feeling the man himself might be part of the problem. He wasn't exactly the most selfless husband. As his wife was being tended to, Mr. Jones lamented how she was putting them behind schedule.

So it was ships passing in the night, a case of poor timing, a little bit of fate that made Mike McCall and Will Savick believe that they were going to be able to take care of their business and get back to the office before anyone questioned their absence.

Mike sent the ambulance on its way with Mr. and Mrs. Jones inside They would have a grueling fifteen-mile winding ride to the nearest hospital. He called for a tow for the RV because it couldn't stay there half on and half off the road. That truck would be coming from half as far as the hospital. Mike settled in, watched the sky and hoped it arrived before everything opened up.

Will Savick had only one stop to make and he had no reason to think his business wouldn't be wrapped up before the rain came, too.

Fritz's Mountain Store
2:45 p.m.

Lightning crackled in the distance. Thunder seemed to roll up from under the ground. The wind whipped around like a caged animal sensing all was not right with the world. Nathan stood behind the screen door and Dove paced in front of it. What Nathan found put Dove and Fritz on the opposites sides of the law. It changed their friendship. It muddied the waters. What Nathan found made everything black and white, good and bad. It made Dove sick but he still had a job to do. Finally, he stopped.

"Nathan?" Dove called. The screen door creaked and slammed as Nathan bolted out of the store. "Go back up the mountain to where you found that eye."

Dove hated talking about it. The sightless eye had come to symbolize so much. The *feel* hadn't left Dove; he had buried it, made himself blind to the evil things happening around him. Dove hadn't wanted to see who Fritz really was. He was having a hard time now acknowledging that his friend got the death he deserved. He hadn't looked at Cherie and admitted she was in pain. He hadn't taken a long hard look at himself and acknowledged that he was at fault for so many things.

One thing, though, was clear now. Tessa Bradley, an outsider, was paying the price for Fritz's sins and Dove's own cowardice. That was going to change.

"But I should be looking inside..." Nathan began.

"I'll do it. I should do it. You do what I tell you." Dove strode back to the store, pausing momentarily to finish his orders. "I need you to just tell me how many people you think were up there, Nathan. Can you do that? I need to know if you can find anything that will tell us which way Tessa Bradley went after that fight. This storm will ruin anything left up there. Go on. All I want is to find that woman before the weather comes in. We've got to salvage something and she's the one who deserves it."

The first raindrops began to fall. Dove looked up then turned his back on Nathan. Determined to keep his eyes open to the truth of Fritz he hurried on to the store. Nathan called after him.

"Do you want me to send one of the Braimen brothers to help you?"

"I don't need any help. I know what I'm looking at now."

Fritz's Mountain Store
<u>2:59 p.m.</u>

Dove took off his gloves and began searching for a pen and paper at the counter in front of the store. He found the paper under the counter. The pen near the register was attached to a string so no one would take it. Fritz always pointed out that 'pens cost money'.

Money.

Right.

Seemed as if Fritz probably had plenty of it squirreled away somewhere. He would have to tell Cherie about this. She'd have to know how Fritz was paying for Bernadette's fancy medicines. He didn't relish telling her any more than he liked the idea of telling Bernadette but it would have to be done.

Dove yanked on the pen. The string broke.

He took a deep breath and did a cursory search of the counter area looking for receipts, ledger books, anything that would fill in the blanks on the drug trade Fritz appeared to have been involved with.

All Dove saw was the same old stuff. The picture of Bernadette on the counter top, a little yellow happy face pasted on the cash register, the first dollar the store had made was tacked to the wall. Dove gave slight note to the winning lottery tickets strung up, the remembrances of the Fourth of July celebrations and thank yous for sponsoring the little league. There was one picture he couldn't ignore. It was taken the day Dove was sworn to office. Fritz had pinned on his star. Cherie was three years away.

Dove looked at that picture: Fritz's gentle smile, his big soft body stuffed into his one good jacket and Dove standing so proudly in front of his friend. It was one of the few pictures of Dove with a full-fledged smile on his face. The only other one had been taken on his wedding day. Dove peeled this picture off the counter top, tore it into pieces and dropped it on the floor.

Pen and paper in hand, Dove went to the back room and pulled one of the boxes toward him. He ripped it open. Inside, he counted a hundred inhalers. In the next there were twenty-four medium size boxes and in each of those there were twelve smaller boxes. Inside the smaller boxes were twelve bubble packs of twenty-four Sudafed tablets. Meth kitchens would cook up the stuff in cabins tucked into these mountains and half the Pacific Northwest addicts would be supplied. God knew how many more operations there were like this, how many other small businesses were used to legitimately order the supplies.

Dove grunted and tugged on another box. It came down hard on him, pinching the pad of his hand against Fritz's desk. It was just the thing to push him over the edge. Grabbing hold of the box, Dove hoisted it above his head and threw it against the wall. It broke open scattering the contents all over the floor. For a few minutes Dove stood there wondering how he was going to tell Cherie about this. What was he going to tell Bernadette? He was a man of few words so where would he find the right ones to talk about this?

Collapsing onto Fritz's old chair, Dove swiveled to the crate and plywood desk Fritz had made for himself. He propped his elbows up and buried his face in his hands. He needed to think.

Think.

Nothing was coming. Not a thought. Not a plan. There was no *feel*. There was only an overwhelming sense of failure.

Think.

Suddenly, Dove knew what he needed. It was simple. It was easy. He sat up and picked up the phone. When Tim answered, Dove asked:

"I need the phone number you found on Fritz when you autopsied him."

Dove picked up the pen and pulled the pad of paper toward him. He was dialing before Tim even knew Dove had hung up. Five times he dialed the number with the Portland area code unaware that Cherie was desperately trying to get him on the phone. Four times the line was busy. On the fifth try a man answered.

"Who am I talking to?" Dove demanded. When there was only silence, Dove gripped the phone tighter and stood up slowly. "This is Sheriff Connelly. I am investigating a murder in my jurisdiction. Who am I talking to, damn it. Answer me. Who am I talking to?"

"You're wasting your time. He doesn't speak English."

Bernadette's Cabin
3:10 p.m.

Cherie left the baby in the car. It was a calculated risk but one she had to take. The baby would slow her down, possibly alert people in the house to her presence if she cried but neither Dove nor Jessica could be reached and Cherie knew she didn't dare call Bernadette. Cherie was on her own and all she needed to do was get Bernadette to safety. If Bernadette was even in there. If she had not been hurt already. Cherie had no idea what she was walking into but there was no choice.

Checking the baby once more, seeing the short ride had sent her off to sleep, Cherie closed the car door quietly. Taking a deep breath, she used the trees for cover as she made her way toward the sick woman's house. She wished she had the presence of mind to grab the cross bow, but she had run out too fast. The only thing Cherie had to help her was her wits and she was determined to keep them about her.

Above her the clouds darkened. A drop of water fell on her forehead. She wiped it away and crouched low, moving forward until she was on the perimeter of the clearing. Hands on the trunk of a tree, she peered around it. The view was good. There was no car in evidence but that didn't mean someone hadn't been left there to guard Bernadette. Whatever Fritz was into it was bad. If the picture in Cherie's pocket was any indication, there were a lot of people interested in Fritz's business including a man without an eye.

Cherie started forward intending to look through the bedroom window but she changed her mind when she saw the shed. The door had blown open, the padlock was hanging loose. Sprinting toward it, thanking the lord for small favors she dashed inside and lay back against he wood slat wall. Her eyes adjusted to the gloom. Inside boxes were piled on boxes. Another time, she would wonder about all this stuff but now all she wanted was a weapon -an ax, a hammer. Frantically, she pushed the boxes aside, praying the noise she was making would be swallowed up by the sounds of the coming storm.

She found nothing. Nothing.

Cherie kicked at another pile of boxes. They were light and tumbled easily into a pile of cardboard and that's when Cherie saw it.

"Oh, God. Oh, God."

Both hands went to her mouth as Cherie backed off, stumbling and falling to the ground. She turned her head away and closed her eyes. When she opened them again, she looked back to make sure she had not been mistaken. There was the body of Peter Wolfson. His eyes were open; his head was smashed in. Peter Wolfson, photographer of the most beautiful woman in the world, had been dumped like garbage in a shed in the woods.

Shaking, Cherie backed out of the small building into the howling wind. The baby was alone, Bernadette needed help and Cherie Connelly was scared to death. Turning her back to the icy rain that had just begun to fall, Cherie fell on all fours. She dry heaved then took three deep, deep breaths. Steady again, she got to her feet, sneaked up to the back window and looked into Bernadette's bedroom.

The room was empty.

She checked through the kitchen window. She stared into the living room, scanning the dark corners.

Nothing.

No one.

Keeping low just in case, Cherie scurried to the porch, lifted the frog statue and took the key to Bernadette's house. She almost had it in the lock when she heard a cry.

It came from her car.

Fritz's Mountain Store
3:24 p.m.

"Who was I talking to?" Dove demanded.

"It doesn't matter, really." Bernadette lolled in the doorway, pale and weak. Dove hadn't heard her come in and, strangely, he wasn't surprised to see her.

"Did you know what Fritz was doing? Did you, Bernadette?"

She lifted her eyes only to have her body crumble. Dove caught her before she fell. She was light as a feather, hollow-boned and small. Her disease was eating her from the inside out. He eased her into the chair. Like a rag doll she sat with her arms out, her knees cocked inward and her feet out. Her head seemed too heavy to hold up so she talked to Dove with her chin on her chest.

"Damn, it's hard to do the simplest thing anymore, Dove. I thought I was going to die coming over here. I hate it. I hate all of this."

Bernadette didn't breathe anymore, she gasped. Dove knelt on one knee in front of her.

"Did you know, Bernadette?" Dove asked again and Bernadette put her hand on his jaw, petting him as if he were a simple sort.

"I knew Fritz was going to do something stupid. That's what I knew. I sure hated him for it, dumb bastard." Bernadette stopped stroking.

"He did it because he loved you." Dove made excuses even though defending Fritz made him sick. "Maybe Fritz thought this was the only way to get the money you needed. It doesn't matter anymore. Tell me what you know and I swear I'll get the people who killed him."

Dove waited, praying that Bernadette still had enough will to help him. Outside the storm was gaining strength; inside, the silence was deafening. Dove could not push her, he understood that, but time was critical. If he could find the person who killed Fritz he could find Tessa Bradley.

Just before he was about to push Bernadette, she lifted her head slowly. Her eyes were bare of lashes but lush with pain and disgust. The pain was her own; the disgust was for Dove.

"God, Dove, you are as stupid as Fritz was if you think you can do anything to these people. You don't even understand what's going on here. This was my doing. This is my stash. My business. Fritz came here trying to put a stop to it. That's why he's dead."

Bernadette's confession hissed out of her like a slow leak as she pushed Dove's hands away.

"What?" Dove sat back on his heels. "Why?"

"Because Fritz made shit in this store, Dove. Because the insurance company cut us off. Because I was dying and I didn't want to die. I wanted him to save me and he wasn't doing anything. Every day, right in front of my eyes, my life was slipping away and he acted like a third grader trying to figure out how to solve a math problem. The equation was simple. Need plus Money. We needed money so I could live."

"Fritz tried, Bernadette. He loved you and he tried hard," Dove insisted.

"He would have loved me right into a grave."

The rain was coming hard now, hitting the glass like bullets. Bernadette looked at Dove with those half-dead eyes of hers.

"Cancer hurts like hell and the doctors won't give you anything to really help, so I found stuff on my own. Meth was cheap and it made me feel strong. Then one day this man tells me that I could have all the stuff I want and make a hell of a lot of money to boot. I could buy myself some time. Maybe I could even buy a miracle. Fritz never even asked where all that stuff in the house came from."

Bernadette's milky eyes weren't seeing much anymore. Dove doubted she even saw that miracle on the horizon anymore.

"I did the ordering for the store, you know. I kept the books. It was so easy. I just ordered all this crap and had it sent to the house. I kept it in that locked shed in the back."

She pushed at the floor so that the chair swiveled toward the window. It was as if she wanted some of the storm's energy. Perhaps, she just didn't want to look into Dove's eyes as she told her story.

247

"My contacts came on delivery days and took it all away. Fritz was never the wiser. Nope, never the wiser." Bernadette's voice tapered off. She took a breath. She coughed. She sighed and kept going. "I must have been tired, Dove. I made a mistake. I put the store's address on an order. When it came here Fritz called the manufacturer to return it. They told him the order matched what was delivered. There was no mistake and no return. They gave him my name. They asked if we had moved since the address was new."

"And he figured it out," Dove interjected.

"Yep. He did. And he said it was wrong. I told him nobody had to know."

Bernadette faced him again. Her eyes were filling. At last, a tear. Dove wondered if it was for her husband, herself or the money.

"The new meds were working, Dove. If I didn't have that money, I wouldn't have the medicine. You think that would have made Fritz happy. Instead he called my people to meet him for a showdown." Bernadette hung her head and chuckled. "Poor, sweet dumb ass. I tried to stop him. Really, I did."

"I could have stopped it. Fritz would be alive if you'd told me," Dove insisted.

"Give me a break. You couldn't stop what happened in your own house, Dove. Do you think I'd trust you with my life?" Bernadette's expression twisted into one of utter revulsion. All those tears were gone now. "Fritz told me why you have that dog. I know why you don't touch that baby. It's because you don't know if that baby is yours. That baby could belong to…"

"That's enough..." Dove snapped but Bernadette rallied.

"It's not enough, Dove. You think you're something special with all that crap about the *feel*. People talk about it like it was real, but you didn't even have a twitch when that man walked into your house and raped your wife.

Bernadette had put the knife in and now she turned it. She wanted Dove to feel the pain she felt. Not the physical pain but the horror knowing that she had caused her husband's death and he had caused much worse. Cherie had to live with the injury he inflicted on her everyday, every time he didn't look at the baby.

"Cherie probably screamed for you when that man was beating her and ripping off her clothes. And where were you? You were here shooting the breeze with Fritz."

Bernadette's head fell suddenly. She nodded and started to slur her words. Her indignation had used up her energy. Now she spoke in that detached way dying people do, like she was already gone and all Dove was hearing was her echo.

"Fritz was killed and you didn't have a clue. I was running drugs for almost a year. A stranger raped your wife and got her pregnant. You haven't got the *feel*, Dove. You couldn't have stopped this anymore than you could have stopped what happened to Cherie and you know it.

"You're dead as a doornail, Dove Connelly. You killed your own self just like Fritz did. He could have looked away. Instead, he walked into this place and threw out his arms and just begged them to kill him. It wasn't my fault he died, same way it wasn't Cherie's that you checked out. Neither of us asked for what we got, but we're strong enough to deal with it because we want to live. That's all we want to do. We want to live."

Bernadette raised her eyes. Dove held her gaze. If she meant to shame him, she failed. Instead Bernadette fired him up. The box he had locked himself into was suddenly opened. He may not have the *feel* but he had the *notice*. He saw clearly what was in front of him and it was ugly and vile and Fritz had deserved better.

"You bitch," Dove said.

"I suppose," she answered.

"Tell me who shot Fritz. Tell me why they took the woman."

"The woman was their business. All I know for sure is that it was the foreign boys who shot Fritz. I don't know where they are. I don't even know their names. One of them speaks a little English, the other is hurt bad but he's still standing."

"His eye?" Dove asked.

"Yeah."

"Did Fritz take that eye out?" Dove asked.

Bernadette shook her head. "The woman did."

Dove stood. He picked up the old fashioned telephone and slammed it down in front of her.

"Call them, Bernadette," Dove ordered. "You tell them to get down here."

"I just don't think that will be necessary, Dove," she sighed.

Bernadette raised a skeletal hand. Dove twirled around, his hand going to his gun as he saw the smiling man lounging in the doorway.

Fritz's Mountain Store
3:40 p.m.

"You are one troublemaker, Sheriff Connelly." Will Savick shook his finger at Dove. The man looked mighty pleased with himself.

"Is Mike in on this? The girl?" Dove asked.

"Hell, no," Savick laughed. "It took me too long to set this operation up. You think I'd take a chance on ruining it by letting the likes of those two in?"

"You're still with Hell's Guardians, aren't you?" Dove raised his chin to indicate the tattoo on Savick's arm.

"Always will be," Savick answered. "We thought we could get down here and clean the place out the other night before anyone knew what was going down."

"Are you running this operation or are you just a flunky?"

"My idea the whole way. Just taking back what belonged to us in the first place," Savick answered proudly. "We had a lock on the trade for years, but then the Mexicans wanted in and the Russians. I found a way to get cooperation from the Russians. Once that happened, the Mexicans bowed out fast. Now that I'm the law, everything runs like clockwork."

"It's smart, I'll give you that." Dove admitted.

"You don't know how smart." Savick took a step inside the storage room. One foot came down straight, the other hit hard because his right leg was an inch shorter. Savick took note of Dove's interest. "Don't bother with any sympathy, Connelly. I wrecked that leg a long time ago, and it don't make no difference for the work I do now."

"You watched that night. You're the man with the limp," Dove said.

"I give you credit for figuring that out." Savick was impressed. He looked at Bernadette. Dove thought Savick's expression softened. If it had, though, it didn't last. Bernadette was of no use to him any longer.

"But you didn't have enough guts to do the dirty work. You just stood back. No blood on your hands," Dove pressed him.

"That's what the boss does," Savick said proudly. "Now, I know this is probably a waste of breath, but I'd be happy to have you join us. Another badge on our side would be a fine thing. Bernadette could deed over the store to your wife, show her how things are done. A little extra pocket money isn't bad considering what a public servant makes. You being a family man and all."

"We're pretty happy with the way things are," Dove answered, sizing the situation up as best he could. Savick was too casual and that made Dove nervous.

"Figured that would be the case," Savick said just before he warned Dove away from his gun. "Don't try it."

"I think I could draw down before you could take a swing. You're not armed," Dove pointed out.

"That's a matter of opinion."

Savick crooked his finger at Dove then pointed behind him. The big man hesitated then decided to take a look at what Savick wanted him to see.

Keeping close to the wall, Dove inched far enough to see into the main store. Waiting on Savick were two men. One was slight with long dark hair; the other was built like a fireplug. That one's head was shaved and the lower part of his face was covered by a blue knit scarf. The left side of his face where his eye should be was covered by a thick pad of white gauze. Dove looked back at Savick. The man smiled.

"I didn't want to take a chance that I might have the urge to use my own weapon on you. Too easy to trace," he explained.

Dove knew he was dead but that didn't matter. The man with one eye was right in front of him. He had put his hands on Tessa Bradley; he had probably killed Fritz. A man just like him had forced his way into Dove's house and hurt the woman Dove loved. Dove wasn't going to die without doing something about all of that and it was time to do it.

He lunged but Savick was too close. One punch sent Dove reeling backwards. He hit Bernadette's chair and twirled into her, falling to his knees. His face was inches from hers and the eyes he looked into were vacant. Dove was on his own.

"Don't do that again," Savick warned as Dove stood up slowly and turned to face him. "These may be hired hands but they are tough sons of bitches. That one — Ante's his name—" Savick gave a nod to the one with the eye patch. "He chased that woman half into the forest with all that blood coming out of his face. Lost his eye and he still went after her. You gotta admire that kind of tenacity. Vilam over there, he saw her get shot and fall over a ledge. They said she was really something. Beautiful and tough. I give her credit for trying but she's probably dead now."

"Why would they do that? Why would they want to kill her?" Dove asked. "What's her connection to all this?"

"Connection?" Savick snickered and a grin spread across his face. "There's no connection. She walked in on our business. My two friends here didn't know what she saw so Ante grabbed her. Pure reflex. I was already gone or I would have steered her clear while they went out the back. Bad timing for that woman. End of story."

Savick took a deep breath. It seemed he almost regretted that things were wrapping up.

"If they let her be, you would have figured this for a simple robbery, the inventory would have been cleared out and this whole thing would have blown over. But you — you were a lot of misery, Connelly. You just never should have come looking for Hart."

"What about Hart?"

"What about him." Savick raised his brow.

"Where did he come in?"

"He wasn't on my payroll. I think it was just like he said. He knew the woman, they saw each other but he was just caught up the same way she was. Wasn't much of a loss when he died. Don't worry about him."

Savick held out his hand. He wiggled his fingers.

"I'll take your weapon. Come on."

Dove understood it all, now. Because Bernadette would do anything to stay alive Fritz was dead, Simon Hart was dead and Tessa Bradley was probably dead, too. Dove would be next and, yet, he wasn't afraid. The *feel* was back. He felt Cherie's love, the baby's innocence and Bernadette's despair. He felt Tessa Bradley was close and that she wanted to live, too. The *feel* was strong one moment, fading away the next. The sense of Tessa Bradley disappeared completely when Savick tired of waiting and took Dove's gun. Dove reengaged. There was still a chance he would get out of this alive.

"My people aren't going to believe I killed myself and Bernadette. They won't give up until they find out who's responsible," Dove warned. "They have prints; they have fibers from your boys there."

"Don't worry. Everyone will be satisfied when this is over."

Suddenly, Will Savick's arm swung the hand holding firm on Dove's weapon. He pumped the trigger twice. The roar inside the store was deafening, drowning out even the sounds of the storm outside.

Dove fell back, calling out as the man with one eye fell first. He barked again in surprise as the long-haired one went down next. His ears were still ringing with the sound of the shots and he had to assume that Savick's were, too because he didn't notice Cherie's car pulling up outside. But Dove did.

Wasting no time, taking advantage of Savick's inattention, Dove threw himself through the screen door and ran.

Fritz's Mountain Store
4:13 p.m.

Cherie was out of the car, ignoring the driving rain as she ran for her husband. Dove saw her screaming. She was trying to tell him something but her voice didn't carry. He hoped his did.

"Back! Get back inside! Go away!"

Slipping in the mud, Dove fell hard on his hands. The rocks cut into his palms, the mud sucked at him. All he could see was Cherie, the stunned look on her face, her indecision. He pushed up into a sprinter's stance thinking of nothing but getting to her. Then Dove Connelly heard the door of the Mountain Store slam open behind him and Savick fire a warning shot.

"I'll shoot! I'll shoot your woman!" Savick roared and pumped off another round. It nicked off the ground near Dove.

Cherie was close enough now that Dove heard her scream. She froze in her tracks. The storm quieted for a minute. The rain fell but the thunder abated and the wind sounded almost comforting as it whipped through the trees.

Slowly Dove got to his feet. His hands were out, palms forward giving Savick no reason to make good on his threat. The rain washed the mud off his hands and ran down his face like tears. His back was to Savick so he kept his eyes on Cherie because hers were tracking Savick. Watching her, Dove could see the other man was circling wide and moving cautiously.

Suddenly from the heavens came a slash of lightning followed by a roll of thunder so loud it shook Dove to the core. The lightning came again and again, all in the same place: the north. It hovered then stabbed down as if it would break the mountain in two. It lit up the sky like the Christmas star on speed. And that's when Dove felt Tessa Bradley.

Look! I'm here!

"Dove! Watch out!" Cherie's scream broke through the *feel*. Savick had come between them.

"You don't need to do this," Dove hollered knowing all he had left was talk. *"We can call it a draw. Those two in there; they were the ones I wanted."*

Savick laughed. He spit. Cherie looked at it. The man chewed tobacco. Now she knew who had been in Bernadette's house.

"You killed Wolfson." Her eyes blazed with hatred. She wiped at the rain in her eyes. Savick flipped the gun barrel her way.

"Both of you get inside. Now."

Dove hesitated. He looked at Cherie. Something passed between them, something only they understood.

"I'm afraid," Cherie called. She held out her hand. Her eyes were steady when she locked on Dove but that hand was shaking. Dove smiled. Good woman. "Dove? Help. I can't move. I'm afraid."

"Get her," Savick ordered. The barrel twitched again.

Dove stepped forward. He took his wife's hand and the minute he did the shaking stopped. They stood in the rain, looking into one another's eyes. They knew exactly what had to happen.

"Come on. Come on," Savick ordered.

Dove saw that Savick was getting nervous now. He and Cherie had to die in the store and they couldn't be shot with Dove's own gun. Knowing that made the next step evident. With one more knowing look at his wife, Dove turned toward the store. Cherie's hand was tight in his. They took three steps. Savick took one to the side to let them pass.

"Hurry up. Hurry up," Savick called.

"My people will know this is wrong." They were almost parallel now and the rain was slanting into Savick's face.

"You give your people too much credit..."

Cherie's hand tightened on Dove's as Savick ranted. With one last, understanding look at his wife Dove swung Cherie hard, whipping her low to the ground. She rolled toward the truck. Dove crouched, grabbed the knife that still rested in the sheath at his ankle and went after Savick.

The first slash hit Savick's leg. The man let out a howl and tumbled back. His bad leg and the rain made it almost impossible to keep his balance but he was a tough son of a bitch. The gun swung as he tried to get a bead on Dove again. Dove lunged once more, slicing and cutting, catching Savick in the hip.

Savick swore and lashed out with his foot. His boot clipped Dove and sent him rolling in the mud. Dove managed to get to his knee just as a bolt of lightning cracked close overhead. In the second of silence between the lightning and the thunder something awful happened that stopped both men in their tracks.

A baby's cry pierced the air. Savick's head whipped toward Cherie's car, a grin of delight spread across his face. Dove looked, too. There was something new in the game. Savick wasted no time. He forgot Dove and went after a bigger prize. He half ran to the car, his bad leg slowing him a little. Faster than Savick, Cherie rushed ahead and threw herself into the back seat, covering the baby with her body.

"Help us, Dove!"

With a roar, Dove went at Savick but the man saw him coming. This time the kick went to Dove's gut and the big man crumpled to the ground. Satisfied Connelly was down, Savick went about his business. He closed on the truck like a jackal, drawing a bead on Cherie as she struggled with the straps that held her child tight. He wanted blood and he was beyond caring where he got it. He wanted blood and he wanted it from the entire Connelly family. Gleefully, he called out.

"She's dead, Connelly. Your kid's dead. Your wife's dead and so are you!"

Cherie shrieked. Dove's cry was louder than thunder. The knife was full out in front of him, pointed straight at Savick's back. Savick turned around. He had the gun pointed between Dove's eyes but Dove didn't care. He would save his woman and his baby.

His baby…

Dove's feet left the ground. Savick's finger tightened on the trigger. He smiled just as a shot rang out.

Marta has gone home, back to her trailer and her little dogs and her cat. I miss her but I don't long for her company. I simply think I was lucky to have met her.

She did not cross the road with me when we came upon it. Instead, she stood on her side and I on mine. I smiled at her and she raised a hand to me. She said goodbye. I said the same.

Now I wait patiently, at peace, curious about what will come next but not anxious about. I am only eager to see what the next moments will bring. The sun has come out and I am bathed in its light. My hands are empty. No rucksack, no stick to hold me up, no lantern. I don't remember when the rain stopped but it's fitting that it has.

I have the car key in my hand. I don't remember putting it in a pocket or laying it aside. I don't remember where it has been but I am glad it is back with me now. I don't think I will need protection anymore but it's nice to know I can fend for myself if necessary.

My watch has ticked off another two minutes. It is now two forty-three. I know this means nothing. My watch is broken and the time cannot be right. I do like that it hasn't given up the ghost. Just like me. I never gave up. Jake will be so proud. I hope Charlotte will be, too.

I hear a noise. It is far away .I walk out into the middle of the road to look. The late afternoon sun is brighter still. It isn't warm but that's alright. It's wonderful just to stand in the illumination. The storm is over so what I hear can't be thunder. It must be a truck I hear coming. Or a car. Whatever is coming, I know it will help me get to where I belong.

Home.

I can't help but smile.

Dove's Mountain
4:53 p.m.

"Sheriff Connelly? You okay? Everybody okay?"

Mike McCall asked as he sidestepped around Will Savick's body, not daring to take his eyes off it for fear the man would rise up again. The deputy's arms were rigid and his gun still pointed at the man in the mud even though there was no sign of life.

"Okay! Okay!" Dove hollered back as he sprinted for Cherie and the baby. From the corner of his eye he saw Mike approach Savick's body and disarm it. Mike stepped back quickly. The gun in the younger man's hand started to lower. Dove would deal with Mike later. It was hard to kill a man; harder though to see someone you love be killed. Dove took care of family first.

"Cherie? Are you hurt? Either of you hurt?"

Clawing manically at the baby's car seat, Cherie's head shook and shook. Over and over again she shook it, her wet braid slapping across her shoulders as the baby wailed. Dove grabbed her and pulled hard.

"Stop it! Stop it! Cherie, stop it."

Dove clasped his arms around her and pulled harder still. She was no match for his strength. Inching his way backward, Dove managed to get her out of the car and into the rain. He turned her, grappled with her and finally held her tight against him.

"Let me go! Let me go!" She screamed.

"Stop it. Enough. Enough. Quiet. Cherie, quiet."

"My baby!" she cried

"I'll get her. I'll get her. Mike!" Dove passed her to the deputy. "Take her inside. In the storeroom only. The woman inside is Bernadette. She's a suspect. Don't let her leave."

"No," Cherie moaned, her knees giving way. "My baby."

"Take her," Dove ordered.

Mike half carried Cherie through the drizzle as Dove went back to the car. With a steady hand he released the restraints and gathered the child to him. Holding her as if he had been doing it since she was born, Dove pulled the blanket from her car seat and put it over her head. He breathed in her scent. Mingled with it was Cherie's scent and his own. They had lived in the same house and they were family. Dove understood that now.

"We're okay. We're okay now. All of us are okay."

He wrapped his jacket around her for good measure. She quieted as he held her close and Dove's heart drained of the regret and anger he had carried for so long. There would be other things to fill it up now. Ducking out of the car, he dashed for the store.

"Oh, God, Dove. Is she all right?" Cherie grappled with his jacket.

"Fine," Dove said. "Our daughter is fine."

Cherie looked into her husband's face, hardly believing what she was hearing. Exhausted, done in by her relief, she fell forward, embracing him and the baby he had sheltered from the rain.

"Thank you," she whispered as he put the child into her arms.

"I have to go," he said. "I feel her, Cherie. I have to try and find Mrs. Bradley."

"Yes. Yes. Go."

Cherie nodded hard, not wanting him to leave but knowing it was something he had to do. Then Bernadette moaned. Dove could hardly look at her but when Cherie took a step toward the other woman, Dove put out a hand to stop her.

"She's responsible, Cherie. She helped kill Fritz."

"It was meant to be. Nothing can be done now." She tightened her hold on the baby and whispered to Dove. "It's alright, Dove. A small kindness."

Dove let her go. Carefully, she held the baby's head and put her on Bernadette's lap. Dove was forgotten. They each had something important to do.

"Can you help me, Bernadette? She needs to be warm. Can you help me do that?"

"I'll call for an ambulance," Mike muttered and turned away from the women.

"And the state troopers," Dove ordered.

Dove was already out the door when he ran into the store and pushed past Mike to get into the front of the store. He ignored the bodies on the ground as he went after what he wanted.

Behind the counter Dove picked up the pieces of the torn picture of him and Fritz. He would keep it close, paste it back together, look at it and beg Fritz's forgiveness for thinking the worst. That's what he'd do as soon as this was over. It just wouldn't be over until Tessa Bradley was found.

Dove's Mountain
5:23 p.m.

Dove crashed through the forest heading to the place where Tessa Bradley was last known to have been. It was the place where the lightning had cracked and seemed to be the heart of the thunder. That would be Dove's touch point now that the *feel* was with him.

He left the car on the side of the road and clawed his way through the soggy terrain. All of Nathan's little flags were washed away. No matter. Savick was dead. Those foreign men were dead. There was no one to prosecute for crimes that had been committed on Dove's mountain.

Fine.

Justice had probably been done better in that store than it would have been in a courtroom. There would be no lawyers to tear Nathan apart on the stand or question his findings, no need to call Tim up to testify about how Fritz died. The only thing left to do was find Tessa Bradley. Dove paused to stand in the spot where she fought for her life.

Wanting to run on, Dove forced himself to wait. He laid his head back. The rain had stopped but water still dropped from the leaves and branches above him. They seemed to sparkle like crystals, shot through with rainbows. The *feel* warmed Dove. He opened his eyes just as the clouds blew away. The glow of the setting sun bathed him in golden/orange light as his soul filled up with the *feel*. He followed it through trees and brambles, leaves and needles. He was surefooted but careful. He walked around boulders and stepped on rocks. He saw that Tessa Bradley's path had not been easy but he knew she had gone this way. He stayed the course because the *feel* stayed with him.

Slowly at first, then more quickly, Dove walked up the slope. He changed directions and went west and north again. She was close. He knew it.

"Mrs. Bradley?" Dove called.

Silence came back at him but there was something in it. Something important. Like a diviner, Dove put out his hands. They itched with the need to grasp on to something. Then he had it. He crouched down and shoved aside branches of dense shrubs that were right in front of him. Dove's foot hit a rock. He pushed it aside and grasped hold of the underbrush. Slowly, carefully, he made a hole big enough for him to get through. Sidestepping through the tangle of brush Dove found himself faced with more brambles and a slight rise in the land. He parted the brambles and found himself atop a ridge that dropped off sharply.

Down he went, slipping on the gravel and in the mud. He inched on down. A moment later, Dove saw the riverbed. It would flow rough when the snow melted but now the rocks were exposed, the water was only a stream. Dove's foot slipped sending a shower of pebbles down the incline. He grabbed onto a bush grown tight into a boulder and steadied himself just as the sun blazed again.

Crimson and gold, heaven appeared to open the pearly gates just for him. In that glorious light, Dove Connelly found what he was looking for and the sight of Tessa Bradley took his breath away.

Lying on her back, her hair streamed out in the water. One of her arms was flung out and the other lay across her body. She was more beautiful than he ever imagined. The hand that was in the water moved; she was waving at him. She was alive.

"Mrs. Bradley!" he called. "Mrs. Bradley."

Dove scrambled down the incline, slipping on the loose rock only to break his fall before he wrapped himself around a tree. He hit the ground hard. Dove stumbled over the stones. His boot splashed in the water. He wanted her to look his way; he wanted to feel her leaning on him. He wanted to bring her back to Jake Bradley and her daughter but, when he got closer, Dove saw none of that was going to happen.

The last light of the day had shown him what he wanted to see: a beautiful woman waiting to be rescued. Reality was not pretty but as it dawned on him, Dove Connelly knew it had been predictable.

Tessa Bradley's see-through eyes were open, filmed over and colorless. She was chalk white and cold, not from the weather, but from the natural consequences of death. Part of her face was gone, eaten away by the forest critters. Her neck was broken, her head turned at an unnatural angle. Her waving hand was nothing more than the current moving her arm as the water flowed gently by.

Dove's chin fell to his chest. He was defeated. He was too late. He could not look at her for a moment. Then, in the stillness, Tessa Bradley's spirit touched him. It was as if she had been waiting, as if they had passed on a road and she had smiled knowing they would never walk it the same way or to the same destination. Dove raised his head. He would do her the courtesy of attending to her death as a professional should.

Walking out wide of her, he took *notice*. His report would read like any other: victim lying face up, broken neck, head resting on a flat rock. Bullet wound to the shoulder. Body decomposing, showing signs of animal activity. Mrs. Bradley's right hand was closed tight, arm lying across her torso. Her left hand was open, arm in the water. Heel broken on one boot.

There, the notice was done but Dove was not. Stepping into the stream, he settled himself on a rock near her head. One foot was in the cold stream but he didn't care. He could see her skull. One ear was gone and part of her cheek. He reached out and touched her hair. It was silky, soft.

He picked her arm out of the water. The diamonds on her watch glittered; the hands had stopped at two forty-three. She had died not long after her escape. Dove thanked god for small favors. She probably didn't feel a thing; she probably didn't even see it coming. He hoped she didn't suffer. He prayed she wasn't afraid.

Touching her right hand, Dove tried to pry open her fingers. Rigor or the climate made it difficulty to move her. Whatever she clutched, she held onto it for dear life. Finally, Dove got it free. He held it up to the light, sat back and took a closer look at the car key.

Dove didn't need Nathan to tell him what was in the crevices of this thing: blood and gore, skin from the man who wanted to kill her, who would have killed her if she hadn't fought back.

But this wasn't just a key. There was a chain attached and on the other end was a gold locket fashioned with delicate hinges. Carefully he opened it. Inside was a picture of Charlotte Bradley, dark eyed and serious. She was no more than three or four years old. Dove thought of his own baby but his mind went no further than that. There would be years to sort out his feelings. By the time she was three or four, Dove would have it figured out.

Closing the locket, Dove put it back in Tessa Bradley's hand and then positioned her hand over her heart. He turned her face so that God looked down on the part that was still beautiful. Finally, Dove rested his arms on his knees. He breathed in the mountain air and closed his eyes.

"Tessa," he whispered.

Or, perhaps, it was only the sound of the wind in the trees.

THRILLERS BY REBECCA FORSTER

The Best-Selling Witness Series

HOSTILE WITNESS (#1)
SILENT WITNESS (#2)
PRIVILEGED WITNESS (#3)
EXPERT WITNESS (#4)
EYEWITNESS (#5)
FORGOTTEN WITNESS (#6)
DARK WITNESS (#7)

BEFORE HER EYES
THE MENTOR
CHARACTER WITNESS
BEYOND MALICE
KEEPING COUNSEL
(USA Today Best Seller)

To contact me and to see all my books, visit me at:

RebeccaForster.com

Made in the USA
San Bernardino, CA
26 June 2017